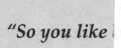 

"So you like

"Only by you." He let his gaze wander down her body. "And apparently you're aroused by having a hostage."

Her face flushed a deep red. "You just forced yourself on me."

"It was a long while before you broke the kiss."

She had no answer for that.

They continued to stare at each other in stalemate, her eyes storms of gray.

For all of her control, there was passion roiling beneath the calm surface of her, and it aroused him more than any woman he'd ever known.

She had an uncommon strength and intelligence—but a woman's desire.

Other AVON ROMANCES

Coming Soon

And Don't Miss These
ROMANTIC TREASURES
from Avon Books

Julia Latham

Secrets of the Knight

AVON

An Imprint of HarperCollinsPublishers

This is a work of fiction. Names, characters, places, and incidents are drawn from the author's imagination or are used fictitiously and are not to be construed as real. Any resemblance to actual events, locales, organizations, or persons, living or dead, is entirely coincidental.

AVON BOOKS
An Imprint of HarperCollins*Publishers*
10 East 53rd Street
New York, New York 10022-5299

Copyright © 2008 by Gayle Kloecker Callen
ISBN 978-0-06-143296-5
www.avonromance.com

First Avon Books paperback printing: September 2008

Avon Trademark Reg. U.S. Pat. Off. and in Other Countries, Marca Registrada, Hecho en U.S.A.
HarperCollins® is a registered trademark of HarperCollins Publishers.

Printed in the U.S.A.

10 9 8 7 6 5 4 3 2 1

To my sister-in-law, Jean Caples: As the years have passed, our friendship has deepened. You're more to me than my husband's sister—you've become my sister, too. Thanks for everything.

SECRETS
OF THE
KNIGHT

Prologue

England, 1480

In the great hall of Castle Bannaster, the seat of Nicholas, Viscount Bannaster, Diana Winslow helped serve the evening meal and reminded herself that being the first female member of the League of the Blade was never meant to bring her glory. In the minds of Englishmen, the League was only a myth, with no proof of its existence, except to those grateful few whose lives were changed by the Bladesmen's assistance. Diana had wanted to fight for justice, just as the shadowy Bladesmen did, and she'd known that someday, only the occasional legend of her deeds might be spoken of in a hushed, disbelieving whisper. But she'd never imagined that her first assignment would turn out to be so difficult!

For three weeks she'd been living as a servant, working to gain the confidence of the other maids. Their master, Viscount Bannaster, was known for

abusing his servants. He had bastard children
that he did not acknowledge, and the vulnerable female members of his staff were terrified of
him. One woman recently killed herself over the
disgrace.

Yet still, no one would go to the shire's royal
court of law and ask for help. He had convinced
them that no law of the land could touch him. Diana's mission was to make them understand that
if they only stood together, they could ensure that
the viscount would be forced to alter his behavior,
that he would be held accountable. The League
never worked in the open; they used their skills
in the shadows, assisting the victims.

Diana carried a tray from table to table, display-
ing choice selections of roasted lamb. Knights,
soldiers, and travelers hungrily jostled each other
for the best meat, almost upsetting her tray. They
paid her no heed, for she was a maid, plain of
face, hiding her only beauty, her long blond hair,
beneath a servant's wimple swathed around her
head and neck. For only a moment, she wished
she could draw her dagger, insist that they show
respect. But her impulsive temper was the one
thing she was determined to master.

She deliberately turned her thoughts to Mary
Gairdner, wondering where the maidservant was.
Mary had already been forced into the viscount's
bed, and the woman's young cousin was about to
follow her into service for the family. Mary didn't

want the girl to suffer the abuse that she had, so she was ready to stand up for herself at Diana's side. There were so many others to convince. The women were not like Diana, who'd grown up training on the tiltyard with her father's knights and considered herself a man's equal.

Yet Mary was supposed to be with Diana in the great hall, helping the other maidservants and valets serve the meal. Where was she? Diana thought, feeling a prickle of unease that never seemed to go away within the oppressive atmosphere of Castle Bannaster.

She looked toward the head table, hoping that the viscount had arrived, but he had not. Sitting there quietly, ignored by the guests of the household, was the viscount's brother, Thomas Bannaster, only a year older than Diana's seventeen years. He was destined for the priesthood, and he spent most of his time with the parish priest, preparing for his future life of service and religious duty. She did not see him often, but when she did, her eyes were drawn to him, leaving her feeling confused and embarrassed. He was not as tall as his brother, or as broad, for he was not allowed to train with the squires and knights. He had dark, wavy brown hair and the most somber brown eyes that she had ever seen. His face, though yet thin with youth, showed his handsomeness with angled cheekbones and a square jaw. And there was something about the way he carried himself that made her think that he did not spend all his time kneeling in prayer.

Mary had told her that it was no secret that Master Thomas was reluctant to enter the priesthood, but he knew his family duty. Two years before, when their parents had died of the plague, young Thomas had thought himself free, being the new viscount's heir. But the older brother he worshiped, Mary had told her coldly, had decreed that Thomas's life still belonged to the church. Lord Bannaster would marry soon, and beget his own heirs. Mary said that she could still remember Master Thomas's brief look of despair before it had been wiped away by one of duty.

Could he yet become her ally? Diana thought. Surely a man of God would not want the women of the household abused. When the two remaining men at the head table departed, leaving only Master Thomas, she approached him with her tray, as if to set slices of meat upon his pewter plate. When he looked up at her, their eyes briefly met, and she felt this strange awareness, as if they were somehow connected. But she had never met him before her arrival three weeks ago. His face reddened before he quickly looked away.

"Master Thomas, sir," she began softly, "were you able to speak with your brother?"

Not meeting her eyes, he nodded. "But I did not achieve the results you had wished for."

He spoke in his deep, husky voice that seemed strangely incongruous with his youth. No one would ever have a problem listening to his sermons.

She gave a start, realizing she hadn't even paid attention to his words. Why was it so hard to *think* when she was near him? "Your brother would not listen?"

"He said it was none of my concern." His mouth twisted. "He claimed he would only discuss it someday when I hear his confession. But I will try again to reach him. Such behavior is against God's commandments."

Hesitantly, she said, "Perhaps you could suggest he should imagine how it would feel if his own mother or sister were abused."

"My brother only sees the world as it is," he said dourly, "and does not concern himself with what might have been."

"Thank you for any help you can give, Master Thomas," she said, bowing to him as she took her leave.

She had not counted on the viscount listening to his younger brother, a novice priest, but she felt frustrated all the same.

And where was Mary?

Diana looked again at the viscount's empty chair, as massive and ornate as his opinion of himself. Her unease blossomed into fear. She wanted to go in search of her friend, but she could not leave her duties, not with the cook, a sharp-eyed man, standing near the doorway leading to his kitchens. So she continued to serve, moving through the aisles between the crowded trestle tables, dipping her tray for people to sample, her attention constantly focused on newcomers.

When at last the cook left the hall, Diana slipped into the stone corridor and began to hurry away from the heat and light. The sound faded until she could only hear her own frantic breathing as she practically ran through the pools of torchlight. She went up another level, using the curved stair-case built into the castle wall. She passed the oc-casional guard or servant, and she nodded with confidence, glad she had brought an empty tray covered with a linen cloth, as if she were on an important errand.

When she reached the viscount's bedchamber, she set down her tray and put her ear to the door, holding her breath to listen. Suddenly, the door opened and Diana stumbled forward, righting herself in time as a woman—Mary—pushed past. She heard the sobs, saw the bowed head and the frantic, pleading glance that Mary gave her before the maidservant broke into a run.

Then the viscount was towering above Diana, looking over her head as he shouted to Mary, "Return at once! How dare you disobey me!"

Diana took a single step back, pressing herself against the wall beside the door, hoping she was of so little consequence to him that he would ignore her. Mary was safe. That was all that mattered.

But the viscount's dark eyes fastened on her, and the sudden interest and satisfaction that flared there made nausea swirl within her stomach.

But she was a Bladeswoman; this kind of beast was what she fought against. She would resist him.

He grabbed her by the wimple, pulling painfully on her hair and yanking her into his bedchamber. When he let go she stumbled, but avoided falling to her knees where she would be even more vulnerable. The wimple unwound about her head, revealing the blond braid.

"Aah," Bannaster murmured, coming up behind her.

She tensed, ready to turn and defend herself, but she knew the subservient role she was playing. All she could do was pretend to cower while he yanked at the tie of her braid, releasing her hair to fall in long gold strands about her upper body.

He gripped her arm and pulled her up against him. Diana lifted her eyes to his, not having to fake her trembling lips.

"With that hair, you're more of a beauty than you've let on," Bannaster said. "Gray eyes, like storm-tossed seas. Aye, you'll be spirited in my bed."

She tried to pull away. "Nay, my lord, unhand me. I am not the sort of woman who—who—"

"Sleeps with a man?" He gave a bark of laughter. "All women are. Now take off those garments, and show me more than the meager offerings of that pasty-faced wench you've just replaced."

Secreted in the girdle about her waist, her two daggers seemed hot against her. She ached to use them, if only as a threat, anything to distract the viscount and escape. God above, she had known coming here was perilous, but to find herself in the same situation as the women she'd been trying to protect was too sad for words.

He grabbed her about the waist and flung her toward his bed. Instinctively, she rolled and came to her feet on the far side. Her hair tangled in her face, and she flung it back.

He grinned, starting toward her, his hand outstretched. "Lively sort, aren't you?"

He was drunk and too confident when he made another swipe at her, and this time she was able to duck and run toward the door, as desperate as any woman who fled from him. She misjudged his clumsiness, for he caught her hair in his fist and yanked. She found herself on her back on the floor, the breath knocked from her.

He was on her in an instant. She had thought his evil made him weak, but he yet had the body of a warrior, a peer who believed himself invincible in his own world. She brought her knee up hard and he blocked it, pulling her hair even harder until her back arched off the floor beneath him to keep her neck from breaking. His mouth was hot and wet on her throat, and she gagged when he bit her. She tried to slam his ears with her palms, but he evaded her, catching both of her arms and spreading them wide.

"Someone taught you to defend yourself," he said, before trying to cover her mouth with his.

She shook her head wildly back and forth to evade him, and all she got for her effort was a hard slap across the face. Her ears rang, as the room seemed to tilt crazily.

God above, she could not faint. It wouldn't matter to this monster. She might awaken and find herself defiled. She began to fight in earnest, butting his face with her head. He reared back as blood began to stream from his nose.

"You bitch!"

She had only a moment to roll out from beneath him and came to her feet, her dagger in her hand. Wearing a bloody grin, he dove at her, catching her around the middle. She fell back, her head hitting a coffer against the wall, but she didn't lose her grip on the dagger. With incredible strength, he held her wrist immobile with one hand, and as she arched and kicked, he yanked her skirts up with the other, falling between her thighs to hold her down. When she dug her heels into the floor to throw him off, her hand inching down to her waist, he only groaned as if he were in ecstasy.

Her head was pounding from the blow, her

heart raced wildly, and she couldn't catch her breath. He countered everything she tried. She felt trapped, like an animal, and in that moment of desperation, she forgot everything but survival.

Yanking the second dagger from her girdle, she buried it between his ribs.

He went still above her, his expression astonished.

"By the devil—" Then he seemed to look beyond her. "Tom—"

Someone lifted him off her and rolled him onto his back. She was able to scramble onto her hands and knees, wild hair hanging in her eyes. She pulled her hood over her head, desperate to cover herself, to hide from what she'd done. It was surely the viscount's brother who now stood above her.

Still on her knees, horrified and confused, she could not look away from the viscount, his body going slack, his expression almost comical in its bewilderment. And then his face drooped as the light went out of his eyes.

She'd killed him, a peer of the realm.

She heard nothing but the blood pounding in her ears. A normal woman might faint or scream; Diana's mind raced to analyze what she should do next. She waited for the novice priest to drag her to her feet, call for the guards, condemn her to hell's fire, anything. Risking a glance at him from beneath her hood, she saw him staring in shock at the body.

Without looking at her, he said harshly, "Just go."

Her mouth fell open. She collected herself enough to whisper, "But—I did not mean—he—"

He closed his eyes as if in pain, his expression a grimace of sorrow. "I know what he was doing, and I do not blame you. He bears the sin. Take your dagger and go before you are discovered by someone else. Speak of this to no one. Flee the castle at the first opportunity."

Bending to hide herself from him, confused and grateful and guilty, she gathered her wimple and both daggers, wiping them clean on a discarded shirt. Lord Bannaster's brother—the new viscount, she realized—never moved. Taking a deep breath, she listened at the door, unlatched it, and looked out. The corridor was deserted. She picked up the empty tray, tucked it under her arm, and walked as slowly as she dared, retracing her steps. All the while, she braided her hair and hid it beneath the wimple. She did not return to the great hall for fear that there might be blood on her clothing or a bruise on her cheek from the viscount's slap.

As she changed into her night rail in the small chamber she shared with three other maidservants, she did not even think of fleeing. That would make her look guilty. Nay, she would remain until his body was found. Mary already wished to leave Castle Bannaster with her, and being born here would enable Mary to convince the guards that her parents needed her in the village. Together they could escape the castle. After all, Diana and Mary would not be suspects; what man would ever believe that a woman could overpower the viscount?

As Diana lay on her pallet in the darkness, her body began to shake. She told herself it was just relief at how close she'd come to dying. But tonight she'd taken a man's life, committing a sin that God might not forgive her for, especially since she could not risk confessing to a priest.

She knew she'd acted only to protect herself. But part of her felt guilty—for not feeling more guilt.

And what about the new viscount? Although she did not think he'd seen her face, he knew that his brother's murderer was one of the castle maids. He was in shock now, but what if he changed his mind about shielding her? What would she do then?

Chapter 1

Yorkshire, six years later

Aching with the cold of winter, Tom Bannaster and his small party of men had been traveling north from London for several weeks, and only the promise of looking over a potential bride made him keep going—and the fact that his cousin, King Henry, had "suggested" he take the journey to meet this particular woman. That in itself made Tom uneasy. But he was a loyal subject, and through the last six years—and four different kings—he'd managed to choose the right path. Not without several stumbles, of course, but when a man had to relearn an entire childhood's worth of lessons, some mistakes were inevitable.

The town of Richmond was a welcome sight to men who'd been urging their mounts ever higher into the flat, hilltop moors of the Pennines. Tom had three men-at-arms with him and they all grinned at each other when they could see the lights of the town on the River Swale, glittering in the distance against the snowy patches of ground.

The tavern they chose overlooked an ancient stone bridge that arched over the river. There was cheerful company, a huge stone hearth that warmed the room, and a plentiful supply of ale.

As Tom bit into a dripping lamb pasty, he thought of the woman he would soon meet. Cicely Winslow was reputed to be a true beauty, the sister of a baron. That the king had suggested her gave Tom pause, but then his cousin understood that he hadn't had good luck persuading a woman to be his wife. By the devil, it had taken Tom a long time to even understand how to treat a woman after his unusual upbringing, and he'd made some foolish mistakes in the last year.

Tom took a swig of ale to hide his wince. He'd thought for certain he could persuade Lady Elizabeth Hutton, daughter of the earl of Alderley, to marry him, joining two great houses and settling Gloucestershire after his cousin's ascension to the throne. But the situation had deteriorated, and before he knew it, he had kept her confined in her tower bedroom at Castle Alderley until he could confer with the king. And even then, she'd switched places with her maid to outwit him. Perhaps he should have relieved his steward, Milburn, for suggesting the plan. But Tom had to bear some of the blame, for he had gone along with him willingly enough, feeling desperate.

And now Tom wondered if his foolish mistakes had only earned him the chance to woo the daughter of a baron in the remote North Riding. Yet . . . Tom had been able to repair some of the damage to his reputation by assisting the king last summer in the delicate matter of traitors to the Crown. Perhaps Cicely Winslow was even a reward, of sorts, a beautiful woman easily won to wife. He wanted heirs, children to love and treat better than he'd been treated. He had thought he would never have a wife or children of his own, and the promise of companionable nights with his family drove him. For even though he'd renounced the priesthood six years ago, and spent the occasional night with a willing woman, his new life had gradually seemed lacking. He wanted to feel . . . close to someone, to feel loved and to love in return.

He thought he was finally ready to put the past behind him. After six years, the suspicion of his people had faded, if not entirely disappeared. But at the beginning of his rule, it had been a different matter. *He* had been the one with the most to gain from his brother's death, although there was no proof that he'd committed the crime. It had taken several years of hard work and proof of his determination to be a decent leader to win the sympathy of his people.

But the king's court was another matter. He knew there would always be men who thought he'd killed his brother out of greed and ambition. And for a long time, their suspicion forced him to pretend to search for his brother's murderer. But although the maidservants had shared suspicion with him, no one had been identified. Even he hadn't seen the girl's face, for he'd been staring at his dead brother while she'd pulled her hood forward to disguise her features.

Perhaps the king thought a happy marriage would further his acceptance at court. Yet it was hard to persuade a noblewoman that he was nothing like the rumors about him. Maybe Cicely Winslow would be different.

Or maybe she just wanted to escape this frigid corner of Yorkshire. Tom drained another tankard of ale, feeling his toes begin to unfreeze at last. He tapped his foot in time to a patron's lute and smiled as several women began to dance. The crowd grew raucous, clapping a beat and roaring approval as the women dipped and swayed their hips. Their garments clung tightly to their breasts, and Tom watched with hearty appreciation. After so many years of being unable to even look at a woman, now he found that he could stare at their graceful forms like a starved man. When one of the women ended up in his lap, he'd had just enough ale to agree to her whispered proposal. He followed her out of the public room and up to the chamber he'd paid for.

When the door closed, he reached for her, but

she stepped away, laughing as she plopped a horn of ale on the small wooden table.

"More drink, milord?" she said, swaying, a lock of her dark red hair loose at her shoulder, her smile full of promise. "The night is far too cold."

He grinned. "Then let me warm you."

When he reached for her waist, she eluded him, uncorking the horn and taking a sip before passing it to him. The wench was right, he thought, drinking deeply. His belly burned with warmth, though the fire in the hearth was meager, and the shutters rattled with the wind.

The woman took the horn away and pulled him to his feet. To his surprise, he swayed as the chamber slowly spun around him, so he kept a grip on her hands.

"I have not had too much drink," he insisted, feeling vaguely astonished.

She pulled him toward the bed and pushed him onto it, releasing his hands. When he would have sat up to pull her into his arms, she retreated, smiling as she began to loosen the laces that trailed down her chest. Tom relaxed back on his elbows to watch.

And then the chamber faded into darkness, and he knew no more.

The first thing that awoke Tom was a deep, penetrating cold, the kind that made one shake relentlessly. He rolled onto his side and groaned.

The depths of his bones felt as if they would never get warm again. He had thought for certain that his party had reached an inn the previous night. Had his fire gone out?

He stopped breathing, his body going tense as memory returned. He *had* reached Richmond and a warm tavern. As he cracked open his eyelids, all he saw was gloomy darkness lit by a single torch in a stone wall. Mice skittered across the ground nearby.

He slowly moved his hand to his waist and found his sword gone, as well as his dagger. Even more wary, he silently lifted his head, but saw nothing except the rough-hewn rock walls and a solid wood door with a grill for a window. The wall was close at one side, and he realized that he lay on a wooden pallet raised above the floor.

Tom sat up and swung his legs over the side, only to hear the rattle of chains and feel the weight of it against one ankle. Someone had chained him. The sensation of being enclosed and trapped tried to panic him, but he wouldn't allow it. He was no longer the child who'd been forced by his family to live a solitary life.

Rising to his feet, he walked forward, but the chain went taut before he was within five paces of the door. He examined the metal shackle at his ankle and found it old but secure. The other end was affixed to the wall. He yanked on it as hard as he could, but it didn't even tremble. The chain wouldn't permit him to test the door, but he could reach a privy hole, only a crack in the rock floor, at the far end of his cell. There were no windows, so he had to face the truth that he might be in a dungeon.

"Is anyone out there?" he yelled at the door, his voice echoing in the stillness.

No one responded, and he found himself wishing that there was at least a fellow captive to answer some of his questions. But he seemed to be the only prisoner. He paced for a while, trying to call to mind everything that had happened the night before. He'd been fine until he'd accompanied the woman back to his chamber. She'd given him something to drink. But damn, had she not drank from it, too? He could have sworn so. If she'd just wanted to rob him, it would have been easy enough after she'd rendered him unconscious. But the jeweled ring of his viscountcy was still on his finger, and his pouch of coins was still at his waist. Why take him captive?

He could find no answers. Without outside light, he had no idea how much time passed as he paced in frustration. He briefly sat on the pallet, but even with the blankets—clean, adequate blankets, he noticed with puzzlement—it was almost too cold for comfort. He realized that if someone didn't return soon, he might very well freeze if left here long enough. Or starve to death, of course, he thought cynically. To keep from imagining the worst, he began to feel along the walls that he could reach, looking for a weakness.

Suddenly, he heard the clank of a door somewhere down a long, echoing hall. Through the grill, he could see a light bob ever closer. He waited tensely near the pallet, hoping his captor wouldn't realize how long the chain was. Let them just step too close and—

He could see shadowy movement through the grill, heard the key scrape in the lock. It seemed to take forever for the lock to turn over. He stood on the balls of his feet, ready to spring forward.

But when the door opened to the outside, he could only see the slim shape of a woman carrying a lantern in one hand and balancing a covered tray on the other. But not the same woman who'd drugged him. This one was tall and held herself proud and stiff. She wore a plain dark gown that only revealed her slim curves. Yet even without being well rounded, she was definitely an appealing woman. Her hair was a light shade of blond, but it was pulled back beneath a felt hat with a turned up brim. Her narrow face was still, hesitant, and she watched him with wary gray eyes.

"Who are you?" he demanded. "Who has imprisoned me here? I am Viscount Bannaster, cousin to the king, and—"

"I know who you are, my lord," she said in a low, even voice. "But I know little else. I am to care for you until my master decides what to do with you."

"Who is your master?"

Her direct eyes lowered at last. "I cannot say, my lord."

"Why am I here?"

"I do not know."

"What is this place?"

"I cannot say."

"Is it ransom he's demanding?" Frustrated and angry, he suddenly rushed toward her, but she didn't even flinch as the chain caught him short of her by several paces. "Damn you, I need answers!"

She hung the lantern from a peg in the wall near the door. "I am told that you will receive them when we're able to give them. Know that this is not a permanent situation."

"And I'm supposed to accept your assurances?" he asked scornfully.

She only bowed her head.

"Where are my men? Why aren't they here?"

"They were not apprehended with you, my lord."

"So they think I simply vanished."

"You and your horse."

"They are supposed to think that I left them?" he said, outraged. "They will not believe that."

She shrugged.

"They will find me."

She made no response.

For the first time, he began to wonder if this had anything to do with his brother's death, or even his foolish imprisonment of Lady Elizabeth. A chill of foreboding rippled down his spine. Did someone want to see him punished, since the law had been unable to? Yet this woman seemed to believe he would not be kept here forever. Unless, of course, she was being lied to, all to enlist her assistance.

"Would you like to eat?" she asked.

At her words, his stomach gave a low growl. His jaw clenched, for he hated to show any weakness. He wanted to fling the tray back at her, insist he would not eat until he was given answers. But these people had the power to outlast him, he knew, and it wouldn't be all that long before he would have to eat or die.

"So what have you put in the drink this time?" he asked with sarcasm.

She only cocked her head in confusion. "I . . . know not what you mean, my lord. I have brought you a wineskin."

"Drink from it."

"Your pardon, my lord?" she said in puzzlement.

"I was already drugged once by orders of your *master*, and I won't be again. Eat and drink while I watch."

"Very well, my lord."

To his surprise, she gracefully knelt down before him, put the tray on the floor, and lifted the cloth. A large bread trencher was covered with stew, thick with gravy and chunks of meat and vegetables. There was another loaf of bread and the wineskin she'd mentioned. His stomach growled loudly, and she glanced up at him. Her face did not lose its impassivity, but he thought her eyes brightened. Was that her version of laughter? Behind those eyes was the intelligence of a woman who was more than a servant.

He narrowed his own eyes at her. How could she be amused when he was being held against his will? She sobered and began to eat, taking several bites of the stew.

"Now the bread," Tom said.

She broke off a piece and ate it.

"Surely you're thirsty," he added with sarcasm.

After lifting the wineskin to her lips, she drank deeply. A drop of red wine slid down her cheek toward the smooth tendons of her throat, and Tom found himself watching its path far too closely. He groaned and closed his eyes. He had spent too much of his life forbidden from looking at women, and now he could never get enough. Even staring at this plain young servant made him want to touch her. There was something . . . mysterious about her, hidden depths that were just beneath the impassivity of her gaze.

He ran a hand through his hair and turned

away. He would not become like his brother, thinking of the maidservants as his playthings.

"Are you satisfied, my lord?"

He glanced over his shoulder to find her standing again, watching him solemnly. "Leave it."

She turned away and reached for the lantern.

Did he want to be alone again? He spoke the first words he could think of. "I'm surprised that you are taking the lantern but leaving the torch. I could start a fire to alert people to my imprisonment."

She paused and faced him once again, hands linked serenely before her. "You could, my lord, but let me assure you that no one would notice. The dungeon is in the rear of the castle, and only my master and I know of your captivity. You could die from the smoke before I return, and that might not be until the morrow."

"So that implies that you're only bringing one meal a day?" he demanded belligerently.

"Whatever my master orders."

He was sick to death of hearing about this absent man, but there was nothing he could do except threaten. "The longer I'm here, the worse it will be for your master."

She nodded. "I am certain he realizes that. Good day, my lord."

Taking her lantern, she left the cell and spent a long time making sure the door was locked—the door he couldn't reach because his ankle chain wouldn't permit it. Impotent anger infused him, and he barely kept himself from flinging the tray at the door. But all that would get him was more hunger, making him too weak to take a chance at escape when it presented itself.

Diana Winslow walked to the end of the corridor in the dungeon and looked up at the stairs leading to the inner ward. Her hand shook, making the lantern swing. She blew out the candle inside it, then sat down weakly on the stairs in the dark. There were no guards on duty but her; no one within the castle—but Mary and Joan—who knew that there was a viscount locked in the abandoned dungeon.

She covered her face and found herself listening for him. But she heard nothing except the occasional clink of the spoon on the tray.

God above, what had she done?

She had panicked, that's what she'd done. When her sister Cicely had gloated over the fact that Viscount Bannaster was coming to court her, Diana had been too stunned at the news to mind Cicely's superior grin. *Bannaster is coming here?* had been all she could think, over and over again. And then more questions had begun to hammer her brain. Why was he coming? Had he discovered her identity at last?

And then Diana had enlisted Mary and Joan, who'd understood her fears. They had been happy to serve Diana for the last six years, and now they, too, worried that the past had caught up with them. Diana would never forgive herself if because of her, both women were also under suspicion in the late viscount's death.

When Bannaster had been farther down the dale, he'd sent word of his approach. Diana had known he'd stop in Richmond that night, for the road into the hills was too unsafe in the darkness. There were only a few inns, making it easy enough to find him. Because Diana could not risk him recognizing her, Mary had offered to disguise herself as a loose woman. She'd lured Bannaster into his chamber, fed him the ale they'd tampered with, and the three of them had managed to drag him down the rear staircase to their cart waiting in the courtyard.

It was too much of a coincidence that Bannaster could have heard about Cicely, not when he lived in Gloucestershire, and spent much of his time in London. Kirkby Keep was a crumbling castle in the wild hills of Yorkshire, far from civilization. Diana had been banished there several years before by her brother Archie. And then Cicely had joined Diana in banishment when Archie's patronizing abilities at court had landed him a bride who was jealous of Cicely's beauty. The two sisters, who had never got along, were now forced to inhabit this small castle that Archie neglected, waiting and hoping that their brother would send eligible men their way. And that didn't happen much.

Bannaster coming to court Cicely, of all the women in England, eight days before Christmas, seemed like such a remote idea that Diana could only conclude one thing. He was sick of bearing the weight of suspicion in his own brother's death. When she'd realized six years ago that he would be blamed, she'd almost returned to take her punishment. A Bladesman, who was her contact with the League, had not allowed it, convincing her that Bannaster's position as the new viscount, and the lack of proof he'd committed the crime, would protect him. And it had—but not from ridicule and suspicion. Everything Bannaster had suffered was her fault.

But . . . he hadn't recognized her. Aye, she'd made sure she looked different, leaving her hair mostly uncovered rather than disguised by a wimple, as it had been before. She wasn't wearing the coarse garments of a servant.

When she'd first entered the cell, she'd held her breath, waiting for him to say, "Aha!" and proclaim her a murderess. But he hadn't; he'd only demanded answers that she couldn't give. Six years ago, over the course of several weeks, she had only seen him at the occasional meal, had only spoken to him a half-dozen times. And even then, he'd barely made eye contact with her. Perhaps he really didn't recognize her, yet was searching for her, or even one of the other maidservants, Mary or Joan.

Or was it all a coincidence, and once again she was being impulsive? She'd worked so hard to conquer that weakness, training steadily in the doctrine of the League even though they had not called on her assistance in six years. They'd told her that she was too impulsive, that they would have to evaluate her again before placing her in a dangerous situation. But she was still waiting, her life of excitement and purpose gone. Now her past mistakes had returned to haunt her.

Could Bannaster really be here simply to look over her sister?

Well, she couldn't let that happen either! God above, Diana had killed his brother! She would have to send word to the League and ask for their assistance. She hated to involve them, but she did not want her actions to jeopardize the secrecy of their mission to help those who needed it the most. Though she did not know where the League was based, she knew how to leave a message that would be sent to the right people.

Pushing tiredly to her feet, she turned and walked up the stairs that led to an outside entrance. The dungeon was beneath one of the corner towers, with its own separate staircase. Feeling distracted, she walked through the inner ward, remembering to nod at the greetings thrown her way by the dairymaids and the stable grooms, and the huntsman at his kennel. Her breath puffed before her, her toes began to tingle with numbness as her feet crunched over the packed snow.

The curtain wall of the castle had been breached at two points in a battle long ago, so in the gatehouse there was no longer even a need to lower the portcullis, the pointed iron gate that would normally guard against intruders. Diana had soldiers take turns patrolling through the night, but that was the best that she could do for security. The keep was nowhere near a well-used highway; what thieves would travel into the dales to steal what little they had?

Much as all the servants had been kind to her, Diana never felt like she belonged. She'd grown up on the plains near York, at the castle where Archie and his wife now resided when they weren't in London. On a whim, her brother could send Diana anywhere he wanted. It was frustrating and humiliating, and although she was hardly the only woman to suffer so, she was a Bladeswoman, trained to take command of a situation, to act and even attack when necessary.

Instead she was as much a prisoner as Viscount Bannaster now was, running her household, it was true, but unable to leave. And of course she had to deal with Cicely, arrogant in her own beauty, as frustrated as Diana was with the way her youth was being wasted.

It was now midafternoon, and Diana entered

the great hall to find dinner cleared from the trestle tables. The castle was drafty with age, leaving threadbare tapestries a last defense against the chill wind that snuck in through every crack and seemed to seep into the very stone. At least there were several stained glass windows cut high into the walls to let in light. An ancestor had once gone to a large expense for a small keep, and Diana was grateful for the meager warmth the light brought.

With a sigh, she slipped up the stairs and into her bedchamber before Cicely could find her. Diana didn't want to hear how excited her sister was about the viscount's visit, not when she knew that he wouldn't arrive—at least not for Cicely.

Her bedchamber was Diana's retreat from the world. She'd brought her favorite tapestries to hang on the walls to keep out the drafts. Her four-poster bed was comfortable, piled with cushions and warm coverlets. It looked like the bedchamber of any woman. Unless someone examined the coffer resting unobtrusively in the corner. It contained Diana's weapons: her daggers and swords, the crossbow she'd become proficient at. Cicely had spent their youth taunting her, but to be different than her sister was something Diana was proud of.

Her skill had brought her the notice of the League and led to the predicament she found herself in now: she was keeping a man against his will in her dungeon.

The present viscount little resembled the eighteen-year-old boy she remembered. He had grown taller, and his work becoming a knight had made him broad with muscle through his shoulders, arms, and chest. Above his wide neck, he had a man's face now, all hard angles. He'd lost that pale, pinched look of unhappiness. He seemed so . . . full of life, bigger than life, a man who'd found his proper place. Those brown eyes she'd once thought somber now snapped with authority and frustration. Yet he'd been living with the repercussions of her actions, just as she had. She'd lost her place in the League; he'd lost his people's trust. Diana had not spared herself from hearing everything that had happened to him. He was not taken seriously at court, though his cousin the king was protective of him.

Yet . . . he would never be punished because of her crime—unless you counted her imprisonment of him. She groaned and sank into a cushioned chair before the bare hearth. Since he'd inherited the viscountcy, he was used to having everything his way. She couldn't imagine he'd take well to being locked up, but what choice did she have?

She knew that no one had ever trained and succeeded to the knighthood as quickly as he had. But after that, he'd made terrible decisions. How could he complain about being held prisoner, when he'd done the same to a woman? He had long since left the gentle ways of a priest behind.

Shuddering, Diana hugged herself against the cold. She would have the servants light a fire for her.

And then she remembered Bannaster, and the cold depths of the dungeon. Though she wanted to avoid him, she would go to him once more.

Chapter 2

I t was late in the evening before Diana was able to slip away from the household. Joan had already prepared a tray for their prisoner and left it in Diana's chambers. Diana took a rear staircase down to the small door seldom used that led to the lady's garden and beyond, to the inner ward. She used no torch, just carried a sack over one shoulder, and the tray in the other hand, moving slowly through the dark, her bright hair covered by a hood for secrecy. Only when she was on the far side of the tower did she breathe easier, opening the dungeon door, careful not to disturb the cobwebs draped across it.

She hurried down the stairs in the dark. The grill in the cell door was the only source of light. Setting everything on a small table, she used the key she kept hidden in the girdle belted about her waist. The sound of movement from inside ceased at once. She gritted her teeth as she forced the lock to turn, fearing it was rusting with age. After pulling open the door, she found Bannaster standing in the center of the cell, the chain piled at his feet, his face pale and furious. To her dismay, the rock cell was even colder than this afternoon. Well, at least she'd remembered his plight before he spent a freezing night. She brought in her sack and tray and knelt down to unpack.

She was prepared when he rushed at her, only blinking when he came up short and cursed.

He stared down at her with narrowed eyes. "You do not show fear," he said coldly.

"There is nothing to fear." A mistake, those words. Too brave for a mere maidservant, as if she were still a Bladeswoman.

He scowled, and she realized she'd offended him.

"When I am free," he said, "you'll remember what fear feels like."

She barely kept herself from asking if those were the threats used by someone who'd once studied for the church. But again, that would reveal herself as more than a servant—and as someone who knew much about him. His garments were still immaculate, as if he hadn't tried hard to escape. But the shackle around his ankle left him little leeway.

"Threatening me will not help, my lord," she said softly. "I fear someone else more." *My own conscience.*

"Who is your master?" he demanded again.

Without answering, she took the cloth off the covered tray. She'd had Joan prepare a selection of stewed beef and mutton, which now rested on another bread trencher. There was a salad of carrots and beans dressed with verjuice, and another wineskin. Before she added a spoon, she looked at the tray he'd discarded and found his earlier spoon missing.

She slid the tray toward him. "My master told me not to give you another spoon if you had hidden the first one."

With another scowl, he started pacing, ignoring the offering of sustenance. "How long do you intend to keep me here? I will be missed."

"I'm glad that you are certain of that, my lord."

"And what does *that* mean?"

She could not keep talking to him if she could not control her words. Why did he affect her so poorly? She calmly pulled the brazier out of the sack, and then produced a smaller sack full of coal.

"You carried all that on your back and managed a tray, too?" he asked.

Some of the fury had left his voice, and to her dismay, he was studying her more closely now. She hid her face by staring intently at her work. "I did not wish you to be cold, my lord. You can light the coal from your torch. There is a small hole high in the ceiling for the smoke to escape."

"The torch is about to burn out."

She slid the sack toward him. "There are several more in here."

"And now you've told me about a possible means of escape."

Did he sound wary beneath his satisfaction? She stared up over his head, to where blackness concealed the true height of the ceiling. "Should you even be able to reach it, my lord, the hole is not wide enough for a man to crawl through. And it leads not to the outside."

He gave what sounded like a growl, then sat down cross-legged to face her. She was so surprised, that she met his gaze without thinking of the effect. As she knelt facing him, eye to eye, to her consternation something seemed to . . . shift inside her. She could not give a name to the strange sensation she'd never felt before. Looking into those fiery dark eyes made her feel unusually defiant, ready to challenge him word for word.

But she was a maidservant, she reminded herself, reining in her emotions.

"Why am I here?" he demanded all over again.

She shook her head, trying to appear helpless.

"You seem familiar to me," he continued.

Her insides tightened, but she was well trained to show no reaction. "Have you been to this corner of Yorkshire before, my lord? Because I have never left it."

"You were born here?"

She nodded the lie quite easily.

"Your master, too?"

She made no answer, only started to rise.

"Wait!"

Impassively, she stared at him. "Aye, my lord?"

"You have not tasted the food."

With a sigh, she sat back on her heels and tried a bite of everything. He remained silent while she did so, watching her every move. She could have sworn he was paying too much attention to her lips, felt almost as if he touched her. After a sip from the wineskin, she began to rise again, feeling relief and the need to escape. Had she become a coward?

"How do I know the poison won't act slowly?"

"You do not, my lord. All you can trust is that my master does not want me to fall unconscious when I leave here. And there's no point in harming you, when he already has you vulnerable."

She thought she could hear his teeth grinding.

Rising to her feet, she said, "I will bring more food on the morrow."

"And how long will we keep doing this?" he said with obvious frustration, rising to stand tall before her. "He cannot possibly mean to break my mind, not when you've given me food and drink and fire."

"Perhaps that is not his intention."

"Then what is? What is this about?"

He stood facing her, hands on his hips, the very broadness of him intimidating. He had been so very different six years ago, still a boy, destined for the priesthood; now he seemed to fill the cell, crowding her out.

What could she have possibly thought she could do with him? All she'd felt was the blind panic of a woman guilty of murder, who'd worried that another suffered in her place. But he didn't look like he'd suffered.

Regardless of the weather, she would have to send her message to the League tomorrow. She could not keep speaking to him every day, with no answers to give, no solution to her dilemma.

"Good evening, my lord."

He almost gaped at her. "Is it good? I cannot even tell if it's evening."

"Then listen for the church bells." She turned and walked through the door.

"Damn you, return to me at once!" he thundered, even as she locked the door behind her.

In the darkness, she fled up the stairs, glad to leave.

Tom strained to the limits of the chain, feeling the shackle cut the skin of his ankle, furious with the sound of his voice echoing in the dungeon. He had not meant to sound as desperate as he felt, but he hated the cold and the solitude more than anything else. It reminded him of all the hours he'd spent kneeling on the stone floor of the church, reciting the prayers he'd had to memorize, feeling like he would never be warm again. Life had gone on outside his small church, his prison, but he had not been a part of it.

He ran a hand down his face, bitter laughter welling up inside him. His mysterious captor didn't need to deny him food and water to break him, if Tom continued to allow his own mind to work against him. He sat down on the pallet, picked up a rock, and began to hit the hinge of the shackle. It looked far too solid to break easily, but at least he was doing something that might lead to escape.

He couldn't stop thinking of the maidservant, and he told himself it was because she was his only contact with the world. But in his mind he saw the grace of her movements, the blankness of her gaze—not the blankness of unquestioning obedience, but something else, almost like a curtain he could not see through. She knew much more than she was saying.

Diana was awake before dawn. She had washed herself quickly in a basin of cold water and was already dressed in her plain garments before Mary arrived. Mary was a buxom redhead who always caught men's eyes. Were she a noblewoman, she would have easily found a husband. But instead she was a maidservant, abused by the late viscount, and so she shied away from men altogether. Diana had thought giving her a home would help heal her, and Mary claimed to be—and seemed to be—happy at Kirkby Keep. Diana, who'd never felt a real desire for the restrictions of marriage, thought Mary should be left to her own wishes. But it was Joan, the other maidservant from Castle Bannaster, now being courted by the huntsman, who said they needed to help Mary find a husband.

Mary closed the door behind her and came swiftly to Diana's side. "I did not see you yesterday eve, milady. Did ye go to him again?"

Diana sighed. "I could not leave him to freeze. I took him a brazier and more torches."

"He could harm himself."

"If he's foolish enough to try. But he will not. He is too intent on discovering all the answers."

"Would you not be, if ye were captured like that?"

Diana frowned at her, knowing that Mary was right. "Are you telling me that we did wrong?"

"Nay, of course not! We had to know his purpose here. But milady, now what?"

"We send a missive to the League. And I go to see how he spent the night."

"He must be very angry, if he be anythin' like his brother."

When Mary shuddered, Diana almost comforted her friend, but remembered in time that Mary wanted no reminders of her past weakness.

"He's angry, aye," Diana said, "but he's not like the late viscount."

Mary cocked her head, green eyes curious. "And how do ye know that, especially after the things we've heard about him? Though I lived in the same castle, I knew nothin' of his mind. He kept to himself, he did, forced to by that family of his."

"There is not the same cruelty in his eyes." Diana willed herself not to blush.

"And ye trust that?" Mary asked, her own eyes wide with disbelief.

"I trust nothing. I promise I'll be careful." Diana sighed. "Will I escape my sister this morn?"

Mary grinned. "Nay, she's already awake, too busy anticipatin' a suitor to sleep past dawn, her usual custom."

With a groan, Diana went to the door. "Then I will bear her delirious happiness."

"And I shall fetch a tray for your *guest* and leave it here for ye."

"My thanks, Mary," she said, giving a tired smile.

The maidservant studied her. "I think ye did not sleep much either."

Diana shook her head. "I did not realize how my actions would . . . weigh on me."

"'Tis not too late to change our minds, milady. We can use the potion again, blindfold him, and set him free."

"And when he comes here to meet Cicely, how am I to hide my face?"

"Oh."

"And he makes me taste the food and drink, so I would suffer the effects of the potion as well."

"A clever man."

Diana sighed. "But I vow to be more clever. Somehow I will set this to right."

Mary looked skeptical, but said nothing as they turned opposite ways at the next corridor. Diana went down to mass in the chapel built into the curtain wall of the castle and then headed toward the great hall to break her fast. Her sister was humming as she followed on her heels across the inner ward.

Cicely Winslow was a true beauty, there was no doubt about that, Diana admitted, objectively studying her sister's light blue eyes, heart-shaped face, and blond curls. Since Cicely was unmarried, she took advantage of the custom for maidens to wear their hair down—impractical as it was for women such as Diana, who worked hard through the day. But to Cicely, others existed to serve her. A year younger, her sister was delicately petite and well curved next to Diana's tall and sturdy build. Their father had doted on Cicely, favored her to the point that she thought special treatment was her due. Behind that sweet smile lurked a selfish woman.

"Ah, if only it were summer," Cicely said, catching up to Diana as they took the stairs up to the great hall. "We could decorate the entire castle in flowers for Lord Bannaster."

"I don't think men care as much for flowers as women do," Diana said, glancing with reluctant amusement at her sister.

Cicely's pert nose rose in the air. "As if you know anything about men."

Diana arched a brow.

"I mean men when they're courting women," Cicely amended mockingly. "Fighting in the mud with them does not make them treat you as a woman."

"That is very true."

They went to the head table, and for once, Cicely seemed to be studying her.

"Do you not regret being trained with the boys?" Cicely asked. "Father only allowed you to do so to spite Archie."

"Who made sure to take out his repressed ire on me when he became the baron."

"Your banishment is old news."

Not wanting to ignore an honest question, Diana at last shook her head. "When you were interested in embroidery, I only cared about how to throw a dagger. When you were learning to sew, I was learning to fish."

"Better if you had been born a boy, than to be so . . . in between."

It wasn't said maliciously, to Diana's surprise. "I used to think so, but now I don't know."

"Because there are so many men courting us?" Her voice was bitter.

Diana only shrugged.

Cicely seemed to shake herself back into her sunny mood. "I won't think about Archie's ill treatment of me anymore. Today I'll have a suitor, a viscount!"

Surely she'd just said his title for the hundredth time.

"When he sees me, he shall want to rescue me from this place, to protect me, I just know it!"

It was on the tip of Diana's tongue to point out that the viscount would see by their shabby keep that there would not be much of a dowry, but she couldn't say it, not even to Cicely, who deserved it.

In some ways, she wished Cicely *would* marry. Diana's days would be peaceful then, without her sister's sulks and tantrums. But Cicely could not marry Lord Bannaster. The terrible secret that bound their families together would come out, and the viscount might make his wife miserable as punishment.

And if Diana didn't have Cicely to distract her, would she eventually become bitter over the League's avoidance of her?

At the head table, Cicely leaned near. "Do tell me that you will wear your best gown today and avoid the tiltyard."

"Are you not afraid I'll steal him away from you?" Diana asked with sarcasm.

Cicely only laughed, and Diana admitted to feeling a momentary hurt beneath her resignation. Nay, she would never steal a man away from her beautiful sister. She had accepted her plain features long ago.

But still, Cicely had always been able to sneak beneath her defenses. Her appetite gone, Diana said, "I will see you at the midday meal."

"Do be certain that the servants clear away the old rushes on the floor."

Cicely had always left the cleaning of the castle to Diana's management. Diana felt a little guilty for ignoring her request, but her sister deserved it.

When Tom heard the first light steps in the hall, he hated his feeling of relief and anticipation. He'd spent hours the previous evening working on the shackle at his ankle, with little to show for it but a few dents in the metal. Then he'd paced until he was exhausted before pulling the blankets about him to sleep. The dungeon cell was too large to contain the brazier's warmth, so when he had awakened, he'd moved about briskly, loosening his stiff, cold muscles.

At last the woman came to him, and although he tensed, waiting, she was still alone. She brought a tray, a bucket of water, and another full sack. As she set the items down near the door, out of his reach, he studied her again. She wore another plain gown, not quite as coarse as a servant would normally wear. Either this was a well-to-do household, or she was more than a servant. Could she be the mistress to his mysterious captor? But would a mistress do such menial duties as caring for a prisoner? It seemed unlikely. Her speech was refined, but a woman raised as a lady's maid could speak so.

"What am I to call you?" Tom asked.

She stared at him, as if his calm voice was foreign to her.

"Shouting at you will not help me," he added. "And calling you 'mistress' seems foolish."

"I am not permitted to give my name," she said after a moment's hesitation.

"This master of yours sounds far too controlling, *mistress*," he said with sarcasm. "But I guess, being his ignorant captive, I should not be surprised. Even his servants aren't permitted to acknowledge their own names."

She pursed her lips and kept silent.

The only way Tom was going to get anywhere with her was to appeal to her sympathies, to make her comfortable with him. No more flinging himself at her like a mindless animal. He would appeal to her womanly qualities, her pity and guilt.

When she set the tray on the ground and slid it toward him, he grinned at her and slid it back.

"Mistress, you know I don't trust that master of yours."

She looked up at him from where she knelt on the cold floor, her eyes luminous and somber. "But I assure you that the food is—"

"If it were only you, I would take your word. But I cannot."

She sighed and removed the linen. Several apples and wedges of cheese lay beside a loaf of bread and a crock of butter, along with a tankard of drink.

"Do you wish me to take a bite of each apple?" she asked dryly.

"Perhaps you should simply share them with me." He spread a blanket and sat down cross-legged on the ground opposite her. "Would you like a blanket to sit upon?"

When she hesitated, he reached for one and tossed it to her. She placed it on the ground and sat upon it, her legs bent gracefully to the side. The tray was almost within easy arm's length of each of them.

"I am only doing this because you're insisting," she said primly.

"Of course. You would not want me to starve."

She took a bite of apple, arched a brow at him, and then tossed the fruit. He caught it and took a large bite from the same spot. She only frowned at him, her expression puzzled. He realized that the sexual suggestion was lost on her. She was not a man's mistress. Ah well, he would try anything he could to sway her. While he munched his apple, she broke the round loaf of bread, slathered butter over half of it, took a wedge of cheese and an apple, then pushed the tray with everything else toward him.

"Hungry this morn?" he asked idly.

"I have not had time to eat."

He buttered his own bread. "Your master keeps you busy."

"A woman's life is always busy, my lord. Did you not have a mother who kept just as busy, or were you sprung from the ground?"

A piece of bread caught in his throat as his laugh turned into a cough.

"Now I shall be forewarned about your dry sense of humor," he finally said, smiling.

She eyed him speculatively. "You are too pleasant today, my lord."

"What is the point of being otherwise? It will just deprive me of company that much sooner."

"I cannot be your companion here."

"I didn't think you would be." He pushed the tray back. "You forgot to taste the ale."

She sighed, took a generous sip, and then once again sent the tray scraping across the rock floor of the cell. For several minutes they ate in silence. Rather than look demurely, meekly, at the ground, the maidservant studied him forthrightly.

"Still debating about my mother?" Tom asked.

"Maybe she was a terrible person who raised a terrible son. After all, if your wise master imprisoned me, I must have done something wrong."

"I do not know that, my lord."

"Or perhaps I did something worth demanding money for."

"Not money."

"Aha, so 'tis not a ransom he's after."

She blushed, and he noticed for the first time that her skin was not as pale as a lady's, indicating that she was a servant accustomed to the sun.

She lowered the apple she'd been munching. "I have said too much," she whispered with a disconsolate voice.

"All you've told me is that this is not a random demand for money. And with all this trouble, I had already assumed as much. So it is something personal between me and your master."

She said nothing, only absently turned the apple about in her fingers. He'd pushed too hard. He was losing her, he could tell.

When she stood up, he said, "Wait, you have not told me what the bucket is for."

She reached for it and slid it toward him. "Water, so that you can wash."

"How thoughtful. Is this from you or your master?"

She remained silent and turned away, but not before he could see a flush of red creeping up her neck. While she removed linens and a crock of soap from her sack, he removed his leather jerkin and doublet. She tossed items toward him one at a time, not paying enough attention to realize that he was disrobing. He got her attention by deliberately juggling the soap crock until she gasped and put her hands out as if to catch it. Then she caught sight of him, garbed in his shirt and woolen breeches. He pulled the shirt off over his head, waiting for her reaction, hoping he was appealing to the deepest part of her womanhood.

Chapter 3

Staring at his nude chest, Diana felt her face flush. What an arrogant man to flaunt himself before her. Or did he have a different purpose? Perhaps he only wanted to confuse and humiliate her, to make her reveal even more than she'd already foolishly let slip.

"My lord," she said coolly, "I am not the sort of maidservant who would bathe you."

He grinned. "I did not even think it. I assure you that I am quite capable." He lathered a small facecloth and began to soap his chest.

And it was a fine chest. She had been raised on the tiltyard, had seen many a man strip to the waist to wash after a strenuous day of training. But somehow this was . . . different. They were alone, the darkness of the earth lit only by torchlight, the air smoky and warm from the brazier. The planes of his body were . . . pleasantly shadowed, showing well-sculpted muscle that displayed his dedication to the knightly arts. A scattering of dark hair across his chest narrowed down his flat abdomen, and she resented where it led her gaze. His breeches were well fitting enough to outline what would normally be covered by a codpiece, and he had the broad, thick thighs of a horseman. Just looking at him made her body feel too hot to be contained by her skin. She needed to leave, to understand and permanently banish her thoughts and reactions to this man.

"I'll give you privacy, my lord," she said, proud of her impassive voice, even while her mind was frantically wondering why he affected her so strangely.

"I do not mean to drive you away, mistress."

She winced, wishing she'd thought to give herself a false name. She hated how he stressed the title, even though it was truly hers. He had somehow taken control of this encounter, and she needed to get it back.

She stepped out into the corridor and brought back two saddlebags, which she placed on the floor next to the door.

He stilled, his smile fading. "Those are mine."

"Aye, they are."

"Give them to me . . . please," he added.

She recognized the effort it took to keep his voice level. She had once again reminded him of his position here as helpless captive. Her guilt was entwined with other reckless emotions he seemed to inspire in her.

"My master instructed me to make sure there is nothing in here that you could use as a weapon."

"He trusts *you* to search it?" he asked with none-too-subtle sarcasm.

She glanced at him, irritated that soap and water dripped down his chest and into the waist of his breeches, dampening it. "He does, my lord."

"And he did not feel the need to search the bags himself."

That was a mistake. She'd allowed her anger to get the best of her. Why did she want to annoy him by searching his belongings in front of him? She'd already emptied them out yesterday, of course, and found flamboyant garments that belonged at the king's court. He must have come directly from London. She remembered him in the black cassock of a novice. How many years had he worn *that* sort of garment?

"I do not know what he did with the bags, my lord," she said evenly. "I only know that I will feel safer going through them one last time before I allow you to have them."

His movements were angry as he rinsed the cloth and wiped the soap from his chest. Wasn't it too cold to be standing about wet and unclothed? She turned away from him and removed several shirts, doublets, and jerkins. His hose ranged from plain silk to multicolored stripes. She left the codpieces untouched in the bottom of a bag.

"Handle my undergarments carefully," he said with cool amusement. "They're delicately made."

She didn't look at him, knowing that even the tips of her ears were red by now. She found another money pouch, a small piece of flint and steel to start fires on his journey, and a rare book of poetry.

"That is a gift," he said shortly.

For Cicely? Diana wondered. That was already a strike against him, for Cicely had little use for education. Her sister preferred jewels.

But Diana wasn't going to allow Bannaster anywhere near Cicely, so it didn't matter.

"May I have my possessions now?" he demanded.

She repacked then tossed both bags to him, and he threw them onto his pallet.

"Your wardrobe is not very practical for your current circumstances," she said.

"It succeeds with the ladies."

"And yet you had to travel here, in winter, to see a woman?"

He said nothing, but his eyes smoldered with rebellion as he loosened the laces of his breeches and pulled them below his waist. She saw the edge of his linen braies beneath, where bone and muscle met in his hips.

"Is this how you want me?" he asked softly. "Totally defenseless?"

For only a moment, she wanted to stay, to prove

that his taunts would not affect her. And then she wanted to touch him, to see what such smooth skin felt like unadorned. To take the wet cloth and run it along his—

She turned and fled, thanking God that she was supposed to be a simple maidservant who would be shocked by his behavior. His laughter echoed, bouncing off the stone walls, almost hurting her ears as she clumsily locked the door.

The last of Tom's forced laughter left his throat, and he began to wash more quickly, feeling that he was turning into a block of ice. Freezing was worth seeing her reaction to his near nudity. Nay, she was no mistress. He'd shocked her, but mayhap he'd helped her see him as a man rather than just a prisoner. She may have the upper hand, but he, too, knew how to get to her. He'd seen the dazed look in her eyes and felt absurdly satisfied.

But how did she know he'd come north to see a woman? What else did she and her master know about him?

Diana arrived back in her bedchamber, still chilled from the outdoors. But she'd been glad of the softly falling flakes of snow—she'd lifted her face and let them take the hot blush from her cheeks before anyone could see her. Then she removed her wax tablet from a coffer and began to compose a message to the League. It had been years since she'd used the special code they'd taught her, the way to bury her message within the wording of an innocent letter supposedly written to a friend. She practiced on the wax tablet, where she could correct her errors, and then she would eventually transfer the encoded message to parchment.

After an hour, she'd only gotten through a paragraph and was trying to figure out the best way to sound as if she hadn't panicked with Bannaster's approach. When someone knocked on her door, she was almost relieved. She smeared the wax tablet, knowing she'd be able to rewrite the paragraph she'd figured out. She called for the person to enter.

Mary and Joan came in, both wearing worried expressions. Joan Carew was a woman with no family, who had been abused by the late viscount and had wanted to live where there were no memories of what she'd endured. Broad-shouldered and jovial, she'd never forgotten how the late viscount had abandoned his bastard children. She had insisted that one part of her duties at Kirkby Keep would be watching the children of mothers who had to work to survive.

"What is wrong?" Diana demanded, coming to her feet.

Mary and Joan exchanged a glance.

Mary said, "Lord Bannaster's men have arrived, lookin' for their master."

"You don't mean that they think he's here."

Wide-eyed, they both shook their heads.

Diana took a deep breath to calm herself. "I knew they would come eventually, since he was headed here in the first place. Does Cicely know?"

Joan shook her head. "She's in the sewin' room."

"Working?" Diana said in surprise. "I wonder if she's brushing up on her skills for marriage." She sighed. "Forgive my lack of restraint where my sister is concerned. I'll go down with you."

"Oh, we cannot go, milady," Mary said. "We kept far away from them. 'Twas the steward who sent me to fetch you, and I brought Joan. After all, we might recognize his lordship's men, and they us."

"Of course, I had forgotten. I do not think they'll remember me."

"Nay, milady," Mary said with a grin. "Ye act quite different from the shy maidservant ye pretended to be six years ago."

Diana saw the curious glance Joan sent between the two of them. Joan knew only that Diana had wanted to rescue the Bannaster maidservants from the influences of the late viscount. If the woman suspected there was more going on, she had been too grateful to question Diana.

Alone, Diana descended into the great hall. Three men were standing before the hearth warming themselves, already holding steaming tankards of mulled wine to fight the winter's cold.

They kept their cloaks wrapped around them, and she saw the occasional shiver even as she approached.

When they noticed her, one man, tall and ferocious-looking with a bushy beard and matching eyebrows, stepped forward. To her shock, he gave her a pleasant smile.

"Good day, mistress."

She blinked in surprise at his refined speech. "Good day, sir. I am Mistress Diana, sister of Baron Winslow."

"I am Talbot, the captain of Lord Bannaster's men-at-arms. Has he by chance arrived?"

"He has not, sir." She used the tightness in her stomach as the motivation for the concern she projected. "But he was supposed to. He did not travel with you?"

Talbot's smile faded, replaced by a look of determination. "He did, mistress, but we stopped at a tavern in Richmond two nights ago, and he disappeared from his chamber. His horse and belongings were gone as well, so we hoped he had come here early. But to be certain, we searched the town yesterday and could find no word of him."

Before Diana could respond, they all heard girlish laughter from the top of the stairs. Every gaze looked up as Cicely appeared with her pretty lady's maid. Both wore light-colored gowns of the most delicate fabric, which moved about them as if they stirred on a spring breeze. Cicely's blond hair was in ringlets partially caught back, but leaving some scattered on her shoulders. Even Diana thought the two women brightened the dreary winter day. Talbot's mouth slowly gaped.

"My sister, Mistress Cicely," Diana said dryly.

Cicely came down the stairs, each step so gently placed it was as if she floated. Her smile showed off gleaming white teeth, and her blue eyes searched the roughly dressed newcomers. Her pleasant expression gradually faded.

"There is a problem, Cicely," Diana said. "Lord Bannaster has disappeared."

Cicely came to Talbot on a wave of the sweetest perfume. "Sir, I do not understand."

Talbot glanced at Diana for help, but she only shrugged, for the story was his to tell.

"We hoped he had traveled ahead of us in anticipation of meeting you, mistress," Talbot said gently, reverently. Then he shook his head, as if freeing himself of Cicely's spell. "But since he is not here, it means he met with foul play." He looked at his two fellow soldiers, who returned his frown, then back at Diana. "We would like to question the nearby villagers, your tenants and soldiers. Do we have your permission?"

Cicely stepped forward, sliding her shoulder in front of Diana as if to upstage her. "Of course you do, sir. If there is anything we can do to help, please let us know. Oh, poor Lord Bannaster. I fear for him in this winter weather."

Diana stepped back, allowing Cicely to pretend that she was in command of Kirkby Keep. Bannaster's men could question anyone they wanted, but they would find no news. Her conscience tweaked her about the effort they would have to expend—and their worry—but it could not be helped.

"Mistress," Talbot said to Cicely, "might we use the keep as our command base while we search the surrounding countryside?"

"Of course," Cicely said.

Diana winced inside. She knew it had been too much to hope that they would base their search in Richmond.

While Talbot and his men began to speak to the servants, Diana tried to escape the hall. She was to train this morn on the tiltyard with her men, and she was looking forward to the chance to concentrate on something other than Bannaster.

Cicely flew to her side and caught her elbow before she could ascend the stairs. "Oh, Diana, this is terrible!"

"It is," she answered solemnly.

"He must be grievously injured to not come to meet me."

Diana arched a brow. "All of his belongings were gone from the inn. Might he not have willingly departed?"

She rolled her eyes. "Of course not! He was coming here to see *me*, was he not?"

"So we were told."

Cicely frowned. "That is not amusing. I hope you are not so petty as to feel satisfied."

"I do not understand."

"I know how jealous you are of the suitors who come for me but ignore you."

"All three of them?" Diana raised a hand when a shocked Cicely opened her mouth. "Nay, that was cruel of me. And I am not jealous, nor do I feel satisfied that a man might be lost in the snow."

Gritting her teeth, Cicely said, "I will see that Cook has a lovely dinner for our guests." She whirled away.

Before Diana ascended the stairs to change, she looked over her shoulder at Bannaster's men-at-arms. She would have to be very careful whenever she visited her prisoner.

When Diana returned from the tiltyard several hours later, she was hot and exhausted and satisfied with the day's training, ready to finish her letter to the League. She would never have the strength to best a gifted swordsman, but she could hold her own. And with a dagger, she was unmatched in accuracy.

She wore breeches and a sleeveless leather jerkin over her shirt, leaving her arms free to move. Her garments stuck to her damp body as she began to remove them. She had the shirt unlaced and was beginning to pull it over her head when a prickling sensation swept over the back of her neck. Her body went still as her gaze thoroughly swept her bedchamber. Something seemed . . . wrong.

She sensed no movement, not even air leaving an intruder's lungs. But someone had been here, someone who didn't belong.

Her eyes darted to her weapons coffer, the only thing of value she possessed. She quickly unlocked it with the key she always carried with her. Her breath caught when she saw a rolled piece of parchment sitting on top of the crossbow.

Someone from the League had been here this day.

She tensed, her first instinct to run below and stare at Bannaster's men-at-arms, looking for clues. Could one of them be a Bladesman? If so, surely she could not have easily kidnapped Bannaster from the tavern.

Her breathing shallow and nervous, Diana unrolled the parchment. It was a cheerful letter written to her as if by a lady she'd once met in her brother's home. With clumsy fingers she pulled out her wax tablet and began to decipher it, transferring each word into proper order. She was concentrating so hard on the task that she didn't even think about the meaning until the whole message was before her.

The League was giving her her first assignment in six years, and it concerned Bannaster. Her stomach knotted. Through the king, the League had deliberately sent Bannaster to look over Cicely, so that Diana could spend time with him. She gave a low groan, rubbing a tired hand over her face. What had she done?

She forced herself to read more. The League wrote that Bannaster had made errors in judgment, and they needed to know that a man so close to the king could be trusted. Or would he be the kind to get caught up in the treasonous plots surrounding the new king? She was to evaluate Bannaster and report back to the League.

She had feared that Bannaster had discovered her connection to his brother's death; instead it was the League who'd brought Diana and him together. Was this also a way for the League to evaluate *her*, to see how she would react with the brother of the man she'd killed?

Diana carefully set the wax tablet down and stared at it blankly. They'd given her a way back into their good graces, and through her impulsiveness, she'd already ruined her first mission in six years. She had spent so long practicing her control—and with a sister like Cicely, she'd had plenty to work with. The League was her only chance at escape from her brother's guardianship, and now it might be permanently out of her reach.

But Diana was not a woman to give in to despair. She had much to prove. She *would* complete this mission, even evaluate Bannaster while he was in her dungeon. Surely his reaction to such stress would say much about him.

And she had to admit, so far his behavior had been understandable. He had tried angry coercion to make her talk, and now he was using more subtle persuasion, appealing to her woman's nature. It would be interesting to see what he would do next.

Then she would have to find a way to free him—in time for Christmas?—and to make sure he didn't marry Cicely. It wouldn't make for good family relations if he found out his new sister by marriage had killed his brother.

Chapter 4

For Tom, it had been a long, long day. He'd spent much of it getting filthy, searching every inch of every wall he could reach. He found a bit of loose stone behind his pallet, and dug at it for several hours with his spoon, making little headway. But if there was a chance that there was another cell next to his, one with an open door, it might offer him an avenue of escape.

But only if he escaped his chain. He spent more hours hammering away at the shackle about his ankle until he was bleeding, but he ignored it, having suffered much worse. He even made an attempt to dig where the chain was attached to the wall, but it was imbedded in solid stone.

Very far away, he could hear the church bells tolling every four hours. It was well past supper when the maidservant came back to visit him. She was alone again, which was making him more and more suspicious. Why did her master continue to hold him without giving a reason?

When she unlocked the cell door and came in, she stopped abruptly and stared at him. He knew how filthy he must look, and that she would know the reason why. He grinned at her with a cockiness that no longer came easily. He wanted to give his anger free rein, but it was not yet time.

She only shook her head, her expression faintly amused, and began to set down all the items she'd brought. He saw more coal and torches, clean linens, water in a bucket, and even a tray of food. How she'd carried it all he didn't know, but she was a tall, sturdy woman.

He imagined how sturdy she'd be in bed, and then shook his head at himself. He was determined not to let himself be distracted, but she was making it very difficult. Why was he so attracted to this quiet, strong woman, when he usually liked his women feminine and dependent on him? He wanted to stay angry with her, to focus on escape, not lust.

Mastering his emotions, he said quietly, "Good evening, mistress."

She straightened from her tasks and stared at him. "Good evening, my lord."

"Your master has not chosen to visit."

She said nothing, her intelligent face impassive.

He smiled. "I'm beginning to wonder if there really is a 'master.'"

She cocked her head, but made no other response to his statement. There were plenty of women he'd offended in his past, considering how little he'd understood what pleased them. But he could not see the women he'd known lowering themselves to such a tactic as kidnapping.

"You have been busy today, my lord."

"I have to find something to do with the hours in the day."

"Many would find solace in God."

He snorted. "I am not one of them. I alone am responsible for my actions—and for saving myself. Will God free me? I think not."

She studied him in obvious surprise as she set his supper tray on the floor. "You betray bitterness, my lord."

"And I am allowed to, after spending my entire childhood and youth studying for the priesthood against my will."

She stilled, her hand on the linen cloth she'd been about to remove.

"Did not your master tell you that?" he continued. "Anyone who knows of me, knows of my past."

"I have heard nothing of you, my lord, here in my corner of Yorkshire. And yet I must say, it was not God who caused your problems, forcing you to study for the priesthood, but men. Should not your bitterness be directed at them?"

She removed the cloth and made to stand up, as if she would leave him. He didn't want her to go.

"It is difficult to direct my ire against dead men," he said. "I inherited the viscountcy from my brother, who died under mysterious circumstances."

She bowed her head. "That is tragic, my lord."

"Yet I escaped the priesthood, so in one sense, it was not tragic for me."

He sat down as he always did for the meals, opposite her, the tray between them. She was watching him again, her eyes the color of the stone that surrounded them, and just as impenetrable. There was a stillness, a serenity about her that he respected, as if she were able to accept anything that happened to her. *Did that come from faith?* he wondered. *Or simply long practice accepting what one had to?*

"Did you . . . regret your brother's death?" she asked hesitantly.

Her face was open with curiosity, and he knew he had to feed it, looking for a weakness.

"You mean am I a heartless bastard who welcomed his death?" He reached for the loaf of bread, broke it in half, then tossed a piece to her. She caught it with excellent reflexes. "I can truthfully say that I mourned him—or I mourned the man I once thought he was. He was not a good man at the end, and there were many who could have killed him." He did not tell her of his guilty feeling of relief.

He saw her stiffen.

"Aye, it was murder, and the villain was never discovered." A necessary lie. But something in him still wanted to protect that poor, unknown woman after all these years.

She slowly spread butter on her bread. "That must be . . . difficult to bear."

"I have grown accustomed to it. There is a part of me that burns for the truth, and another part full of resignation that I might never have my answers. But I have not given up." It was what he told everybody.

She nodded, her eyes concentrating on the task of eating, as if she could not meet his gaze. He imagined that she was unused to men speaking freely to her, especially if she was the maidservant she claimed. He didn't like discussing his past with a stranger, but if it would help him sway her to his cause, he would bare his sins.

Diana felt strangely trapped, knowing she should listen to everything he willingly said. She was surprised that she actually felt guilty for having to report what he said to the League. But she would put aside her feelings to serve justice. If Bannaster could gain the League's approval, then perhaps she would not feel so guilty for leaving him the main suspect in his brother's death. Somehow she had to find a way to lead him to speak more of himself.

She reached forward and speared a bite of boiled mutton to eat and noticed that only then did he take a bite of the same. After chewing, she said, "Even though you didn't want to be a priest, was it difficult to leave that life behind?"

He studied her with narrowed eyes, his jaw moving slowly. She felt uncomfortable, knowing that he was an intelligent man. Her questions certainly weren't what a normal maidservant would ask.

He sipped from the wineskin, before finally saying, "I cannot tell you how much I wanted to forget about being a priest, and be like normal men. But normal men had spent much of their lives on the tiltyard, and I had been punished for picking up a sword."

She said nothing, just watched him with wide eyes as if she were delicately shocked.

"I knew I could not command my people if I didn't have their respect, so I threw myself into training. Although I was eighteen, I had to begin as the lowest squires, who were usually boys, barely away from their mother's skirts."

"But you were now the viscount," she said breathlessly, as if she admired him. She did admire his determination.

"And I had to become a knight. I trained harder than anyone else, all hours of the day until it was too dark to see. But I began to earn their respect."

Yet you didn't earn the respect of other peers, she thought, knowing that that was partially her fault.

Had the suspicion she'd cast on him led him to make desperate choices?

"And you were dubbed a knight?" she asked.

"It is what I set my mind to do." He looked up at her and smiled. "And now I have a most important goal, and you and your master are keeping me from it."

She watched him bite into a juicy pear. "And what is that, my lord?"

"You already know it. Somehow your master knew that I came north to court a noblewoman."

She should not have revealed that to him, but it was too late for regrets. "According to my master, it was not difficult to decipher. The clothes you brought, the gift, how far away from home you've traveled so late in the year."

"So he knows where I'm from." Bannaster nodded, as if that confirmed something for him.

Perhaps it did, but he already knew that this kidnapping had a personal motive, so exploring that could not make things worse.

"I am only telling you what was said," Diana murmured in a low, shaky voice, as if she feared that she might be punished.

Bannaster used that charming grin on her, the one that had surely helped earn him forgiveness for his many transgressions. "Aye, 'tis a woman that brings me into this godforsaken northern clime."

She tried to duck her head as if embarrassed.

"Forgive my boldness, but I am surprised that you are not married."

Something in his eyes turned dark and blank. "It was not for lack of trying," he said lightly. "But it always came to naught."

Much of it through his own mistakes, she thought with sarcasm.

"So as every man must, I'm trying again," he added.

"Who is she?"

His smile spread wider. "I think that is not information I wish to give to your master. But understand that I need to reach her, that you need to release me."

Diana rose to her feet, leaving him the tray. "My lord—"

Frustration evident in his face, he too vaulted to his feet. She could hear the chain rattle as it stretched taut, saw his hands tighten into fists, but his face showed only concern.

"I will not let him hurt you, if you release me," Bannaster said in a low, urgent voice. "I will take you away from here, if you want to go, even give you a better way to support yourself. I could find you a husband."

She lifted her chin. "And how do you know that I do not already have one?"

"You do not, mistress," he said, his tone gently chiding.

She could not stop her blush, remembering that

she'd gaped at his near nudity when he'd been washing.

She backed toward the door, making her voice sound pleading. "Do not ask for my help again, my lord. I am . . . bound to this place; it is my home."

She turned her back, ignoring him as he kept saying, "But mistress, please talk to me."

Once she'd slid his supplies within his reach, she left, closing and locking the door behind her. Her fingers ached every time she had to use that stubborn key. She marched up the stairs, then quietly crept back down to hear how he behaved after her rejection. Would he shout his frustration? Throw the tray at the wall? Was his temper ungovernable?

But he did none of those things. There was only the sound of movement. What was he doing?

At the cell door, she crouched, glad she was wearing a hat over her blond hair. Slowly she raised herself just enough to peer through the bars of the window grill. To her surprise, she found him moving about the cell, acting as if he had a sword in his hand, thrusting, parrying, jumping over the invisible blade of an imaginary opponent. His face was a mask of angry concentration, as if he were using the movement of his body to overcome his frustration.

And he could move his body, she thought, feeling a little weakness deep in her stomach as she remembered the ripple of muscles down his abdomen. He had worked hard to have the skills a lord needed to train and lead men, and she could only admire him for that. He could have just accepted his inheritance as his rightful due, spent his money on a good life, but he'd wanted his men to know that he deserved it.

Another day passed, and Diana began to brace herself each time she entered the dungeon. Bannaster's kindness and patience were only making her feel more and more guilty—and frustrated. Since he'd found no way to escape, she was his only hope. He would use his charm—and on most women, it would be successful. She could not understand how this was the same man who'd locked a woman in a tower while he went to secure permission to marry her.

Yet . . . was she seeing the true Viscount Bannaster? He was obviously playing a part to sway her. She would have to learn to see beneath the act, to watch for kernels of fact amidst the pleasant persuasion of his words.

Oh, how had she gotten into this mess?

By nightfall, Bannaster's men had returned from another fruitless search for him. They were worried for his safety, Cicely alternated between angry frustration and bitter self-pity, and Diana felt trapped.

* * *

It would have to be this morn, Tom thought with determination. He awoke with the bells, knowing that up in the world, everyone would be at mass. If the maidservant followed her usual practice, she would bring him food afterward, when the rest of the castle had begun their daily work.

Tom paced, listening to the chain rattle behind him, his ankle suffused with a dull ache. He felt like an animal, trapped, desperate for light and fresh air. Though this was only the morning of his third day here, he almost didn't remember what the sky looked like, what freedom felt like. He worked endlessly on the shackle, and he was making some progress denting the hinge, but not fast enough. His entire world had narrowed until it contained four rock walls—and the woman.

He didn't even know her name, he thought with bitter amusement. Yet she filled his thoughts, when he wasn't thinking about a way to escape. He could picture how she moved, confident yet demure, so controlled. Her very nature made him imagine her in bed. Was she hiding a fiery passion? Did those eyes she kept downcast smolder?

With a groan, he ran his hands through his hair and kept pacing. Last night, he had washed and changed into fresh clothing, but part of him didn't know why. He would run out of clean garments soon. Yet he couldn't bear to look like the animal he was imagining himself becoming.

He heard the echo of a door open and close, and he tensed. He had given up even the thought of the woman's master coming to see him. Nay, 'twould be *her* again, taking care of him with more consideration than a prisoner usually deserved.

But her kindness—her desirability—did not sway him. He had a surprise planned for her. He had spent the last two days trying to persuade her to his side with every ounce of charm he possessed. He had spoken of his past to ensnare her sympathy, hoping she could not sleep at night thinking about him alone in the dank, cold dungeon.

But her behavior toward him had changed not a whit. So it was time for more drastic measures.

He was waiting for her in the perfect spot, the chain arranged just so, when the door creaked open.

A simple veil, dotted with melting snowflakes, hid more of her hair than was normal, and once again he felt a flutter of curiosity. Had he seen her before? She was not a woman whose beauty would make her stand out, but there was a quiet confidence to her that was rare in most of the women he knew—and doubly rare in a servant, except for those who held high positions within a household. *Was she a lady's maid to a noblewoman?*

She brought her usual supplies, and as she set them down near the door, she eyed him, for he knew his silence must surely confuse her.

When she bent to push the tray toward him, he moved swiftly, catching her wrist. In that frozen moment, her wide eyes met his.

Wearing a fierce grin, he said, "You should have paid attention to the chain."

And then he yanked, and she stumbled into his arms as the wooden tray flipped upside down. Her back was against his front, his arms around her. She was so warm and he was always so cold. Before he could even search for the keys at her waist, she drove her elbow into his gut. When he hunched in painful response, still bent over her body, she caught him by the hair and flipped him over her shoulder. He landed hard on his back on the rock floor in time to see her flee to the safety of the door.

Rolling over and coming up on his hands and knees, the chain clanking, he knew he gaped at her. His breath came hard, his scalp and his stomach ached. But as he rose to his feet, he studied her with a new intensity.

"You have had a man's training," he said with conviction, feeling stunned.

She shook her head fiercely. "I reacted with instinct to your attack."

"Nay, you're lying."

They stared at each other, he trying to determine the truth, she obviously attempting to show nothing with her expression. But she seemed uneasy, as if her behavior had revealed too much.

He was getting closer to the truth, he thought with eager triumph.

"Mistress Diana!" came a woman's urgent voice from the corridor outside his cell.

Tom saw the shock on the maidservant's face only a second before she fled the cell and shut the door, leaving most of the supplies out of his reach.

Diana. She had seemed so dismayed that he would hear her name. And in that instant, something in his brain clicked into place as he thought of her refined speech, her vague references to her supposed master, and the purposelessness of his capture. Fury erupted in him.

He shouted, "Diana Winslow?"

Sister to the baron—to Cicely, the woman he'd come to court?

Chapter 5

When Diana slammed the cell door shut, she found Mary standing at the bottom of the stairs, her face a mask of surprise and dismay.

They both heard Bannaster shout, "Diana Winslow?" For that brief moment, he had not bothered to mask his anger.

Diana winced. She wasn't surprised he had deduced her identity so quickly. He was no fool.

Mary covered her cheeks with both hands, eyes widening in horror. "Ye hadn't told him your name?"

Putting a finger to her lips, Diana leaned back against the frozen wall as she shook her head.

Mary came closer and whispered, "But I only said your Christian name, milady!"

"And apparently, 'twas enough for an intelligent man," Diana said softly, glad that Mary had brought a lantern, because she'd left hers hung inside the cell. "Come, we will leave and let him suffer the punishment of seeing the comforts that he cannot reach."

"Punishment?" Mary echoed.

"His meals had become too much of a routine, and I grew lax. He misled me about the length of the chain and grabbed me to wrest away the keys."

Mary stopped on the stairs to touch Diana's arm. "You are unharmed?"

"I fought back and escaped, betraying my skill. I should have been more subtle, but my body just . . . reacted to the threat." *It wasn't just the threat of defeat either,* Diana mused, facing the fact that for a single moment, while his arms and his body had enfolded hers, she had not cared what they were to each other, had only felt the heat and strength of him. God above, what sort of sins kept occupying her mind?

"And then I said your name," the maid continued, closing her eyes on a wince.

"'Twas not your fault," Diana assured her.

Before they reached the door to the outside, Mary caught her sleeve. "Milady, I came for a reason. I should have waited until ye'd left the cell, but I panicked. Bannaster's men are movin' through the inner ward again, talkin' to our people. I didn't want them to see you come from behind the tower."

Diana nodded. "I am grateful for the warning."

"Ye don't think they . . . suspect somethin'?"

"I think they're just desperate."

"And I have made things worse," the maidservant said, glancing over her shoulder to the dungeon below.

"My behavior had already made Bannaster suspicious. He might have drawn his own conclusions soon enough."

Mary bit her lip but said nothing as Diana pushed open the door. The winter wind caught it, but she held it firmly, glancing out to see no one.

But when they emerged from behind the stables and headed for the lady's garden, following the path made earlier in the snow, they heard a man's voice call, "Mistress Diana!"

Diana gave Mary a warning frown, smoothed the stressful lines from her face, and turned to give the soldier a pleasant smile. "A good morn to you, Talbot."

"It would be, if I did not have to keep bothering your household."

He looked behind them as if he were curious about where they'd been, but knew it was not his place to ask. She felt a cold shiver move through her. If it were discovered that she had imprisoned a viscount, she would have to answer to the king himself.

Of course, Bannaster had imprisoned an earl's daughter, Diana thought bitterly. He had not suffered much in the way of punishment—unless one counted being unable to find a proper, subservient wife.

"I'm keeping you out in the cold," Talbot continued contritely. But his gaze was sharp. "Why do you not wear a cloak?"

Before Diana could respond, Mary said, "My mistress be different from other women, sir. Did ye not know that she trains in weapons side by side with our men? The cold does not harm such a strong woman."

Diana wanted to roll her eyes, but it seemed that Mary had succeeded in distracting Talbot, for his wary eyes widened in surprise.

"What is this, mistress?" he asked with amused disbelief. "Your maid speaks true?"

"My father indulged my love of all things military. I am no match for a soldier such as yourself, of course," she added, hoping flattery would distract him.

"But ye should see her with a dagger," Mary said with fierce pride.

"That I would like to see," Talbot said.

Unclenching her jaw, Diana said, "Perhaps when the weather eases, sir. But tell me, how goes your search for Viscount Bannaster?"

His amusement faded, and his sober worry only added to the unease that continuously roiled in Diana's belly since she'd taken Bannaster hostage.

"Not good, mistress. We have heard not a clue

of his whereabouts. I have sent one of my men back toward London, just in case he returned that way, but I do not believe it of him. He would never simply leave us with no explanation. Nay, he has definitely met with foul play. But he is alive somewhere," Talbot murmured, as if convincing himself.

"Of course he is," Diana said firmly. "Who would harm a viscount? His very title protects him."

"Only in some ways, mistress. But to many, that title makes him a target."

"To an anxious heir, perhaps. And who is that?"

"A distant cousin, mistress, who resides in France and has no wish for the title. He wants Lord Bannaster to have a son almost as much as my lord does."

Diana forced herself to smile. "Now come inside out of the cold, Talbot. At least we can give you that comfort before you continue your search."

"I have seen that you invite the villagers to enjoy the comforts of Kirkby Keep."

As they walked up the stairs to the doors leading to the great hall, Diana glanced at the soldier. "They are my people," she said, wondering what he implied.

"I have been to the village, mistress, and although it is well cared for, it has obviously seen better times."

When she opened her mouth, he continued before she could speak.

"And it is not simply because of the winter season. Nay, it is obvious that you have not had the means. Your walls are breached. I can see wild grass beneath the snow on fields that should have been planted this season past."

Diana felt embarrassed, even though their troubles were not her fault. She didn't know how to answer him.

"Does not your brother see to his property?"

There was kindness in his bearded face, and it stabbed her with guilt and remorse for things other than the state of the castle and its countryside.

"My brother has much property, Talbot," she said, knowing her voice sounded cool. "He does the best he can." *For the property that matters to him*, she thought with bitterness. Keeping Diana from his sight was not enough; did her brother hate her so much for having the favor of their father? Or was he simply making sure that she could not feel at home here, because of the neglect her presence brought these people?

Perhaps she was misjudging him, and he was having more difficulties than he'd ever let on.

She had to force her mind from her brother. She had Talbot to distract—and later, notes to write on what she'd learned about Bannaster.

* * *

Gathering in his anger and submerging it, Tom sat down on the edge of his pallet and drew a blanket about his shoulders. His mind whirled in several directions, wondering at her ability to overcome him physically, but mostly focusing on her name.

Diana.

Was it truly Diana Winslow?

When he'd been captured in Richmond, he had only been a half-day's journey from Kirkby Keep, a remote manor. How many other Dianas of noble descent could there be?

Perhaps the baron had taken him hostage so that he could not court the man's sister. But Tom had been in London only weeks before, and Winslow had been there. It would have been easier for the man to confront him in London.

Tom leaned his head back against the wall, letting the cold rock cool his fevered brain. Nay, his capture had happened just after he'd sent word to Kirkby Keep to expect his arrival. His reputation could well have spread this far north. He'd done foolish things trying to help his king, perhaps cost himself the king's respect.

Tom had hoped for a fresh start with Cicely, but she might prefer spinsterhood over marriage to him. His plans were crumbling around him, all because of the past, the beginning of which had been out of his control.

But why was Cicely's sister seeing to his care,

rather than a servant? Of course, Diana was well capable of defending herself against him, unlike most women.

The last chunks of coal were burning in the brazier, and he looked longingly at the sack Diana had left out of reach. He had upset her; he only hoped he wouldn't freeze before she finally came to him again, before he could have answers.

There was one way he'd found to keep warm, to ease this frustration that never went away. He picked up a rock and began to bang on the hinge of the shackle.

By supper many hours later, when his arm ached, sweat ran in his eyes, and his ankle was freshly bleeding, the old hinge broke. Triumph burned through him.

The cell was dark. Diana winced as she hurried along the dungeon corridor. Setting the lantern down on the small table, she carefully held Bannaster's supper tray propped against her hip as she unlocked the cell door. As the door swung wide, she picked up the lantern and held it aloft.

"Bannaster?"

In the gloom, she saw him unfold his long frame from the pallet and shield his eyes. The chain rattled as he stood. It was dreadfully cold in here, and her breath misted before her. She stared at his supplies still resting undisturbed right next to the door, and the tray of food upended, its contents scattered across the earth floor out of his reach.

She faced him again, chin lifted.

"Aye," he said quietly, "I know the lack of heat and light was my doing."

"I cannot fault you for trying to escape," she answered. "I would have done the same."

"I know you would have." He looked down her body in an appraising way. "Your gown conceals an unusual strength."

She felt a momentary pride, as if at last a man appreciated what she'd made of herself, how hard she'd worked. But she quickly realized that he was only looking for weaknesses he could exploit. "Women are strong, my lord," she said coldly. "Ask the villagers who work in the fields. Ask the woman who's just given birth."

"Do not try to tell me that you are not a special woman . . . Diana."

Hearing her name on his lips chilled her, as if he were one step closer to discovering *every* way they were connected. "That is my name."

"Diana Winslow?"

She did not answer, only took the sack of coal and torches from the floor and pushed them toward him. He made no move to retrieve the items, as if he could sense how skittish she was and wanted to placate her.

"There is no need to deny your identity," he said.

The fact that he showed no anger made her even more cautious.

"Take the coal and light it. You must be chilled."

He bent, pulled the sack toward him, and removed the torches. As he lit kindling in the brazier and began to place coal above it, she used a cloth to wipe up the spilled food. He tossed her the empty coal sack to use for the refuse.

"Your true identity is not a difficult deduction," he said at last. "How many other noblewomen with your name can be in the North Riding? And I was kidnapped after I'd sent word to Kirkby Keep that I was on my way." He paused. "So what do you have against me? Or is it your sister who leads you?"

She sighed. Continuing to deny him would only delay the inevitable. His theories were certainly a more acceptable reason for her to imprison him. And she did not want Cicely involved. "It is my duty to protect my sister," she said in a low voice.

"Ah."

He sat down in his usual position, as if awaiting his meal.

"Let me see the length of the chain," she said.

He lifted it for her, showing all its length. She pushed the tray toward him, then sat back on her heels.

"You do not eat with me?" he asked.

"It is no longer necessary. You know I do not mean to poison you."

"Do I? Perhaps you believe that poisoning is the only way to keep me from your sister."

Was that tension she heard in his voice, thrumming through his words, though he strove to keep his voice mild?

"If so, I would have been done with it already. After all, no one has discovered even a clue to your whereabouts."

His smile faded. "My men are here, aren't they?"

She cocked her head. "Believe what you will."

"I know they would not abandon the search. I have been in here for four days now, while they comb the countryside in this weather."

Diana found herself unable to meet his gaze. He was poking at the heart of her discomfort. "You are correct. They are loyal men."

"Yet you'll continue to allow them to waste their efforts. Let me go," he said earnestly.

His brown eyes were so direct and persuasive when he wanted them to be.

He continued, "I will tell no one what you did in the mistaken attempt to protect your sister."

"You of all people should certainly understand my motivations for your imprisonment." She knew her voice was too silky. She was letting him get to her.

His gaze sharpened. "So that is the reason I am in here. You have heard stories of me."

"Are you denying them?"

"I haven't heard you speak them yet."

"You have a terrible reputation, my lord," she said firmly. "I do not trust you to treat my sister well."

"Most women would simply convince their sister of that, so she could reject me by the usual methods. But not you."

Diana continued to hold his gaze impassively. It wasn't helping that he was partially right.

"Nay, you are a woman who has been trained to defend herself," Bannaster continued thoughtfully. "Such a woman might respond like a man, protecting her sister with force. How did you manage to imprison me by yourself?"

"It was not difficult, my lord," she said coolly. "You were lured easily by the promise of a woman's bed."

"Of course, you were not alone."

"And then you were careless."

"Not anymore," he said, tossing her a loaf of bread. "Take a bite."

She tossed it back. "Then eat it not. 'Tis your choice. But I, too, have learned from my mistakes."

He leaned back on his hands with a casualness that she suspected was feigned.

"I imagine you *have* learned," he said. "After all,

I almost had my hands on those keys of yours. And although I did not manage that, I still had you in my arms."

Diana stiffened, feeling suddenly warm, even in the cold dungeon. "But not for long, my lord."

"Nay, that is true. But long enough. I liked the feel of your body, long and firm—and powerful."

"Powerful enough to defeat you." She let her gaze rake him. "And you wonder why I do not feel that you are worthy of my sister."

He laughed. "I haven't even met her yet, nor declared myself to her. Should I not notice a woman when I'm holding her?"

She stood up. "Enjoy your solitary meal, my lord."

He rose to his feet, taller than she. "How long can you keep this up, Diana? What do you think you can possibly do with me, other than release me?"

His words pounded at her insecurities. Of course he was right.

"I shall think of something." She whirled away and strode to the door.

Tom had known that timing would be everything. He did not want to alert her by jingling the chain too soon. But as she pulled the door shut behind her, he already had his belt buckle in his hand, and he raced forward as silently as possible, but for the faint sound of the shackle falling from his ankle. He shoved the flat piece of metal into the doorframe, blocking the lock. He knew she'd been having difficulty locking and unlocking the door.

He flattened himself against the wall, listening to her turning the key in the door and hearing it jam. He closed his eyes and waited, counting on the fact that she thought him chained to the wall. He heard her groan, and then a delicate curse, before her brisk footsteps faded away.

Tom waited, wondering if she would come right back, perhaps with a servant in tow. He might have been able to escape in just that small space of time, but he had plans for Diana Winslow. He would exercise patience.

Chapter 6

Tom waited an hour before making his move, and during that time, Diana did not return. He was already wearing his traveling jerkin and breeches, which were now so filthy as to mask the fine quality of the fabric, so he would blend in well enough with the castle servants. His hat was too elaborate, so he rooted through the saddlebag for the coif he usually wore beneath his helm, and pulled it over his head. It hung down beyond his ears, disguising his hair. No one would know him, except his own men and Diana, none of whom he planned to approach. If he were careful, he thought he could remain unseen, and find out what was really going on at Kirkby Keep.

He pulled open the door, walked out and closed it behind him with deep satisfaction. He was in a narrow corridor with stairs leading up. He ascended until he reached a door. He opened it only a crack, and with the darkness of a winter's evening, he could see nothing but the meager glow from the occasional torch. A light layer of snow covered the ground. The air smelled so cold and fresh after the coal-tinged air of the cell, that he inhaled deeply and with gratitude.

He moved slowly around the tower and paused to get his bearings. To his surprise, torches illuminated a breach in the castle wall, which was still filled with fallen rubble. He passed the stables, for he could hear the quiet sounds of horses in the night, and men speaking softly to them. He wondered if his own horse was there, but doubted it. How would Diana explain the acquisition of a new animal, especially one with such extensive training as to be an expensive purchase?

He saw the gatehouse built into the wall and realized that the portcullis was raised, and that anyone could pass through, if they could dispose of the guards. He thought he would feel more like fleeing, after spending days in a dungeon, and now having freedom so near. But the Winslow sisters were a puzzle, and he could not let it go unsolved. And the king had sent him here. Maybe there had been another reason.

The keep itself was built out from one curtain wall, three stories high, he estimated. Torches ringed the wall itself, and men stood on guard to watch over the breaches. But on a winter night, there would be little to guard against.

Tom moved back toward the stable, then turned as if he'd just left that building and was headed across the ward to the keep. No soldiers questioned him, and he was able to ascend the stairs behind two men who reeled drunkenly, as if they'd been out searching for a privy. They opened one of the great double doors and Tom stepped in behind them, staying near the shelter of their backs. Though no castle was truly warm in winter, a fire roared in the hearth, and he shivered as if shaking off the perpetual chill of the last few weeks of travel and then imprisonment.

There were dozens of people inside, and the sound of laughter and cheerful voices. He saw no sign of his own men, and for that he was grateful. He didn't want to be noticed just yet. Several trestle tables remained in place, and were the setting for games of Tables. Little groups of spectators watched at each as the players moved their pieces along the game board. Tom stood beside the closest table to the door, trying to keep away from the center of the hall.

He saw Diana almost at once. She was standing near the hearth, engaged in conversation with several men. She gestured as she spoke with diligence, a woman sure of her power. If her brother had not arrived at Kirkby Keep—and it was highly unlikely—then he assumed she was in control of the household as the eldest sister. The men listened with respect, and one pointed something out, causing them all to burst into laughter.

Tom couldn't take his eyes off Diana. Her face came alive with merriment, showing white teeth as she laughed. No missish simpering for her, only the bold laughter of a strong woman. Nothing covered her hair, and though it was drawn back at her neck, it moved and shimmered like golden silk.

Shouldn't she feel guilty? he wondered, anger pooling in his gut. For all she knew, he was alone in a dungeon in winter, while she was here, enjoying the warmth and camaraderie of a winter's evening with friends.

Before he'd known who she was, he'd played into her hands talking about his days training as a priest, and about his brother's murder. She had wanted to judge him for his past, for his mistakes, to prove to herself that she was justified in holding him captive.

He was watching her face so intently that he noticed the slight darkening of her expression as she glanced toward the staircase. Tom followed her line of sight and saw a beautiful woman descending, wearing a blue gown that set off the brilliance of her blond hair. Her face had the purity and serenity of a Madonna painting, with its pale cream complexion and delicate features. It was surely Cicely Winslow. King Henry had not exaggerated when he'd proclaimed her a beauty.

But why did Diana look so guarded at Cicely's arrival? Wasn't this the beloved sister she was trying to protect, whose very purity would be sullied by a crude man like Tom?

Cicely ignored Diana and glided gracefully to a group of women seated together as they sewed or embroidered. She touched one woman's shoulder, smiled at another, said something to a third, and they all laughed together.

Tom had spent so much of his childhood on the outside, not even permitted to look at women, that now he always indulged himself. And Cicely was enjoyable to look at. How would it be to have a wife like that, so elegantly beautiful, surrounded by her sweet ladies?

But his gaze kept sliding back to Diana. She did not join the other women, but remained with the men, listening with intensity, gesturing occasionally as she spoke, then giving that smile that seemed so rare.

A cheer erupted from the table he was standing by as someone won the game. Tom slid farther into a shadow to escape notice. The next challenger sat down, the onlookers resettled themselves, and Tom's tension eased enough to let him look back at the Winslow sisters.

Cicely had left her ladies and walked smoothly toward the minstrels. One man strummed a lute, and the other played a pipe. Instead of waiting for the song to be done, Cicely stepped right up to them and motioned for their attention. Though a dozen people were dancing, the minstrels obediently ceased to play and looked up at Cicely expectantly. Tom wondered if an announcement was pending, but since she spoke softly, he could not hear. They began another song, Cicely motioned to her ladies, and another dance commenced.

The previous dancers backed away as if on cue, and more than one face showed the briefest look of resignation or irritation before turning away.

Curious, Tom glanced again at Diana, who had missed nothing. Her eyes were narrowed as they studied her sister, and she shook her head as she turned away.

To his surprise, he thought Cicely glanced at her sister with . . . satisfaction. Was this some sort of game between the sisters, and they didn't care who got in between them?

But Diana didn't respond in any way, only went back to her discussion.

"Pardon me, sir?" said a man to Tom's left.

Tom gave a start and turned to see a short, broad man who openly studied him. Tom wasn't sure what he'd do if he were discovered, because he wasn't ready to leave the castle yet.

"Aye, milord?" Tom said, knowing that the man did not look like a nobleman, but hoping to confuse him.

The man cleared his throat. "'Tis clear ye're a stranger here, and we don't get many of those."

"I'm Tom, milord. I'm a traveler passing through, grateful for the food and warmth for a night."

The other man nodded. "That's our Mistress Diana, always carin' for folks."

Tom noticed that the man did not question which sister would give a traveler respite.

"I never saw the mistress," Tom said. "Is that her dancin'?"

"Nay, 'tis her sister, Mistress Cicely. Mistress Diana is the woman standin' near the hearth."

Tom nodded, glancing between both sisters as if curious.

"Surely ye can see the shared hair color," the other man said, then snorted. "'Tis about all they share."

"Do they not have a brother?"

"Aye, the baron. This is not his home castle, so he is seldom here."

"Surely this is where those lovely ladies were raised. They be so at ease here."

The man shook his head. "'Tis no secret I'm re-vealin' to say that the mistresses only came here a few years ago, sent away from their brother. I heard that the new baroness be jealous of Mistress Cicely's beauty, but as for Mistress Diana, who came here first, there is something bad be-twixt she and her brother. 'Tis a shame, too." He clapped a hand on Tom's shoulder. "If ye need another ale, I'll tell you who to see. I'm Hatton, Kirkby's blacksmith."

"A fine evenin' to you, sir," Tom said, bobbing his head.

Hatton turned back to watch the game, and Tom didn't want to draw attention to himself by seeming too curious about the sisters. Cicely did not seem very well liked. The woman was all smiles as she glided through the steps of the dance, moving in a circle between the other dancers. Even knowing what he now knew, Tom could feel the pull of her beauty.

Yet she was not married. It made him wonder. Diana was a year older, he remembered, and she, too, had no husband. Did their brother not wish to ally himself with other families?

At last the dance was over, and to Tom's surprise, Cicely walked toward the tables where the game boards had been set up. He didn't mind seeing her close up—

Until he realized that while he'd been studying Cicely, Diana had approached and began to play at the next table. Tom quickly turned his back, grabbed the nearest tankard of ale, and lifted it to his mouth to obscure his face.

He could hear Diana's voice now. Gone was that quiet tone she'd used with him to prove her status as servant. She spoke with casual authority. Tom was able to hang back, yet see between the various watchers to catch glimpses of her face. Aye, she was intelligent, and he was reluctantly impressed by the visible change in her behavior. She seemed to deal with people directly. What would they all think if they knew she'd imprisoned a man in her dungeon?

And who here had assisted her, he wondered, looking around at all the laughing faces. At least one other woman had helped Diana drug him and take him a half-day's journey from Richmond. What man here did his mistress's bidding?

He noticed that Diana won a game as she nodded gracefully to acknowledge the applause.

Cicely was watching her sister with a feline speculation. "Few men here can best you at this game, my sister."

"I have practiced many years," Diana answered simply.

"Perhaps Lord Bannaster will succeed where others fail."

Tom was so surprised to hear his name on the fair Cicely's lips, that he almost missed Diana's faintly shuttered expression. But all she did was give a brief nod of her head.

One of Cicely's maidens had approached, and she plaintively said, "Where is this viscount, Cicely? You thought he would be here days ago."

"His men will find him," Cicely said with conviction. "He is surely injured, else he would have been here."

"But the snow—"

Diana rose. "My sister shares your fears, Edith. We will surely hear from the viscount when the weather eases. The roads are treacherous, and he is from the warmer south. He might be waiting for the passage to ease, wherever he is."

For one moment, Tom wanted to step forward, to reclaim his identity. Diana was holding him captive, telling lies about him, digging herself in deeper with her sister and her people. How could she imagine it would end?

Yet he saw the respect her people accorded her, which they evidently did not feel for her sister.

There was something deeper going on here. Diana had claimed that her entire reason for capturing him was to protect her sister—a sister who seemed distant from her. But of course, that did not mean she wouldn't still take care of a member of her family.

Or was Diana deliberately keeping him from Cicely, out of spite?

He needed answers, and the only way he was going to get them was to keep control over Diana Winslow, staying one step ahead of her. He would not turn her household against her by proclaiming what she'd done, not until he knew how his announcement would be taken.

At last Diana left the table, spoke a few words to the same man she'd conversed with earlier— *the steward?*—and ascended the stairs to the next level. Tom watched Cicely's face, saw the anger and frustration she didn't bother to hide as she watched her sister's departure.

When the next game of Tables began, and two soldiers headed for the inner ward, Tom left with them, hanging back once they were outdoors. Their voices faded and Tom was left alone in the cold. The wind took his breath, and he deliberately staggered for the benefit of anyone watching him, as if he'd had too much to drink.

He headed back for the rear tower with the dungeon at its base. His cell was at least warmer than the outdoors. He shook the brazier to dislodge ash, added more coal, then hovered near it until he was warmer. Closing the shackle about his ankle once more, he secured it with a leather tie, just in case Diana paid him an unexpected visit.

As Diana opened the cell door without the key, it discomfited her to know Bannaster had been unlocked through the night, but he was just rising from his pallet. He wore only a dirty shirt and breeches, his hair was sleep-tossed, and his face was darkly stubbled with several days' growth of beard. But yet he was a fine man to look upon.

Hands on his hips, he studied her as if waiting to see what she'd do. She was still unused to so much attention from a man, but how could she blame him, when she was the only person he saw?

He stood stiff and tall, saying nothing, watching her with a new intensity. When she turned back to get her sack of coal and torches, he moved with her, the chain rattling, almost as if he were stalking her.

How foolish of him. He only had the reach of the chain.

Yet this morn, the small cell seemed as if it could barely contain him. Yesterday eve he'd almost been flirting with her, a new tactic. So was this more of the same?

When she pushed his tray toward him, he didn't sit down, only looked at her.

"Surely you are hungry, my lord," she said demurely.

"Tell me again why you're keeping me here, keeping me from meeting your sister."

She put her hands on her hips and faced him. "I already told you. You are not the sort of man she should marry. She needs someone . . . safe."

"Safe?" His laugh was harsh. "Tell me again what you think I've done to merit this treatment. I might not even like your sister."

"Unlikely. All men like her well enough."

"Is that sarcasm I hear?"

She said nothing, not wanting to reveal more.

"Go ahead, Diana," he said in a lower voice that almost bespoke a growl. "Tell me again what I've done. You said I have a terrible reputation."

"You do."

"Tell me what you've heard."

She paused, moistening her lips, when she knew full well she wasn't truly nervous. But his gaze went right to her mouth, as if he studied too deeply whatever she did. It made her feel . . . uncomfortable, uneasy, like her blood was suddenly too warm in her body.

If he wanted some of the truth, she would give it to him. "You're a man who would hold a woman hostage when she refused to marry you."

He began to move then, pacing back and forth, his intense brown eyes never leaving her face.

"And where did you hear that story?" he asked.

She was ready for that, for she could hardly proclaim her source as the League of the Blade. "To amuse us, my brother sends court gossip."

"Instead of visiting you."

"What do you mean?" she demanded. What had her brother said or done while in London?

"You alone are trying to protect your sister, not your brother. I know he's not here. Obviously he cares little enough about his sisters to accompany me and introduce me to Cicely."

"My brother is not the topic. You are."

"Then tell me what stories he wrote about me."

"You wanted to marry the daughter of the earl of Alderley, and when you discovered she was already betrothed and awaiting her groom, you took her hostage while you went to persuade the king to nullify the contract between their families."

"Fact number one, I did not keep Lady Elizabeth imprisoned, because she and her maid changed places."

Diana rolled her eyes. "You held a *woman* imprisoned to have your way."

"You're keeping me imprisoned, and that's the worst thing you can say about me?" he asked with exasperation.

"Not the worst."

"Did you ever wonder at my motivations?" he demanded. "And yes, my goal was to marry Lady Elizabeth. And her maid was in a luxurious bedchamber, not a dungeon cell! My cousin the king had just taken the throne, and there were still unsettled shires throughout the country. My holding that part of Gloucestershire would have done much for the peace of Henry's realm."

"Not to mention make you an earl," she said, trying to keep the triumph from her voice. What was it about this man that made her want to best him?

"Aye, it would have done that as well," he agreed, almost too pleasantly. "But then I would have had even more sway to aid my cousin. I needed a wife, I do not deny it. Were my methods misplaced? Aye, I agree to that—now. But at the time, my only guide was the knowledge that my father and his father before him both persuaded women who did not belong to them to wed. It is how things are often done."

"And you didn't have any other guide than your family's past, did you?" she said slowly, a new realization dawning. "Because you'd only been raised a priest. Did you have any contact with the king's court in your youth?"

He frowned, crossing his arms over his broad chest. "None."

"Did your father not discuss his decision with you, show you a nobleman's duties?"

His frown grew even more ominous. "I see not what this has to do with—"

"You did not know what to do, did you?" she asked in disbelief. "You'd had no training in anything but the church, and then your whole family died. You became the viscount at just eighteen years of age, and then you spent so much time learning the art of war, that you had none to spare for the art of diplomacy."

He took a threatening step toward her, and the chain tightened as he was forced to halt. She didn't move, only raised her chin. Her breath was coming too fast, and she felt far too excited verbally jousting with him, making discoveries. Had his capture of Lady Elizabeth really only been an ignorant mistake? But there were darker rumors.

"I had men to counsel me," he said coolly.

"Then they didn't counsel you well."

She thought she saw the briefest flash of regret in his dark eyes, but the wall that hid his emotions went up again. He was once more the proud viscount, a man who'd worked hard to deserve such a title.

"If it helps you to make a decision about me," he continued, "I have been punished for these mistakes."

"How?"

"I am unmarried as of yet, am I not?"

There was a bitter twist to his mouth, and she found herself wondering if he was lonely—or only angry at not having his way.

"It will only take time before people begin to forget," she said. "That is not much punishment."

"Time is not enough for you, is it? Or are you upset because your sister is just desperate enough to consider me?"

He was right, which made her angry. One moment, she found herself almost admiring him for trying to better himself, and the next he could make her furious again.

But he was her prisoner, a man she had to examine to satisfy the League.

She would make herself indispensable to them again, so that she could be free.

Chapter 7

Talking about his mistakes was not so terrible, Tom told himself. He was able to counter her arguments, show his motivations, perhaps change her mind.

Until Diana said, "But that's not all you did to those two women."

And then he was inundated by the vague memories of one foolish night, where in his frustration he'd imbibed too heavily. Two women had almost suffered the consequences.

Diana was watching him far too closely, and he suddenly didn't want her to know the kind of man he'd almost let himself be. Oh, he'd learned from that night, had been appalled at what he'd almost done, and had never again drank like that. But his resolve didn't end his guilt.

He couldn't pace, he couldn't look away. All he could do was meet her watchful, suspicious gaze. "Aye, I won't deny that terrible night. I'd had far too much ale."

"You tried to force yourself on Lady Elizabeth."

Her voice was so flat and emotionless that he almost flinched.

"Nay, whoever told you that was lying," he said with conviction. "I wanted a kiss, a seduction, but it never even came close to that."

Because he'd been stopped, thank God. He didn't like to remember that night. When one woman had eluded him, he'd tried to seduce her friend. He'd been so close to becoming like his brother.

But who had told Diana? he wondered sharply. Anne and Elizabeth—and both of their new husbands—would never have spoken of it. A soldier or two, perhaps a servant, had seen his behavior, but their words would never have reached Diana's brother at court.

He studied her too closely, for suddenly she seemed to retreat from him. What was she hiding?

"You must have learned something from your mistakes," she said grudgingly. "My brother also told me that you had done a good deed this summer past in London, helping identify traitors to the king."

"Nay, a brave woman did that. I only offered brief assistance." He knew his voice sounded absent as his mind played over this newly revealed information of hers. Her brother could have had knowledge of the foiled plot of traitors, but it was not commonly known, and the baron was not one of the king's councillors.

Who could know all those things in his past, but the League of the Blade? They played a shadowy part in what they wanted to, and then all word of them disappeared, sometimes for years. But when a king—or members of his realm—needed them, they eased their way in. They'd helped to reunite Lady Elizabeth and her betrothed, so they'd seen Tom at his worst. And then last summer, when the king's life had been threatened by traitors within his own court, the League had been there as well.

Did Diana know someone within the League? Had they contacted her about him? Had they finally decided to determine if he had murdered his brother?

He couldn't demand the truth from her without revealing his suspicions. She might not even know it all. He would have to bide his time and discover his own truths. But he couldn't do that from within this dungeon.

He looked down at the food she'd brought him to break his fast. With a rattle of his chain, he sat down cross-legged, as if prepared to eat, when instead he was plucking the tie from the shackle at his ankle, and reaching for the belt buckle tucked into his waist.

When she turned away, he said, "You cannot keep me here forever."

"I know," she said softly, not facing him. Then

she seemed to stiffen, and shot him a determined look. "But you will not marry my sister."

He only arched a brow and grinned, making her stomp to the cell door. As she pulled it shut behind her, once again he was there to block the lock, and as she jiggled the key in frustration, he prayed she would not come back inside and see him unchained. He didn't want to fight her, not here, not like this. He needed to know her secrets; he needed to make her trust him.

Diana felt . . . awful. She hurried across the inner ward, barely paying attention to where she was going. The sun was shining, reflecting off the snow and ice, almost blinding her. She told herself that her spying for the League was really going to help Bannaster, if he deserved it. The League wanted to know if he'd changed, matured.

But a man who would attack a woman—two women, according to the League—did a man really change from that? He'd admitted to being drunk, confirming part of the League's account. But he hadn't wanted to discuss it, had minimized the severity of what he'd almost done. She had never really thought him a man like his brother, but forcing women had been the late viscount's specialty.

Diana couldn't believe it of Bannaster. Not the true, terrible malevolence of knowingly hurting a woman. But he'd looked . . . guilty, uneasy, as if the memories were not pleasant. *He* had *changed . . . hadn't he?* Throughout her years of collecting stories about him from the League, she knew that at least his servants respected him, which certainly hadn't been true of the late viscount.

"Diana?"

Diana stumbled to a halt, face-to-face with Cicely. What was her sister doing out in the cold?

"Where do you keep disappearing to?" Cicely demanded with suspicion, her cloak swirling about her.

"Since when have you kept track of my movements?" Diana asked, glad that her voice sounded so very normal. "Ah, you needed something done within the keep."

"The servants hate me," Cicely said, frowning, "but they listen to you."

Diana began to walk toward the keep again, leading her sister away from the tower. "Perhaps if you treated them better—"

"I am so tired of such a refrain!" Cicely said. "I am their mistress."

"And they would not disobey you."

"Nay, but . . . it always takes them so much longer than when they obey you."

"And you are in a hurry?" Diana's breath misted before her face, and she shielded her eyes against the glare.

"Well . . . I do wish the great hall to be ready for our important visitor."

Diana said nothing.

"He *is* coming to meet me," Cicely insisted.

There was a new desperation in her sister's voice, and Diana found herself actually feeling sorry for her. Perhaps Cicely would not be so miserable if she had what she'd always wanted, a husband and children of her own. Even Diana understood what it was to want to truly belong somewhere.

Patiently, Diana said, "I feel like this is fate's way of telling you that Lord Bannaster is not the right man for you."

"But there are no other men!" Cicely said, her voice almost shrill. She caught Diana's arm, pulling her to a stop. "I cannot lose him!"

They stared at each other as if across a great distance, neither understanding the other. But Diana understood Cicely's need to distract herself with whatever happened to be closest.

Cicely's eyes narrowed. "You did not say where you've been going each morn."

And she'd decided to distract herself by annoying Diana.

"And where do I always go?" Diana asked with exaggerated patience. "To train with the men."

"But they are not yet at the tiltyard."

Diana had been prepared for Cicely's questions from the beginning. "Sometimes I practice alone."

"Surely you have not suddenly had the good sense to be embarrassed by your unwomanly behavior."

Diana arched a brow in amusement. "Of course not."

"I do not see a sword."

Pulling the dagger swiftly from its hiding place within the girdle about her waist, Diana was too satisfied by the squeak of surprise her sister emitted.

Cicely rallied herself. "And you are not in your absurd version of male clothing."

"I must be prepared to battle wearing many different garments. When I protect you from a thief as we journey, you will be grateful for my forethought."

Cicely only groaned and walked more swiftly. "Come. I wish the cook to be prepared at a moment's notice for the viscount's arrival."

At supper that night, Diana was feeling distracted. Bannaster's men had returned that afternoon, cold and tired and discouraged, adding to the lump in her chest that was her guilt. From her place at the head table, she watched them pick through their food with tired, sad movements, as if they had begun to realize that their quest might be lost. And Bannaster had been right—what if one of them was injured in this useless pursuit she was putting them through?

To her left, Cicely's worry had coalesced into an anger she took out on her food, slicing her meat almost viciously with her knife. Bannaster's impending arrival had brightened her every manner, and now his absence was making her behavior even worse. Diana feared the servants would soon be cringing from the slicing of her tongue when she spoke to them.

There was a sudden pounding at the double doors, and then they were thrown open, knocking back the young usher who'd gone to investigate. Several soldiers rose at the loud intrusion, and then in shock, Diana did the same.

Viscount Bannaster walked into the great hall, snow perched on his cap and dusting the shoulders of his cloak. He was carrying his saddlebags.

God above, how had he escaped? And was he now ready to denounce her before all? She thought of all she would lose and her stomach curled into knots, even as her chin lifted to face him with pride.

She could not speak his name, for she wasn't supposed to know his identity. She glanced at Cicely, who stared at him wide-eyed. She knew her sister was closely examining his garments, his noble bearing, his handsome features, but was hardly daring to hope.

"Lord Bannaster!" Talbot, the captain of his men-at-arms, came to his feet, his voice full of relief and gladness.

Cicely gasped, and then gave Diana a smug, victorious look, as if the resolution of his disappearance had been a battle between them.

Bannaster strode forward through the rushes on the floor, down the row between the trestle tables, straight for the dais and the head table, although he did not look directly at Diana. She felt frozen in place, full of dread, knowing her mission for the League had failed, knowing that her own security, meager though it was, would now be lost. What punishment did the king hand out to a woman who imprisoned one of his relatives? She sank slowly into her chair, her back yet stiff, watching as Bannaster's three men-at-arms surrounded him, asking questions all at once. Out of the corner of her eye, she saw Mary and Joan standing near the entrance to the kitchens, trying to hide their expressions of stunned dismay. Diana vowed to protect their part in her foolish plot.

The grin never left Bannaster's face as he stood among his men, and he finally laughed and held up his hands. "Wait, wait, allow me to meet my hosts, and to explain everything to all of you."

Meet his hosts? There would be no meeting, just a revelation—and her imprisonment. She clasped her fingers together in her lap to still their trembling. She'd taken a risk, and lost.

Talbot and the soldiers fell back behind him,

and Diana absently noticed their fierce looks of triumph and relief. Their belief in their lord had been answered.

Cicely had risen at her side, and now the smile she bestowed upon Lord Bannaster could guide a man in from the cold.

"I am Thomas, Viscount Bannaster," he said, sweeping his cap from his head and bowing low.

Up close, Diana could see his stained garments, but knew that Cicely would not care about that. No one would, once they knew what she'd done. She gritted her teeth, waiting for the incriminating words, but still he did not look at her.

Cicely walked around the table but remained on the dais, which brought her face to an even height with his. She curtsied low, with a smooth grace that Diana had always reluctantly admired.

"I am Cicely Winslow, my lord," she said in her sweet, quiet voice that still managed to carry through the stunned hall.

He took her hand and brought it to his lips. "I have heard much of your beauty, mistress, and glad I am to finally behold you and see the truth of those words."

He was taking the time to flirt? Diana thought in disbelief.

"Where have you been, my lord?" Cicely asked. "Your men have been frantic with worry for you."

"I did not mean them to suffer on my account," he said. "My journey is quite a tale."

He still did not look at Diana, whose throat was tight. It took all of her effort not to shout at him to just denounce her and be done with it. Would he take pleasure in putting her in the same dungeon where she'd held him?

"But I hear you have a lovely sister," Bannaster said to Cicely.

Diana saw the frown that Cicely shot over her shoulder, hidden from Bannaster's view.

"My lord," Cicely said, sweeping her arm gracefully toward Diana, "may I present my *older* sister, Diana."

She stressed "older" quite purposefully. Diana rose to stand behind the table as if it were a barricade. At last Bannaster looked at her, and she found herself clenching the table. She waited, her head held high, knowing her impulsiveness had brought her to this end.

Once again, Bannaster bowed low, then lifted his head and held her gaze as he straightened. Those dark brown eyes were mesmerizing, and she saw a hint of challenge, a hint of amusement, that perhaps others did not see.

"Mistress, it is a pleasure to meet you." His voice was almost . . . silky with satisfaction.

Somehow she kept her mouth from sagging open in disbelief. She didn't know what to think, what to say, and of course, Cicely did not give her the opportunity to speak, which was a good thing. Diana's tongue was surely stuck to the roof of her mouth, so shocked was she. Where was his speech against her? Or was he just dragging out his torture as a means of revenge? And how had he escaped?

"So tell us, Lord Bannaster," Cicely was saying. "We are all so anxious to hear what has kept you from us, from your men."

Bannaster partially turned until he could also be heard by his men and the rest of the hall, since everyone had been silently gaping. "In my haste to meet the two beautiful Winslow sisters"—Diana saw Cicely stiffen when Bannaster didn't single her out—"I could not sleep, so I left Richmond before dawn, knowing that my men would soon follow behind me."

Diana watched Talbot and the other soldiers glance at each other uncertainly. Were they wondering at the stupidity of a nobleman who would travel alone instead of waking his guards?

Why was Bannaster making up lies?

"But a storm made me lose track of the road, and I wandered exhausted for hours. Somehow I found a crofter's cottage, and the family took me in and cared for me. They say I developed a terrible fever, but I remember little of what happened. Only yesterday did I come to myself, and I spent the day regaining my strength. Today they drove me here in their cart because I had lost my horse in the storm. They refused to come in and be rewarded with a meal, claiming that they only did God's work helping the unfortunate."

While murmurings of sympathy circled the hall, Diana stared at him. She wanted to say how fit he looked for a man recently ill, but surely her voice would rise with disbelieving hysteria. He had created a fictional story, rather than reveal her treachery. She couldn't relax or feel safe, for at any time he could turn on her. What was his plan?

"My lord," Cicely was saying, "how dreadful for you! I do wish we could show our gratitude to those kind people who took you in. Know you their names?"

He shook his head. "They wanted nothing from me, and I owe it to them to respect their wishes."

Diana wanted to roll her eyes, but she could not take her gaze off him, as if he were a snake hesitating just before the strike.

"My lord, you must be ravenous," Cicely said, taking his hand and leading him onto the dais. "Your hands are so cold. Someone build up the fire! Please come sit with me and eat."

Diana knew her sister well; Cicely meant to put the viscount on the other side of her, away from Diana. But Bannaster smoothly moved in and sat in the seat next to Diana, forcing Cicely to sit on his left side.

"Mistress Diana," he said in a carrying tone, "you have no idea how good it feels to finally be here, enjoying your *hospitality*."

She only inclined her head, knowing that he was also enjoying his new feeling of power over her.

He sat back and looked between the sisters. "And to be here amidst such loveliness, why it is as if I am dreaming."

Diana could not keep quiet. "There are no beautiful women in London?" she asked quietly.

If Cicely could have thrown daggers with her eyes, Diana would be impaled.

Bannaster laughed, and to Diana's dismay, his rich, deep voice seemed to burrow inside her, unsettling her. As if she was not already distracted enough!

"Mistress Diana, you are far too clever for me," Bannaster said. "I can see that simple praise will not work with you."

"And why would you need to praise me?" Diana asked. "My sister is the one you are here to see."

He looked overly surprised. "Was my missive not clear?" He gave a winning smile to Cicely, then turned back to Diana. "The king has sent me to meet both of you."

Diana narrowed her eyes and waited for the rest. This lie was surely part of his plan against her.

Bannaster took both of their hands, and she fought the urge to pierce him with her nails. She hated feeling vulnerable.

"I eagerly look forward to seeing if I would suit either of you as a husband."

Diana watched the way Cicely blinked in surprise and confusion. He almost sounded as if he were letting *them* make the decision about his suitability, but it was only misdirection. He knew he had set up a competition between the sisters, at least in Cicely's mind. Diana would be forced to contend with Cicely's fury—and Bannaster's courtship. Why was he doing this? It seemed a foolish way to punish her and torment Cicely.

But to Diana's surprise, Cicely rallied from her shock, and her smile could beckon a man to lose himself in her.

"My lord," she murmured, "how sweet of you to include my sister. I thank you for your kindness toward her."

Diana barely resisted the urge to smile in reluctant admiration. Cicely had controlled her own fury, shown generosity, and made Diana appear pathetic all at once. Her sister had certainly won the first contest of what would probably be many, Diana thought with resignation.

The servants began to swarm the head table with offerings of food, sumptuous platters piled with lamb and oxen, tarts made with Kirkby's autumn bounty of fruit, and vegetables spiced and roasted. Diana could not help watching Bannaster's enthusiasm for the food, and he overloaded his plate. It wasn't as if she'd starved him, she thought, feeling annoyed.

While he ate, Cicely saw that his wine goblet was refilled, that the butter was close at hand when he wanted bread, and that her sweet smile was always in his line of sight. If only Diana could tell her sister that she was welcome to every bit of Bannaster's attention.

But of course that wasn't true, she reminded herself, her wariness changing into growing determination. If Bannaster had decided to keep her secret, for whatever reason, then she would use it to her advantage until he chose to denounce her. Her mission for the League wasn't over. Bannaster had just given her the perfect excuse to be near him while she formed her opinions about him for the League. Annoying Cicely was only a happy coincidence.

Oh, that wasn't a very sisterly thought, Diana admonished herself. They were adults now. Diana had always been more than ready to tolerate her sister, but Cicely continued to take out her frustration on her. It did not make for a harmonious family.

She suddenly felt Bannaster's hand on her thigh. She stiffened and swiftly glanced at him, but all she saw was the back of his head as he continued to converse with Cicely. She tried to push his hand away, but he would not be budged. If she used greater effort, people would see her struggle.

She felt furious and helpless. And to her dismay, she noticed the pressure of each of his long fingers, far too close to where no man had ever touched. Did he think she would offer him something sordid if he would keep her secret? His hand slid between her thighs through her gown. She reacted instinctively, grabbing his smallest finger and bending it backward. When his hand retreated, she let it go, noticing that he never stopped listening and responding to Cicely.

When Bannaster was finished eating, Cicely said, "My lord, your journey to visit me had great hardships. Now let me show you civilized entertainment. We have the finest minstrels, and if you'd care to dance—"

Bannaster held up a hand and shook his head. "If you do not mind, I wish to retire, mistress, and save such a generous offer for another evening."

"Oh, of course you are still recovering from your illness," Cicely continued, obviously hiding her disappointment behind sympathy.

"But I want you to enjoy yourself," he said. "There is no need to shorten your evening."

"Thank you, my lord," she said, looking at him with admiration.

"I will escort you to your bedchamber, Lord Bannaster," Diana said. "I, too, am retiring early." She ignored her sister's shocked fury, which wasn't well concealed. Cicely would think Diana was only doing this to have the viscount's undivided attention. And Diana was, but not for the reasons Cicely would assume.

Bannaster gave her a polite smile. "You have my thanks, Mistress Diana. I am so tired that I might wander about and lose my way."

"You seem to be good at that," she murmured, then held her breath, wondering what he would do to her for her insolence.

He only grinned.

She turned away, knowing he was behind her, following too close, watching her. How obvious was he being, before all the castle residents? But of course, he had just told them all he would be looking her over, like a prized horse to be bought. Every maidservant and valet was grinning at her, thrilled that a viscount was noticing her—even if he was only looking at her backside. Diana's anger and fear subsided in the face of her people's concern for her. She had come here as almost a stranger a few years ago, and they had become like family to her. If only she could feel safe here, but she knew she was at Kirkby Keep only on her brother's whim, and he could change his mind whenever he wanted.

And now another man controlled her fate.

She ascended the main stairs, then walked down the torch-lit corridor, past several servants, to the circular stairs going up to the next floor. She had earlier won a battle over Cicely, who had absurdly wanted the viscount to have a bedchamber near theirs.

On the next floor, Diana gestured to a closed door.

"Should you not open it for me out of courtesy?" he asked, still wearing that perpetual smile.

Shaking her head, she did so. Someone had come up the moment he had arrived at Kirkby Keep, for candles were lit, and a cheerful fire already eased the castle's chilly dampness.

The door slammed behind her. Bannaster grabbed her about the waist and shoved her up against the wall. Stunned, she hadn't imagined he would punish her physically. He pinioned her hips with his, spread her hands wide when she would have hit him—and then covered her mouth with his.

Her vaunted ability for self-defense fled, her mind went blank, and she forgot everything that had gone between them, except the pull of awareness. There were only his lips exploring hers, his tongue teasing and winning entrance to her mouth. He tilted his head and deepened the kiss, pressing his body the entire length of hers. And though he was still almost cold to the touch, she burned where his hard flesh met hers. Her breasts ached where they were flattened against his chest; a feeling of hot need pooled low in her belly.

He pressed his thigh between hers, sending a searing wave of desire pulsing through her, and she moaned her defeat into his mouth.

Chapter 8

She tasted like the sweetest wine, Tom thought, lost in the pleasures of her mouth. Her tongue met his with little reluctance, although there was a touch of innocence that surprised him. And then he couldn't think anymore, because his mind was overwhelmed by sensation. Her body was long and firm, not as delicately soft as most women were. Her small breasts pressed so alluringly to his chest, making him long to explore each sweet curve.

He had only meant to kiss her, to dominate her, to show her who had the power now, but all of his intentions faded away beneath the onslaught of powerful passion. Her hips were destined to cradle him; the urge to rock into her became overwhelming, and he slid his thigh between hers.

Her moan, so low and erotic, was his undoing. He released her hands, sliding his fingers across her arms and shoulders then down her torso, just touching the edges of her breasts, the goal being her round hips. He wanted to cup them, lift her, press deeper and—

Her fist slammed hard into his stomach, and he stumbled back, gasping. When he caught his breath, she was still standing there, wiping her mouth with one hand and wringing the other one, the one she'd hit him with. Her eyes were wide, and he thought he glimpsed fear over what she'd just done to him.

He didn't have to ask why she'd done it. She'd imprisoned him to keep him from her sister—and for God knew what else—and at his first kiss, she'd melted.

He'd melted, too, which was dangerous. How could he forget what she'd done to him, what she was capable of? He could not let his anger be submerged beneath lust. He slowly straightened, ignoring the ache in his stomach, and they faced each other like combatants once again.

He knew he had to eventually earn her trust to discover her secrets, but for right now, she had to be kept off balance. She would believe that he meant to reveal her deception, and she would not trust his denial.

And perhaps she deserved some punishment.

"I've been wanting to do that for days," he said in a low voice.

He thought her breath came too fast, which pleased him. But she still met his eyes in challenge.

"So you like being held captive?" she retorted.

"Only by you." He allowed his gaze to wander down her body, saw that her breasts rose and fell even faster. "And apparently you're aroused by having a hostage."

Her face flushed a deep red. "You just forced yourself on me."

Although a buried part of him flinched, he said, "It was a long while before you broke the kiss."

She had no answer for that. They continued to stare at each other in stalemate, her eyes storms of gray. For all of her control, there was passion roiling beneath the calm surface of her, and it aroused him more than any woman he'd ever known. She had an uncommon strength and intelligence—but a woman's desire. And he would prove to her that she wanted him, and she would admit it freely.

"How did you escape?" she suddenly demanded in a low voice. "Speak quickly, for the servants will be bringing you a bathing tub soon."

He smiled and reached for her hand. "That will make our next kiss more pleasant."

Eluding him, she spat on the floor. "That is what I think of your kisses. Answer my question."

He laughed. "I broke the shackle, of course, after many hours of effort. As to the rest, you'll just have to imagine how I escaped your dungeon."

She narrowed her eyes. "The door wouldn't lock yesterday and today."

"I wonder why." He cocked his head and frowned.

"So you could have escaped *yesterday*?"

He shrugged.

"What were you *doing*?" she asked, looking appalled.

He only smiled.

She stalked toward him until they were face-to-face. She was showing him a lack of fear, and he greatly admired her for it. He just didn't believe it. She *had* to be afraid of him and what he could do to her.

"You had your chance to denounce me in the great hall," she said, "to show everyone what I'd done to you, to see me punished. Why did you not?"

He spread his hands wide. "I didn't realize I had to accomplish everything in a certain order."

"That is not an answer," she said, scowling.

He liked the way her blond eyebrows arrowed down over her forehead in a fierce display. He wanted to smooth his fingers over them, to tease her into a softer expression. He remembered the laughter he'd seen on her face when she hadn't known he was watching. When he realized the way his thoughts meandered, he silently scolded himself.

"If I wanted you in a dungeon, I could put you there personally," he said, keeping his voice playful. "Why should I let another do it for me?"

She groaned and whirled away from him. "I do not understand you! You know I want to keep you away from my sister. You could have her all to yourself by revealing what I've done. Yet you claim that the king sent you to look over *me*, as if anyone would believe that!"

"You are an eligible noblewoman. Why would I not compare you and Cicely?" He narrowed his eyes at her. "I cannot believe you would feel yourself inferior to your sister."

Frowning, she waved her hand as she faced him again. "Of course not. But I understand who was gifted with beauty in our family."

Tom stepped close to her again, knowing she was too proud to back away. If she took too deep a breath, her breasts would brush his chest, yet still she faced him down. He could inhale her elusive scent—no obvious perfumes for Diana—and he only grew harder.

"How do you know what I consider beautiful?" he asked softly. "And what makes you think beauty is all I am looking for?"

"I care not what you value in a wife, Bannaster. We both know I would never marry you, and although my sister is desperate for *any* man to take her away from here, I will make sure you do not win her."

"A slur and a challenge all in one sentence," he said, caressing her soft cheek with the back of his fingers before she jerked away.

"Take it as you will," she said coldly.

"Then understand that you will not drive me away, whatever you say or do. I need a wife, and I will take my leisurely time deciding if one of the Winslow sisters is what I'm looking for. And I will also decide how much you deserve to be punished for what you did to me."

He was looking forward to her retort when a soft knock sounded at the door.

"It will be the servants with your bath," she said between gritted teeth.

"As the eldest daughter, is it not your responsibility to personally make certain it is done correctly?"

She rolled her eyes. "That is an ancient custom long abandoned."

He imagined the two of them wet and naked, writhing in a bath. She met his gaze with a hint of uncertainty. Was she imagining it, too?

He dropped his voice. "I could insist."

But she was not cowed, only lifted her chin. "You will not. Shaming me before my people is not the punishment you want for me."

He gave her a slow smile. "Aye, you have the right of it. But it is so tempting to have you touch me."

"And is that how it is to be between us? You will force me?"

His smile died. She already knew too much about his secret fears. He could not let her think she had such mastery over him. "I will not have to force you into my bed. You have already shown me that."

There was no mistaking her blush this time. She went to the door and opened it, beginning a parade of servants. Two carried in a deep bathing tub, and more followed with buckets of steaming water. Tom sighed with eager satisfaction. It had been too long since he'd properly bathed. Without another word, Diana left his bedchamber.

When he at last sat soaking blissfully in the tub, having sent away the last maidservant who'd volunteered her assistance, he could not help but remember the scene that had greeted him in the Kirkby great hall. Though Cicely Winslow was truly a beauty, he still saw glimpses of the selfish woman inside her.

But it was Diana he had concentrated on, Diana whose face had gone pale and still upon seeing him freely enter her hall. He'd done his best not to look at her, drawing out her worries, making her wonder what he had planned, but when their eyes had met, something new had come alive inside him. He had spent the rest of the evening waiting to get her alone.

Though he desired her, he knew he had to stay focused on what was important, discovering if the League had decided to pursue him.

But he was also still looking for a wife, and he

would not rule out the Winslow sisters. Cicely could mature with the right tutelage, and would be a bride who would be grateful for his name, his riches, and his protection. She would bring a beauty to his home that all would envy.

But Diana . . . Diana with her secrets, her daring, her physical skills beyond that of a woman, she was the one who drew him the most. For now. Once he understood everything about her, surely the mystery of her would no longer sway him. He would be himself again, ready to make the correct decision for his future.

Diana was sitting in the great hall waiting for the morning meal. Bannaster had not joined them for mass, disappointing Cicely, who'd looked stunning in a green gown with matching ribbons threaded through her loose blond hair.

"Where do you think he is?" Cicely demanded anxiously, staring at the staircase as if willing him to descend.

Diana forced herself to smile at the maidservant who brought her bread and butter. "I know not. But he is obviously not a humble man, for he does not care to thank God for his health and recovery."

Her sister frowned. "But . . . could he be excommunicated for the sin of avoiding mass?"

"An excommunicated husband. I would imagine his entire household would suffer." Diana watched Cicely closely, hoping to plant any doubts she could.

Cicely broke off a piece of bread. "Nay, it shall not be so. When I marry him, I will convince him that he must appease the church for the sake of our children."

Diana sighed and ate methodically, knowing it would take much more than religion to dissuade Cicely from a handsome viscount.

Last night's argument with Bannaster kept playing over and over in Diana's mind.

As did that overwhelming kiss.

She shook her head to rid herself of the weak feelings that even now threatened to overtake her at just the thought of her body pressed to his. What was wrong with her?

He threatened her in more ways than with just his body. She could not forget that, with one word, he could send her world crashing down around her. Her brother, Archie, would be so livid over her actions reflecting on him at court that he might disown her.

Or would she have rather gotten Bannaster's revelation of her misdeeds over with right away, avoiding this never-ending ache of uncertainty and dread? After all, it was only a matter of time.

And in this brief time, she had to perform her duties to the League flawlessly, because if her brother banished her—and he would do so, given any solid excuse—she would need the League's help.

Yet how could she even think, when her mind was assaulted by images of Bannaster in his bath? And her touching his glistening skin? What was she supposed to say to the League, that she was overcome with lust?

With a groan, she lowered her head to her arm.

"What is wrong with you?" Cicely asked angrily. "You have gotten everything you could want. You're stealing his attention from me—"

"I did not ask for it—" Diana didn't lift her head.

"Don't think I shall make it easy for you. With no effort at all, I will have him fascinated with me."

"No doubt," Diana grumbled.

"You are to keep your distance whenever I am with him."

Diana sighed.

"And wear your oldest gowns—or some of your male breeches! That would be perfect."

Diana lifted her head to gawk at her sister. "I will not dress to alter my appearance!"

"Then you admit you want him!" Cicely said with triumph.

"I do not. You shouldn't want him either. He does not have a good reputation, Cicely."

"I cannot believe you are already trying to dissuade me!" she said, aghast.

Diana rolled her eyes. "I want you to think this through. Do not accept just any man."

"He has a title, wealth, handsome looks, and youth. What more could I want? And I deserve him," she added heatedly, as if daring Diana to disagree with her.

"There are other things that make a successful marriage. You have to be able to respect your husband, and I'm not sure you can do that with Bannaster. Did you know he tried to force a woman to marry him?"

Cicely shrugged and smiled. "Foolish woman. He won't have to force me."

Before Diana could retort, her sister gasped and hissed, "There he is. Go away, Diana!"

Diana couldn't help but look at Bannaster as he descended to the great hall. She recognized the garments he wore from his saddlebag, but during the night a servant had obviously prepared the garments for Bannaster's morning debut. He looked every inch the London nobleman, wearing a wine-colored tunic thrown open to reveal a deep blue doublet over his white shirt. He wore a matching codpiece and hose, the finest leather boots, and a hat with a feather sleekly jutting back. He had shaved for what must be the first time in a week, and rather than make him look younger, the revelation of his smooth, square jaw only emphasized his sensual lips.

Sensual? Diana thought, aghast. He was a court peacock, come to impress the simple northern folk.

But he *was* impressive, she thought reluctantly. Glancing at Cicely, she saw that her sister's eyes shone with awe and gladness. Diana felt a pang, almost wishing she could allow Cicely to have what she'd always wanted.

But it could not be Viscount Bannaster, for so many reasons—not the least of which was how he had kissed Diana just last night. Was his intimate attention to be part of her punishment? She shuddered.

"A pleasant morn to you, my lord," Cicely called with girlish enthusiasm.

Didn't she know that she sounded too eager?

Bannaster gave a broad grin, his white teeth shining, dark eyes merry. Diana had to stop letting his merriment affect her.

As he approached the table, she saw his eyes take in that Cicely sat beside Diana's place at the end of table. Short of asking Cicely to move, he could not sit between them. When he did not hesitate to take his place beside her sister, Diana breathed a sigh of relief. She could not allow Cicely to become suspicious that there was more to her relationship with Bannaster.

Diana listened to Cicely monopolize his attention with questions.

"You were so brave to travel north just before

Christmas, my lord," Cicely said. "Were the roads too terrible?"

"Only at the end, Mistress Cicely," he said after swallowing a spoonful of thick, steaming pottage. "But I could not let that deter me, not when I knew that two beautiful women waited to meet me."

Diana refrained from rolling her eyes as she chewed her bread.

"The holidays will be so much better with a guest to entertain," Cicely said. "Do say you will remain with us for the next several weeks."

When he thanked her enthusiastically for the offer, Diana wasn't surprised.

"Do you have family at home waiting for you?" Cicely asked. "Will they not miss you?"

His face sobered. "Nay, mistress, my parents and brother died several years ago. 'Tis the only reason I am the viscount now instead of a priest."

Cicely gasped. "Your brother was the viscount before you? He must have died terribly young."

Bannaster glanced at her swiftly, and Diana realized that he thought Cicely knew some of his past.

"An unnatural death," he said soberly. "Someone murdered him, and the culprit was never caught."

Was that what he told everyone? That long ago night flashed before her eyes, her helplessness in the face of the late viscount's cruel strength, her desperate defense, and in the end, his death. She had freed women from their fear of him, freed Bannaster from the impending priesthood, but she wondered if he thought his freedom a fair trade for people thinking him guilty. Surely he regretted helping her—and he'd really regret it if he knew that *she* was the one who'd benefited.

"What a terrible tragedy!" Cicely turned to glance at Diana as if she was uncertain what to say after such a sad tale.

Diana was watching Bannaster carefully, and he did not further explain that he was considered a suspect. She could not blame him. Yet if she had to use that against him, to persuade Cicely not to marry him, she would.

What kind of person was Diana turning into?

"I do not wish to dwell on your painful memories," Cicely said. "You could tell me of your home, how it is different from mine."

"You were raised here?" Bannaster asked.

Cicely blushed and didn't look at Diana. "Nay, we were not. But our brother is newly married, and you know how irritating we women are when forced to live together. But for now, this is my home, small though it be."

"Mine is larger, yes, but there is a charm here that I find endearing." He took her hand and squeezed it.

He did not elaborate on his home, and Diana reluctantly realized that he thought he was sparing their feelings. Did he not know that Cicely would love to hear of his home's grandeur?

"Perhaps you ladies could show me Kirkby Keep."

"I would be glad to, but Diana cannot."

Diana arched a brow and waited with interest for the explanation.

"She does not know the household as I do, because she spends considerable time with the men."

That could be taken several ways . . .

The smile Bannaster gave Diana held only a hint of deviltry. "I understand that you are the eldest, Mistress Diana, so you must oversee the castle."

"Oh, 'tis not that," Cicely said before Diana could speak. "She developed the unusual habit of preferring the training rituals of men to the more feminine pursuits."

Bannaster looked interested rather than shocked, and Diana recognized Cicely's consternation that her plan was not working. But she knew her sister well, and Cicely would not give up the fight.

"Mistress Diana, you train on the tiltyard?" he asked.

"I do."

"Did you need to learn to defend yourself? Surely your brother has been more than capable."

He was watching her too closely, as if looking for something. He had already had one demonstration of her talents when he'd grabbed her in the dungeon.

"Our brother is quite capable," Cicely quickly said, "which is why our mother was concerned about Diana's . . . preferences."

"Yet my father gave me permission," Diana added.

"And it made our brother furious," Cicely said.

Diana wanted to wince. Bannaster was intelligent enough to deduce that there was tension between father and son, which was the reason she'd been given permission. They had little protection from their brother, and Bannaster could use that against her.

"So shall we begin our tour of Kirkby Keep?" Cicely said, rising to her feet.

Diana didn't think Bannaster was quite finished eating, but he politely followed Cicely's lead. When Cicely had turned away, he gave Diana an assessing look, ending with a slow smile. Diana understood that he would not be leaving her alone this day to train in peace.

Then let him come to watch her, she thought. If the fact that Cicely had eccentric relatives would help him abandon his courtship of her, so much the better.

His reaction to Diana's abilities would say much about him as a person. Would he feel threatened by a capable woman? After all, she'd been training longer than he had. Her own men accepted her abilities and treated her as a comrade, but more than once, a visitor had left the tiltyard in protest at her inclusion.

But to her, Bannaster seemed too intrigued. She felt . . . tense and worried and too eager to see his reaction.

Chapter 9

As Tom followed Cicely about the castle, he could see the deteriorating condition, and found himself growing angrier and angrier with Lord Winslow, who had put his sisters here, instead of with him at the family seat, or in London. He hated to see a man neglect his duties.

Yet for all of the castle's weaknesses, it was obvious that the residents and villagers of Kirkby Keep were mostly cheerful, going about their tasks with efficiency. Was that Diana's doing? He did not want to admire her beyond the attraction of her body, not after what she'd done to him, and what he planned for her. But it was more and more obvious that her people appreciated her, simply by how often her name was mentioned. He could not miss the way Cicely flinched at her sister's name—or the wariness in everyone's eyes when they saw Cicely.

Again, Tom had to wonder about the relationship between the sisters, and why Diana would so want to protect Cicely from marriage to him.

The tour was also a good method for discovering if anyone had recently moved to Kirkby Keep—perhaps a representative of the League. As Cicely took him through the outbuildings buttressed against the curtain wall, from stables to blacksmith to the dairy, he was able to subtly ask how long the workers had lived there. She did not mention anyone who had been a resident for less than three years. If the League of the Blade had maneuvered to have him sent here, where were they? He had no way of knowing, of proving that the League was involved. But how else would Diana have heard of the mistakes he'd made at Castle Alderley? There had to be some way to find out.

He was as patient as possible when Cicely wanted to show him the women's weaving and sewing chamber, but at last he was able to say, "And where is your tiltyard?"

It was as if she'd been waiting for him to ask, for she granted him a lovely smile and led the way down through the castle. Perhaps among the knights and soldiers, a Bladesman lay hidden, watching for whatever Tom would reveal about his brother's death. Though he was innocent, he knew to remain on guard against anything that might implicate him.

Outside the air was milder than it had been for

several days, with the sun occasionally shining through patches of clouds. Snow plopped from roofs and dripped into puddles.

The tiltyard itself, in a far corner of the inner ward, was a muddy mess. But that didn't matter to Tom, a man who'd been deprived most of his life of what men considered their just right: the ability to defend themselves and their families. He had spent his childhood hiding as close to the tiltyard as possible, gazing longingly at his brother's exploits, back in the days when he'd thought his brother to be a man who deserved admiration.

But even his sadness at his brother's sins had not dimmed Tom's reverence for the art of military training. Several dozen men trained at various disciplines, from sword fighting to wrestling to daggers. Men galloped their horses to joust at the quintain, which spun in a circle and knocked them to the ground if they missed the target.

He spotted his own three men easily, regardless of the mud that coated many of them. They were in a group feinting with daggers, trying to knock their foes to the ground.

At first, he did not see Diana, until Cicely helpfully said, "My sister is with your men-at-arms. She feels the dagger suits her best."

And then Tom saw her, and his awareness focused and heightened. Though she was tall for a woman, the equal in height of several of the men, she had the slightest figure. She wore the breeches and leather jerkin of a soldier, which skimmed the trim curves of her body and ended at her mid-thigh. Her bright hair, bound to her head, was covered by a cap. The breeches emphasized the lean muscles of her thighs in a way he'd never seen on a woman before.

He inhaled sharply when he realized that she moved in a circle against his captain, Talbot. The man was a head taller, his shoulders twice the width of hers. Tom should not let himself be concerned, but he must have betrayed himself, for Cicely eyed him as she spoke.

"Fear not for my sister," she said with exaggerated weariness. "She has been battling men her superior in size since childhood. She thrives on it. Why she would prefer this to the beauty of embroidery, I will never know."

Cicely's voice seemed to fade away. Tom's breath caught with admiration as Talbot thrust his dagger forward, and Diana nimbly let it pass beneath her arm, delivering a hard elbow to Talbot's chin. He staggered back and grinned with good nature at the cheers from Kirkby's men.

At least Diana was battling a man who would respect her accomplishments. He could think of plenty of men who would not take well to being bested by a woman. As Tom continued to watch her feint and thrust, whirl and duck, he found himself growing more and more aroused. He told himself he was being a fool, that this woman put him in a dungeon, that she yet held secrets and meant to use them against him.

But those concerns seemed trivial to the thought of having her in his bed. And right there, regardless of her status as his adversary, Tom determined that he would have a willing Diana beneath him. He wanted those long muscular legs wrapped around him, to bury himself in the heat of her body.

"Lord Bannaster?"

He suddenly heard Cicely's voice again, and realized that she was giving him a cool, penetrating look. He flashed her his most brilliant smile. "Aye, mistress?"

"You seemed . . . distant."

"Our visit here has reminded me that it has been many weeks since I've trained properly. Your men are very skilled, and I am certain I will enjoy testing myself against them during my stay."

"But . . . surely my sister has offended you. For that I ask forgiveness."

"Her conduct does not reflect on you," Tom said evasively. "We all do what we think we must. Yet . . . I do not understand how your sister was permitted to train with soldiers. Surely your mother had plenty for her daughters to do."

"She did," Cicely said.

Tom could see her grappling with what to say, and he thought perhaps that although Cicely considered her sister her adversary, she did not want to be too obvious—or too cruel.

"I will admit," Cicely continued, "that my sister did all that my mother required." She stopped, as if stunned to reveal something she hadn't meant to. "But Diana is willful and stubborn. She was not content to master only a woman's lot in life. She selfishly wanted more. Our brother, Archibald, caught her practicing with a dagger when she was twelve, and he thought he was being mocked. Such things came more difficultly to him, and he had to work hard to please our father, who did not often approve of him. To punish Archie for his anger at Diana, Father allowed her to train with the boys when her duties to Mother were finished." She stopped and took a deep breath, as if shocked at all she'd said.

Tom glanced from her to Diana, better understanding the nuances of a family where a brother could send his sisters to a dilapidated castle, rather than see them properly wed. Winslow's childhood jealousy of his sister had not abated, only altered as his power had grown.

"It sounds as if there was tension in your family," Tom said, which was clearly an understatement. "Sorry I am to hear it."

"Aye, my sister has never wanted to understand how her behavior affects us all."

Tom rather thought their father's childishness toward his son had much to do with it, but he was

not about to say that. He turned back to watch
Diana, who was being buckled into breast and
back plates. He heard Cicely give a weary sigh. He
knew she had wanted him to see what she considered her sister's folly, but if he spent too much
time here, she would become suspicious.

He did not want to reveal his obsession with
Diana. She was a woman with secrets he had to
discover, a challenger who needed besting. And
as for Cicely—he didn't know what she could be
to him, but he would keep his options open. Reluctantly, he turned away from the tiltyard and
continued his tour of Kirkby Keep.

Diana knew when Bannaster left the vicinity
almost as well as she'd sensed his arrival. It had
taken everything in her not to direct a challenging
stare his way, or to let him know that she would
not meekly accept his attempts at controlling her
or the situation between them.

But this unusual fear she felt could easily de-
bilitate her, if she wasn't careful.

With a sword in her hand, she worked alone at
the movements of combat, thrusting and parrying
without an opponent, improving the strength in
her arms and legs.

She did not know what Bannaster thought of
her abilities, although when she'd bested him in
the dungeon, she'd known he'd been impressed.
Why did it matter to her what he thought? An-

grily, she plunged her sword into a man-shaped target stuffed with hay. She had never cared what people thought of her strange proclivities for the manly arts. She had seldom given consideration to the need for a husband, so busy was she with the running of Kirkby Keep and her secret training as a Bladeswoman. She had never thought she would have a normal life.

So why did Bannaster's arrival suddenly have her wondering if she could have a husband, considering the direction she'd gone with her life? She suddenly felt . . . disturbed and confused, as if her certainties were beginning to fade.

What was wrong with her? She captured one man in a dungeon, and suddenly her life's goals seemed upended? Or was she simply afraid that when he finally decided to punish her, any chance of a normal life would be gone? She took out her confusion on the target, hacking and thrusting until both arms ached from her occasional two-handed grasp. Her face ran with perspiration, even in the winter's cold.

"Mistress Diana?"

Catching her breath on a grunt, she pulled her sword free and without thinking, turned to face the person who'd called her. Her captain of the guard, Nashe, took a quick backward step away from her sword.

Diana lowered the point. "Forgive me, Nashe. You needed me?"

His craggy, homely features were crinkled in worry. "Ye seem rather . . . focused on your trainin', mistress. Is somethin' amiss?"

To Diana's surprise, her other soldiers and knights were trying too hard not to stare at her. Bannaster's men were openly gaping.

"Nay, I simply felt the need to test my strength," she said, straightening and handing him her sword. "But I am finished for the day. Would you have this cleaned and returned to my chambers?"

"Aye, mistress."

Diana couldn't miss the curious light in his eyes, but she ignored it, turning and crossing through the mud of the tiltyard. She'd performed for Cicely's demonstration, and although she felt no embarrassment at being Bannaster's entertainment for the day, she didn't understand what she'd felt as he'd watched her. She'd wanted him to see her skill. Why would she care about his opinion?

Deep in thought, she crossed the great hall, staring at the floor, speaking to no one. She ascended to her bedchamber, where hot water was already waiting in a bucket. Her staff was well trained, she thought, trying to shake off her strange mood. They knew she preferred to bathe at night, so they only left washing supplies for her after she trained.

But today would have been a day for a bath,

Diana thought, gingerly removing her mud-caked garments. She had taken several falls, and her clothing had paid the price. Not to mention her new bruises.

Placing a wide basin near the fire, she stood in it, washing her face and body with a soapy face-cloth, before pouring warm water down her to rinse. Even near the hearth, she shivered with the cold. As soon as she could, she wrapped a clean linen about her body and began to scrub the dirt from her arms. When she was bending over, working on her particularly muddy calf, she heard the door open and close.

Without turning her head, she said, "Mary, I might need more water. I am rather filthy this day."

A masculine voice said, "Give me the cloth. I'm told that I'm good at scrubbing."

Diana straightened so quickly she almost lost her balance, and even then had to grab at the cloth, which was coming loose at her bosom. Bannaster leaned back against the door, grinning at her, his gaze moving with deliberation down her body.

Never in her life had she felt so exposed and vulnerable, and the fear was as metallic as blood in her mouth. Here in her own castle, she'd forgotten her League training, and thought herself far too secure to take precautions against an intruder. Her lapse in judgment had her once more alone with Bannaster, giving him the edge. She didn't try to cover herself, which would have been a sign of weakness. All she had left was a pride she didn't know if she was entitled to feel.

"Leave my bedchamber immediately," she said in a cold voice.

"I do not wish to."

But at least he hadn't yet moved toward her. "Surely you need to be at my sister's beck and call."

He arched a dark brow but did not lose that infernal grin. She had meant to make him seem unmanly, but instead had made herself seem almost—jealous, and he knew it. *Damn him.*

He gave a soft laugh and slowly walked forward, moving sinuously, gracefully, a man in control of every muscle. She suddenly wondered what it would be like to face him on the tiltyard, to test her strength against his.

She hated the heat that burned in her, the way she wanted to press her thighs together, not in fear, but against the strange, slow throbbing that had begun in the very core of her. She couldn't let him see his affect on her, so she straightened her shoulders and let him look, knowing there was just a thin, precarious cloth between her and complete nudity.

"If I recall," he began in a conversational tone, as he strolled in a circle around her, "when I was in the dungeon, I was the one doing the washing while you watched."

She looked over her shoulder at him. "You forget

the fact that you took delight in stripping before me in an unwelcome manner, forcing me to view what should be done alone. And once again, today you betray your vulgar sensibilities by invading a lady's privacy. Do not think you can blackmail me into returning your attentions. I would rot in the dungeon first."

He was getting too close to her as he moved about her. She could feel the brush of his upper arm against her shoulder, the lower edge of his tunic against the cloth that covered her.

"Get away from me," she said in a soft, deadly voice, trying to keep from pleading. "If you think my lack of garments will keep me from throwing you out on your ass in disgrace, then—"

"And then everyone will know that we were alone together. Would you be trying to force me into marriage?"

"I would not marry you if you were—"

"You mistake my intentions, Diana," he interrupted mildly, coming to a stop before her. "I watched you battle men today, and I was quite impressed with your skill. Yet such training must take a toll on a woman's delicate skin, and I can now see that it has."

She gave a deep sigh as she restrained her temper, loosening the cloth too much at her breasts. She was forced tighten it again, and it felt like too revealing of a movement. "What are you talking about, Bannaster?"

He touched her shoulder with one finger, and she almost hit him to counter the way her skin seemed to tingle. But then she realized he was tracing a faint scar.

"How did you do this?" he asked.

She twitched her shoulder away and stepped out of the basin. Though her wet feet stood on the carpet, the cold made gooseflesh rise. She knew Bannaster did not miss the way her nipples now tightened against the cloth, but she would not let herself turn away from him. She had to meet an enemy face on.

Though she did not owe him an answer, she would rather keep him focused on her very unfeminine skills. "A dagger slipped between the plates of my armor."

If he decided to press their intimacy further, she could not have him thrown out, not with what he knew about her. It would be a challenge to distract and defeat him every time they were alone.

And she rose to every challenge, especially with him. She did not want to think what that said about her.

"It does not look like they burned the wound closed," he said, still staring at her shoulder.

Or from so close, was he able to look down on her breasts?

"My mother stitched it."

"I imagine she never thought she'd be healing her daughter from such a wound."

She caught herself before she could flinch. Though her mother had obeyed her husband's word, Diana had known her mother disapproved and worried for her. What would she say now? Sometimes the ache of her absence struck Diana so forcefully, it almost took her breath.

She was relieved when Bannaster started to circle her again.

"Leave now, Bannaster, so that I can dress."

"I am not stopping you."

The amusement in his voice grated on her.

"I am only looking at the marks on your body. There is a terrible bruise on the back of your arm."

It was a strain to ignore his brief touch on the bruise. "Courtesy of your man, Talbot," she said dryly.

"Ah, he has done much the same to me. But surely your brother must have inflicted worse, when you were first allowed on the tiltyard."

She briefly closed her eyes. He was not content to disturb her every sense with his nearness, he wanted to get into her mind, too.

"Cicely surely spoke of this already," she said. "She would not be able to resist telling you about how I came to behave like a man."

"That you and Winslow did not get along? That your father used you to punish your brother? Aye, she told me."

She felt his fingertips low on her calf, and she

was so surprised she could not hide her gasp. But she would not flee. She kicked back, but he eluded her.

"It little mattered to me what my father's motives were," she said between gritted teeth. "And Archie was a fool for thinking my goals had anything to do with him. I needed to test myself, to learn what I wanted. But Archie could not see that, because he always thought his needs were all that mattered."

"Were not your needs all that mattered to you?"

She glared at him. "I did not deliberately hurt others to achieve them. Did you not once share my goals? And did not your brother's suffering free you to pursue them?"

He was facing her now, studying her impassively. "Your mother wasn't hurt by your unladylike dreams, Diana?"

She flinched. "And your brother's death conveniently freed you to pursue yours."

They stared hotly into each other's eyes, and Diana, stunned, could not imagine what had gotten into her. Her killing of his brother had freed him from his brother's yoke. How could she taunt him with the suspicions of being a murderer that he'd had to live with these last six years? But he made her lose control, forget everything but sparring with him.

Then he was circling her again, coming to stand

behind her. "I do not mean to fight with you like this. I simply was curious about what marks the life you've chosen have left on your body."

"I care not what a man thinks of me."

"Not even a man who might be your husband?"

She frowned at him over her shoulder. "You do not want to marry me."

"I did not mean myself, of course," he said with great innocence, touching his chest in self-deprecation. "But someday, you will reveal yourself to your husband."

She deliberately faced forward again, as if his presence behind her back did not threaten her. "I do not plan to marry, but if I did, the man I chose would accept me as I am."

"You do not plan to marry?"

She could hear the real surprise in his voice, and she realized she had betrayed too much. He would wonder at her goals, and she could not have him discovering whom she worked for.

"Then it is the nunnery for you?" he asked, laughter in his voice. "Nay, wait, you must mean to spend your days as a maiden aunt in the home of your sister."

Her body trembled with anger, her fists clenched.

"There is another wound here," he said in a deep voice, his breath on the back of her neck, where several curls fell from her upswept hair.

His fingers ran along the top edge of the cloth, then dipped beneath. Diana lost her control and swung her elbow back, but this time he must have expected her reaction, for he caught her elbow, swung her about and pinned her arms behind her. She was pressed hard to his chest, and she realized as she struggled that the cloth about her body had come loose. He held her too close for it to fall, but her right breast was naked, pressed flat against the fine garments covering his chest.

For a silent moment, the only sound was their harsh breathing as they struggled against each other. When she tried to kick him, he lifted her off the ground so that her legs swung uselessly, her blows glancing off him rather than hurting him. He held her arms on just this side of pain, and to her shock, he began to bend her ever so slowly backward, forcing her head to drop back, revealing the vulnerable length of her neck, her bare shoulders—and her naked breast.

She ceased her useless struggles. The air was cool on her damp flesh. She couldn't take a deep enough breath, couldn't scream, couldn't do anything but submit. And it was so wildly exciting that she was overwhelmed, overcome, caught in the raw feelings that only he had ever brought out of her.

She felt his hot breath only a moment before he licked a wet path across her nipple. The shock of pleasure made her jerk in his arms, sending mild pain through her shoulders, and a deeper, fiery arrow into her belly, where their hips were so tight together they could have been mated.

"Bannaster—" she said on a gasp.

She didn't know what she meant to say, but nothing else emerged, for he took her nipple deep into his mouth and suckled her. She moaned and shuddered and was lost.

Chapter 10

She tasted like heaven, smelled like rose petals from the soap she must have used. Tom's need for her burned in him, making him forget everything but the feel of her in his arms, the way she shuddered as he held her off the ground and pleasured her breast. She no longer fought him, so he released her arms so that he could take her hips and press himself between her thighs. At last he felt her arms enclose his shoulders, her hands slide into his hair. With incredible strength, her legs wrapped around his hips, and she surged against him now, reaching for the pleasure he could give her. He groaned against her, slid his lips across to her other breast, using his teeth to pull the cloth away. He worshiped her with his mouth, tongued the hard points of her nipples. Her soft cries were almost his undoing. His palms cupped her bare ass, his fingers so close to the hot, moist center of her. He wanted to rip the clothes from his body, leaving nothing between them.

"Is this how it will be?" she suddenly gasped.

When she pulled herself upright, her legs still clasped about his waist, he lifted his head, met the wild storm in her eyes, let his open mouth brush hers.

"This passion?" he said hoarsely. "Aye, do not deny that you have felt it from the beginning."

When he kissed her, she spoke against his lips. "But is this true passion, when you have to force it from me, when I am not granting you the gift of my willingness?"

He lifted his head and looked down at her, feeling anger mix with desire. "Regardless of how this started, you are clutching me now."

He didn't like the thread of insistence in his own voice, as if he had to convince himself. This was not how he wanted things between them. When she unclasped her legs, he let them slide down his, knowing she felt the shudder he could not control. She turned away from him, and he had the brief, intoxicating glimpse of her bare back, so strong and lean, before she pulled the linen cloth higher and secured it about herself.

"You know this will go on between us," he said in a low voice. "I gave the morning to Cicely. After dinner, it will be your turn to spend time with me."

Her eyes took on a furious glint.

"Your people will want to know that I took turns courting both sisters, especially you, their favorite."

"I am not their favorite. They have only known me a few years, but I treat them with respect. Are you capable of such a thing? Or will it be Cicely's turn next to feel the pressure as you attempt to seduce her?"

"I will not—"

"Let me give you fair warning. Where she is concerned, your clumsy intentions will be met with enthusiasm regardless."

"Clumsy!" He knew she only provoked him, yet he seemed to have no control over any of his emotions when he was with her.

"What you start with Cicely, she will insist you finish. You know that she desperately wants a husband and will take any man."

He gave a harsh laugh. "I will not attempt to seduce your sister, never fear. You alone hold that place for me. She I am thinking about marrying, so I will court her as a tender maiden should be courted."

He saw the way she winced, and even now, knowing he might be hurting her, he could not relent.

"But you don't want what a normal woman wants, do you, Diana?"

"Leave here at once."

Her low voice was full of such fury, that he felt himself tense, waiting for an attack.

The door suddenly opened and a red-haired woman entered, closing the door behind her and then freezing with her mouth agape. Tom paid no heed to how they looked: Diana's spare covering, his own rumpled garments. He had recognized the maidservant immediately.

"So you are your mistress's loyal servant," he said with sarcasm, "the one who will offer herself to unsuspecting men and drug them if her mistress decrees it."

The girl pressed herself against the wall as if he would attack her, and Tom finally understood that he was losing control. He turned from them both and ran a hand through his hair, not recognizing himself. It was as if he was that pathetic boy again, the one who wanted more than he knew he could ever have.

"Mary only obeyed me," Diana said, each word spoken with emphasis. "Do not punish her."

He turned back to them. "Mary, my argument is not with you. You have nothing to fear from me—but your mistress, ah, that is another matter."

He gave Diana a last, knowing look and walked from the chamber.

Diana barely felt Mary's trembling arms as they closed about her.

"Oh, mistress, what did he do to you? How will we ever sort this out?"

Diana patted the woman's back and then stepped away, hugging herself against the cold that she'd forgotten to feel when she was held

in Bannaster's arms. She was unsteady, full of a
yearning she'd never felt before, as if she wanted
something that only he could give her.

"It is all my fault for not knocking," Mary continued, as she moved about the chamber, hanging a small cauldron over the fire to reheat water,
then folding the bathing linen with trembling
hands. "Ye could have sent me away, and he never
would have seen me. But then you—then he—oh,
mistress, what if he remembers me from Castle
Bannaster? He'll realize ye were there, that ye're
connected to his past."

"I saw his expression, Mary," Diana said sooth-
ingly. "He only remembers you from the tavern.
Did you not say that he was seldom at Castle
Bannaster, that he spent most of his time studying with the priest?"

Mary nodded, her gaze unfocused, as if she
saw the past. "I well remember what his brother
liked to do to women. Did Lord Bannaster . . ."
Her voice trailed off as her tears started.

Immediately, Diana put an arm around her,
knowing that although Mary had rebuilt her life
after the late viscount's abuse of her, in some
ways she would always remember. "Nay, Mary,
you mustn't remember those dreadful times.
This Lord Bannaster is not like his brother. But
he yet fears his nature, and I can use that to
control him."

"Control him?"

"I must, surely you see that? At any moment he could reveal what I did to him, and yet he's decided to find a different punishment for me."

Mary glanced too quickly at the cloth covering Diana's body. "Punishment? But I thought ye said—I mean, the way he looks at you when he thinks no one can see him—"

With a last pat of her shoulder, Diana turned away so that Mary couldn't see her confusion. Stepping back into the basin, she used the cold facecloth to scrub the mud at her ankles. "I do not think he intends to punish me in the way his brother would have. He hasn't decided what he means to do. He's trying to discover why I imprisoned him. Now that he's living among us, it is too easy for him to see my relationship with Cicely. He now knows that safeguarding her could not be my only motivation. I have to be so careful, Mary."

"Aye, ye do, mistress," Mary said soberly, bringing her the hot water. "For I think ye might be feelin' things for him, though ye do not want to."

Diana rinsed the cloth, grateful for the heat. "Oh, Mary, I do not know what is the matter with me."

"Ye can resist him, mistress, though it won't be easy. He is a handsome man, but ye'll get over his looks in the end."

As if his looks even seemed to matter, Diana

thought despondently. Nay, everything about him called to her, but she could not tell that to Mary. She only heaved a sigh and nodded, trying to take her maid's kindness to heart.

"You need not fear him, Mary," Diana said a little while later, as the maid was helping her dress. "'Tis me he rightly blames for his imprisonment."

"I can see that, mistress, and I thank you for your kindness. But I do not want to leave you to fend him off alone."

"I am strong enough for it," Diana said, tightening the girdle at her waist. She slid her dagger home, out of sight, but where she could feel the reassurance of it. "And I will feel better knowing that I don't have to worry for you."

"Very well, mistress," Mary said.

Diana could see the doubt in her eyes, but there was nothing else to be done. Thomas Bannaster was her problem, and no one else's.

She wondered what he had planned for the afternoon, and how she might be able to thwart him.

Yet . . . she could not ignore him, could she? Not with the promise of shelter within the League if she succeeded in her mission. Mayhap she already knew enough to send them the first news of him. She would begin composing a missive that night.

But what would she tell them? That even though Bannaster stalked her, determined to discover her secrets and punish her, she could not stop thinking about his body, his mouth on her breasts, the way her pleasure had risen higher and higher with his hips between hers? Now she was left aching and angry and bleak, worried how she'd respond the next time they were alone.

But she would find *something* to write about.

Late that morning, Tom was welcomed to the tiltyard enthusiastically by his three men-at-arms, and cautiously by the Winslow soldiers. But Tom had spent his adulthood proving himself, and he knew he was capable of it. He had changed into rough clothing—still stained with the dirt of the dungeon—and they found him a hauberk to protect his torso. With a sword in his hand, he felt better, more in control of himself. And what helped his eventual acceptance was that the Kirkby soldiers didn't know him as a former novice priest, only as a nobleman.

After an hour of using his muscles, proving to himself that he was still the man he'd fought so hard to be, he recognized that he was trying to forget some of what had happened in Diana's bedchamber.

He had gone there with the intention of keeping her off balance, so she'd always wonder what he was doing, when he might appear. After all, she was his link to uncovering if the League's presence could be found at Kirkby Keep.

But Diana the warrior had been transformed into Diana the woman, with alluring curves and smooth, damp skin beneath only the thinnest cloth.

Yet he'd seen the scars and bruises of training.

As Tom faced Talbot on foot, swords clashing, his mind was foolishly too far away.

Why did she train with the men? What purpose could it serve? It would not help her find a husband. His own training helped him lead his men and prepared him to defend what was his, whether it be country or castle. But Diana had soldiers to serve her. And although she was the mistress of Kirkby Keep, military skills were not necessary.

He'd gone to her bedchamber with questions, with a purpose—and that had all fallen apart. He'd been unable to control his need to touch her, to provoke her. And when she'd tried to defend herself, he'd used force to have what he wanted, the taste of her on his lips, her body in his arms, her surrender. It made him feel ill. He took out his frustration on Talbot, swinging and slashing with his dulled sword, driving the man back until Talbot stumbled and fell.

Tom reached down and Talbot clasped his hand, coming to his feet.

Talbot shook his head, pointing his sword into the ground and leaning on it. "Your illness has not weakened you, my lord," he said, his breath coming hard.

Tom thought of the hours in the dungeon spent exercising to keep up his strength. "Glad I am to hear it."

And thoughts of the dungeon took him back to his concerns about Diana. He could not behave in such a way again. He would learn nothing if she were constantly wary of him. Oh, he still planned to seduce her, since he already knew she had a weakness for him. She would fall under his spell without force, and he would discover the truth about her connection to a Bladesman.

Her cloak pulled tight around her against the cold breeze, Diana watched Bannaster sword fight from behind a corner of the stables. The first time she'd ever seen him, he'd been a pale, quiet boy with the higher calling to God that had set him apart from his own people. Now with a sword he fought with an intelligence and skill that allowed him to defeat larger, heavier opponents.

Leading men in battle was what he'd been meant to do, she realized. He was able to outthink an opponent, anticipate the next move, and counter its effectiveness. And he had learned to do all of this in only a few years, instead of the lifetime it had taken most men.

She could not help but admire him, she reluctantly admitted to herself. He'd accomplished his transformation from novice priest to viscount, all while under suspicion of being a murderer. Nothing had been able to stop him.

That was something she could tell the League, that he had perseverance and dedication. But of course, he'd displayed that quite recently, when he'd chosen to marry a woman who didn't want him. What good was perseverance if he used it for the wrong purpose?

As the midday meal approached, they finished their training, and in the usual custom of filthy men, they began to remove their outer garments to wash. They stripped to their breeches, and if it were summer, they would have doused themselves with buckets of water. But in winter, they only hastily scrubbed themselves of sweat and dirt. Diana told herself to leave, but she could not stop watching Bannaster. It wasn't as if she hadn't seen his nearly nude body before. He'd made sure to display it to her when he'd washed in the dungeon. And only just this morn, she could have sworn he would have removed all his garments if she had asked him to.

She'd been held in those well-muscled arms, had wrapped herself about him with desperation, and had rubbed herself against him with no shame.

God above, she thought, briefly closing her eyes in pain. Give her strength to finish this assignment without doing something foolish.

She opened her eyes again, and experienced

a sudden chill. Bannaster had turned his back, revealing a mass of old scars, ruthless lash marks that had her own men glancing at his healed wounds in surprise before quickly looking away.

Who had dared to so viciously punish the son of a viscount? The blood loss must have been staggering, and men often died before recovering from such trauma. But Bannaster still had an easy grin for any man he talked to, as if his past no longer had any affect on him.

At dinner, Bannaster once again maneuvered to sit between Diana and Cicely. Diana decided to speak to her sister later, using his behavior as proof that he was not serious about Cicely, that he would not make a good husband. For after all, why would he sit beside Diana except to cause trouble?

But of course, Cicely wouldn't take it that way. She'd simply think she had to try even harder to win the viscount, setting herself up against Diana any way she could. Diana would have to think of other ways to prove that Bannaster was unworthy.

But it was hard to at dinner, where he regaled them with tales of life at court and had Cicely giggling or gasping with delight. Even Diana had to fight to remain impassive rather than smile.

How could she want to smile at him, when she

still could not forget what he'd deliberately made her feel just that morn? And did he do that to any woman he fancied? She did not like to think about that, for jealousy was not something she'd ever attributed to herself.

"Lord Bannaster," Cicely finally said, "have you given thought to your plans for the afternoon? Tomorrow morn I imagine you'll want to accompany the men on the hunt for our Christmas feast, but today . . ." She trailed off, batting her eyelashes at him, obviously hoping for an invitation to share his company.

"I do have something in mind, Mistress Cicely," he said, sliding his chair back a bit to include both women.

Diana stiffened with wariness.

To Cicely, he said, "I feel it is only fair that since I spent the morn in your company"—he turned to Diana—"that now I should spend equal time with your sister."

Diana saw Cicely's eyes widen, then narrow into angry slits behind Bannaster's back.

"That is not necessary, my lord," Diana said, imagining the next step in his punishment of her. "I have much to do in anticipation of Christmas."

Cicely opened her mouth, but Bannaster spoke first.

"Which is why you need time away to relax. Remember, the king asked me to get to know you both."

"I would not want you to do something only because you've been pressured to," Diana said between gritted teeth.

Cicely's gave a smile, as if she thought their disagreement could only work in her favor.

"Nonsense. Mistress Cicely has done an excellent job of showing me the keep. You could guide me through the surrounding grounds. And if you feel the need to work," he added when she started to respond, "we can search for holly and mistletoe to decorate the great hall."

At the word "mistletoe," Diana thought Cicely's red face would explode.

"The huntsman has asked me to look at the tree he's chosen for the Yule log," Diana quickly said. "You could accompany me there if you wish." He would have no chance to be alone with her, something that would satisfy both her—and her sister.

He grinned. "A perfect solution." Then he turned back to Cicely and soothed her ruffled feathers by giving her all of his attention.

Hunting for mistletoe indeed, Diana thought, trying to hide her scowl.

Chapter 11

Tom would have preferred to have Diana all to himself, but he knew that their afternoon together was partly for the benefit of her people, who thought he was courting both sisters. So they set off accompanied by the huntsman and his apprentice, who rode before them on the path into the woodland that rose upward on a long slow slope toward the distant heights of the moors.

Diana remained silent, riding astride on her gelding as a man would. Her skirts slid high enough to reveal almost the top of her boots, but she seemed unconcerned. And Tom found himself looking at her legs far too often, hoping to see more.

As if he hadn't seen much more, just that morning.

His uneasiness intensified. She had spoken little to him since then, and he understood why. But he didn't know how to broach the subject of their encounter, how to show her that he had not meant to use force with her.

That he wasn't his brother.

"This is a fine horse," he said nonchalantly, squinting up at the sun through the bare branches of the trees overhead.

"Aye."

He glanced at her, but she didn't look his way.

"I had a horse when I journeyed here," he said, aware of the two men riding not far in front of them. "I know not what happened to it after my *fever* set in."

At last she met his eyes, and the intelligence there still struck him far too pleasurably.

She said, "Perhaps a kind farmer found it and stabled it with his own until the owner could be found."

He gave her a half-smile, understanding that she'd had his horse taken care of. She could hardly stable it with her own grooms, who would ask awkward questions. "That is a thought. Perhaps I can look for it after the holiday."

She only nodded and faced forward again.

The sun was warm enough that Diana was not wearing her hood. She wore her hair pulled back with a ribbon, and the blond curls blew gently in the breeze. She constantly drew his attention, and the more he resisted, the harder it became to do anything else but look at her, at her pure profile, at the way her eyes concentrated on the Pennines so far ahead.

The terrain sloped ever upward, with tumbles of rocks breaking up the path. The horses had to pick their way slowly, and Tom maneuvered it so that the two of them fell behind, out of earshot.

"Mistress Diana," he said, speaking more formally than he'd intended.

Her glance was sharp. "We should ride faster."

"Give me a moment." He regarded her soberly. "This morn I overstepped the bounds of a gentleman. I want you to know that I will not force my attentions on you like that again, regardless of our adversarial positions."

She was studying him far too closely now. "You will not force your attentions on me 'like that'?" she echoed. "What does that mean?"

"Whatever you have done to me, you did not deserve to be forced into a romantic encounter."

"Romantic?" she said with sarcasm. "I found no romance in having my arms twisted behind my back."

He felt a flare of anger. "It is difficult to treat you as other ladies, when you have not behaved as one toward me."

She opened her mouth, but he didn't let her speak.

"But I will not use the fact that you held me prisoner as an excuse for my behavior. Mistake me not—I still plan to seduce you."

Her mouth briefly fell open before she mastered herself.

"But when I'm done," he continued, "you will want me as I want you—freely, and without force. And you'll find pleasure in my bed the likes of which you've never known."

He saw her inhale, but that was the only sign that she might be struggling to master her temper.

"You are a strange man, Bannaster," she finally said in a low voice. "You take what you want, and then you apologize. Does your conscience bother you from past transgressions?"

He ground his teeth together. "I have learned from them, aye, just as all of us learn from our mistakes."

"Or is it not just your conscience, but your bloodline that worries you?"

He narrowed his eyes. "Say what you mean."

"Even here in the north, we have heard tales of your brother. It is one of the reasons I do not wish Cicely to marry you, and you continue to prove my point. Why should I trust that you can withhold your temper, your desires, when your brother couldn't? After all, you're telling me that part of my punishment will be you attempting to seduce me."

Diana knew she dared much, broaching the subject of the late viscount so soon after Bannaster had seen Mary. But here was something the

League would want to know about him, and she had to risk her questions.

Although she *had* been stunned at his apology. It showed that he had a conscience, at least. She hadn't been expecting it, had tried to keep abreast with her men, in case Bannaster tried to separate her from her guard. She'd been almost frightened to be away from Kirkby Keep with him. If only she knew his plans for her—besides seduction. How much longer could she keep waiting for him to denounce her?

"My brother never even attempted to control his basest impulses," Bannaster finally said, obviously having to grind the words out. "It took me a long time to recognize the kind of man he was, to try to make right the things he'd done wrong. When I was a novice, I always hoped that if I prayed hard enough, God might change him. But like in so many other things, my prayers went unanswered. And after his death, there was yet so much damage to the women of Castle Bannaster."

"Someone answered your prayers as far as your brother was concerned," she said dryly.

"Not God." He glanced at her. "So you don't think it was I who killed him?"

She shrugged, conscious of being on dangerous ground. Sometimes she thought she felt guilty for not feeling guilty enough for her part in the viscount's death. She'd killed a man, after all, though it had been to defend herself. But it was this Lord Bannaster who'd borne everyone's suspicions for what she'd done.

For several minutes, she concentrated on ducking beneath the branches of low-growing trees. She gathered her cloak closer to her neck, for within the woods there was little of the sun's penetration. She didn't want to talk about the viscount's death, but recognized that she must, to allay his suspicions.

"You do not seem like a murderer," she said. "How did you make right what he'd done to his serving women?"

He did not meet her eyes, looking forward to avoid the hazards of the narrow trail. His cloak, lined with fur, streamed back over his broad shoulders, and his cap was pulled low across his brow.

"There were several women with bastard children," he said at last. "I made sure that they would never want, that . . . the children would be protected for life."

Does he think of them as his nephews and nieces? she wondered. Noblemen had bastard children all the time, only some of which were recognized.

"I also made it known that the women he'd hurt would have a place at Castle Bannaster for life," he continued. "But several wanted to leave the ugly memories behind, and I found employment for them at other properties of mine, or at neighboring manors."

"Are you looking for applause or approval?" she asked.

He seemed surprised. "Nay, 'tis no one's business but my own. I merely answer your questions."

"Are you using your kind treatment of those women to prove yourself a fit husband for Cicely, while at the same time admitting you intend to pursue me for illicit reasons?"

His smile was grim. "You give no quarter, Diana, do you?"

"I have none to give. I told you I would protect my sister, and though you may not be a murderer, and you may have done well by the women your brother harmed, I cannot approve of what you're doing here."

"I am not married or betrothed to your sister. What I do before then matters not."

"You have much to learn about women, Bannaster. But then you have only had a few years' experience with the female sex. Sometimes it shows." She tapped her horse's flanks with her heels and rode ahead, leaving him to the tail of their small procession.

The hillside leveled off, and the woods became darker, the oak trees larger and older. The huntsman began to point out trees for her inspection, and although she would have preferred concentrating on her worries about Bannaster, she knew her duty.

And it was almost Christmas, after all.

At last they all settled on an oak tree growing on relatively flat ground, with ample room about it for the huntsman and his apprentice to stand while they cut. The huntsman brought forth a long saw, with wooden handles on each end, that had been well wrapped when it hung from his saddle.

"You will cut it now, though you have few men?" Bannaster asked in obvious surprise.

The young apprentice, Peter, only a boy on the cusp of manhood, sniggered.

The huntsman arched a brow, and the boy looked suitably cowed.

Diana smiled. "Peter, why do you laugh?"

He must have little fear of his master, for the boy grinned. "He likes to prove his might in fellin' a big tree, mistress."

The huntsman only shook his head as he removed his cloak. "Someone has to cut it, mistress, so the boy might as well learn a lesson. I will send men and oxen to drag it back to Kirkby Keep."

Diana glanced at Bannaster, who watched with interest as the huntsman and his apprentice took the saw between them, stationed themselves on either side of the massive trunk, and began to saw, each pulling the blade toward them with a powerful burst of motion. Though the boy was not his master's equal, Diana was impressed at his determination.

At last Peter's energy seemed to fade, and the huntsman called a rest.

Bannaster approached them. "May I take the boy's place? Unless of course you, too, need to rest."

The huntsman eyed him quite boldly, then at last gave a nod. "If you're up to it, milord."

It was clear he did not believe a nobleman could match a simple workman's stamina. While Peter brushed snow off a flat rock and sank on it to drink from his horn, Bannaster removed his cloak. He and the huntsman took up the rhythm of the saw. The rough sound echoed in the stillness of the forest, along with the heavy breathing of the men. Diana kept waiting for one of them to signal a rest, but neither did.

She smiled at Peter, asked him about his reading lessons with a widow in the village, but never took her eyes off the men. Well, she could not lie to herself—she was watching Bannaster. The rhythm of his body was hypnotic, his legs spread in a wide stance, his shoulders moving back and forth as he drew the saw toward him, and then pushed it away. Sweat ran down his face, but he paid it no heed, just watched the saw's motion. At last she sat down beside Peter, who only grinned at her.

Eventually she saw the huntsman's legs begin to tremble, and it wasn't long before he called, "Hold."

Both men straightened slowly, stiffly, then exchanged weary grins.

"Shall I replace his lordship, master?" Peter called.

At that, the men chuckled.

"Nay, Peter," said the huntsman, "give me a moment to rest."

Diana tried to feign indifference as Bannaster removed his tunic, revealing his shirt plastered to his damp skin. It hung low over his hips, where his breeches gave his lower body warmth against the cold. But to her unease, he took Peter's place on the rock at her side and leaned back on his elbows. His chest heaved with his breathing, and she thought heat rose in waves from his body.

Silently, they both watched the huntsman, who stood looking at the deep gash they'd put in the tree. It was halfway through the trunk, but they still had far to go before the tree would fall.

"Peter," Bannaster called, "would you fetch my drinking horn?"

The boy detached it from his saddle, and brought it with a shy grin.

Diana glanced at Bannaster, who accepted it even as he ruffled the boy's hair. She didn't want to notice how he pulled out the stopper and guzzled with great thirst. She watched the movement of his throat; even saw the trail of a drop of ale where it slid down the muscles of his neck to be lost in his neckline. When he looked at her, she turned away.

"Come, Peter," called the huntsman, who lifted the saw with his apprentice.

When they were out of hearing, Bannaster said with faint sarcasm, "You do not wish to take a turn? To prove yourself?"

She frowned disdainfully. "I have no need to prove myself, unlike some people."

He chuckled and then drank some more. "I could not watch those two do all the work."

He eyed her, and she didn't like his grin.

"Regardless of your work on the tiltyard," he said casually, "you can be quite feminine when you want to be."

She sniffed. "I imagine you are not terribly choosy when it comes to such things."

His brows rose. "Are you equating yourself with just any woman, even a doxy on a London wharf? And I'm supposed to be attracted to anything in skirts? Not very flattering."

"I did not say all that." She spoke between gritted teeth. "And you were the one who not an hour ago said it was difficult to treat me as a lady."

"I wonder why," he murmured sarcastically, before rising to his feet. "I can take another turn," he called to the huntsman.

Diana was left to fume. Why did she keep baiting him, or responding in kind to his remarks? He held her fate in his hands.

It wasn't long before the trunk of the tree gave a

mighty crack, and Bannaster pulled Peter back as it began to fall away from them, tearing down limbs from other trees as it passed. The boy grinned up at him, and they shook hands in satisfaction.

Diana knew that this tree would easily burn throughout the twelve days of Christmas. And hopefully, during that time, she would understand Bannaster, complete her mission, and send him on his way without a wife—or a mistress.

And convince him to bury her secrets. But to do that, she had to know where she stood with him. She could no longer act the coward and wait for his revenge.

After supper that night, instead of sedate board games and conversation, Diana had engaged the services of minstrels come to play while the great hall was decorated for Christmas. Villagers and farmers crowded the hall to share their evening meal, glancing with interest between Lord Bannaster in his London finery and Cicely wearing her own lovely wardrobe. Diana wore her usual somber colors, having no one she wanted to impress.

And wishing to dissuade one man's interest.

How dare he claim he would seduce her and that she would succumb quite willingly! And then in the next breath, proclaim his intention to keep company with Cicely as well! At least he had said he would not attempt to seduce her, which would surely lead to a marriage, if her sister had any say in it.

She glanced over at Bannaster where he stood beside her sister, leaning down to listen to something Cicely was saying over the sound of the minstrels who launched their first merry song, with pipe and harp and tambourine.

Knowing Cicely, she might very well be the aggressor in a seduction. As far as Diana knew, Cicely was yet a virgin, but her sister was already thinking of Bannaster as her last chance for the right marriage. What would she do out of desperation?

Nay, Diana was no longer going to wait. She would discover his plans. She only had this last evening to get through.

Servants and villagers began to put up ladders, decorating the mantel and tapestries and staircase balustrades with holly and ivy. Diana looked at the happy faces and tried to remember what it was like to enjoy the innocence and peace of the season, but her worries and concerns were too much a part of her this year. She was drawn from her reverie by the sight of her maidservant, Mary, standing in the arched entrance to the kitchen corridor, her face full of worry.

Diana approached and smiled, asking a question whose answer she already anticipated. "This is everyone's favorite time of the year. Why do you not participate?"

"Mistress, his lordship recognized me from his kidnapping," Mary said softly, as if Bannaster could overhear her over the noise of cheerful voices and Christmas music. "I wish not to prod his memory further."

"And Joan? What is her excuse?"

"She will remain in the kitchens when his lordship is here, mistress. If he sees us both . . . if he remembers us together at Castle Bannaster . . ."

When she trailed off, Diana nodded, her own unease a cloud over the holiday. "I understand. I wish it were not necessary. This is a season for joy, after all."

"Mistress, I will feel joyful when he is gone," she said meaningfully.

"And I, too."

"How was your afternoon of . . . courtship?"

Diana gave her a narrow-eyed glance, but Mary was not teasing her. "He apologized and said that our encounter this morn would not happen again."

"Did he really?" Mary said with hope.

Diana had not meant to say more, but Mary was the one person she'd always told the truth to—as well as her fears. "But he said . . . he said that he would still try to . . . persuade me."

"Into marriage?" Mary said, aghast.

Diana only shook her head.

"Oh." The maidservant frowned. "That is the way of it then. He desires you."

"And I know not why, after what I've done to him," Diana said softly. "But . . . I fear he means it as a punishment."

Mary glanced at her in surprise. "Ye know not why, mistress? Ye're a lovely woman, for one."

Diana rolled her eyes.

"Ye have not your sister's classic beauty, but there is great attraction in creamy skin, handsome features, and intelligent eyes. Ye've got all that and more. A man will often forget his anger if he can have the one who's wronged him quite willingly returnin' his attentions."

To Diana's surprise, her cheeks felt heated, as if she were actually blushing. "And I'll have to let him try," she whispered. "He . . . can control me, Mary. And you know what my . . . masters have asked."

"Ye do not yet have enough to answer them?"

Diana shook her head, looking around her again just to be certain they were still alone. In front of the hearth, Cicely and Bannaster had begun to dance, their hands linked as they whirled between other couples.

Her sister's happy face made Diana's heart constrict. "I cannot prove that he's changed, that he can be trusted."

"Ye will, mistress, in time."

"And until then, I will have to suffer his presence and fear my fate."

"Is it sufferin' ye feel?" Mary asked softly. "Or

is it anguish, for perhaps he draws ye like no man afore."

Diana hugged herself and leaned her shoulder against the wall. "I hope my worries are obvious to no one but you."

"No one here knows you as well as I."

"No one has cared to," Diana found herself saying.

"Until him," Mary answered, jutting her chin toward Bannaster.

Diana groaned and closed her eyes.

"He comes," Mary hissed.

She was gone when Diana straightened. She met Bannaster's amused gaze and hoped she portrayed indifference. But it was already so difficult. How could her feelings alternate from anger and suspicion to reluctant and frustrated longing? How could just his touch transform her? Yet so many deeds and lies separated them, and she did not wish to overcome them. He would be here for days if not weeks—and then he would leave, perhaps with her sister as his bride.

And Diana would go on alone, with her secret status as a Bladeswoman, which set her apart from other women. If Bannaster left her her freedom.

"Your maid runs from me like a frightened rabbit," he said, a smile tugging on his lips.

No one was near them, though Cicely watched from a distance, her face a pleasant mask, her eyes cold.

"She is afraid of you, even though it is I on whom you concentrate your revenge."

With a sigh, he leaned back against the wall at her side. "You do not dance?"

"What do you want?" Diana demanded.

He took her hand and bent over to kiss it, his lips warm. "You know what I want."

He spoke against her skin, and she thought she felt the touch of his tongue. She pulled her hand away, and he raised laughing eyes to her.

"A dance."

"It is not as if we declared a truce after your apology."

"Nay, but what will your people think, if their noble visitor neglects one sister in favor of the other?"

"That you are not noble, but a conscienceless bounder."

He tsked softly. "I cannot have them think that."

She glanced down at his garments. "You care too much about appearances."

He put a hand to his heart. "A direct hit. You, too, would enjoy fine clothing, if forced to wear a black cassock for many years."

She could not help her curiosity. "When you took the vows of a novice?"

"Even before," he answered. "My parents believed that I should live the life of a priest from an early age, so that I would not regret the lack of luxurious comforts when I had to leave them behind."

"What are you saying?"

He shrugged. "From my earliest memories, I had no carpets to warm my chambers, only a simple blanket on my bare bed, prayer books instead of poetry."

She thought of the book he'd meant for Cicely, that he had yet to present to her. "You are exaggerating."

And although he smiled, she thought with growing horror that he was not.

"You . . . were not treated as a viscount's son?"

"I had his protection," he answered blandly, turning his head to look upon the merriment.

Protection? She'd seen the scars on his back.

He gave a faint smile when a ladder was put up near the hearth to hang mistletoe. "After all, I was to be his family's entrance into the church, where there is much power for a well-connected nobleman."

"But to insist that a child live as a priest . . ."

She thought again of his disfigured back, wondering how old he'd been when it had happened, but could not think how to question him. He'd become the viscount at eighteen, and surely no one had abused him since then. She thought she now understood better his need for fine garments.

He shrugged. "My father insisted I would not

need the friendships or schooling of childhood. My mother went along with his authority."

"Often a mother has no choice," she found herself saying softly.

Bannaster looked at her with interest. She didn't want to sympathize with him, did not want to share a common background. But if this awkward discussion made him confide in her, made him reveal more of himself . . .

"What did your mother do?" he asked in a neutral voice.

"She was good to me," Diana said simply. "It was I who rebelled at what I saw as her too-simple life."

"You are still headstrong, I think, if *my* experience is proof."

She frowned at him uncertainly, and he threw his head back to laugh. She could have winced when this drew Cicely's cool regard once again.

"You sound as if you almost admire me," Diana taunted against her own better judgment.

He snorted. "I admire much about you," he said, boldly looking down her body, "but not the impulsive part of you that led to my imprisonment."

Aye, she had always been impulsive, she thought with regret.

"And your father?" he continued. "Surely you admired him, since he accepted your silly wish to be like a man."

She stiffened. "It is not 'silly' to want to defend

oneself, to improve one's strengths. And he did not give me permission for my own benefit, as I already told you."

"That must have hurt."

She flinched, hating that he was right.

There was an awkward silence between them, as they both watched the minstrels begin a new song. Bannaster suddenly took her hand in the way of friends to lead her forward.

"Dance with me," he said, his smile full of merriment and deviltry.

"You are giving me no choice," she said between lips curved in a false smile. "What will you do if I refuse? Reveal my every secret?"

He took both her hands now, and spun her once, until she was forced to hold tighter lest she fall. His warm hands were hard with calluses.

"Not like this," he said, drawing her closer in the way of the dance, before letting her pull back to arms' length again. "I will use my leverage for a far better reason."

His arm slid about her waist and she had to accept it as they moved in a circle with other dancers. She saw the many approving looks cast her way, and she let herself believe that there were people who cared for her happiness. Would they defend her if they knew how this man threatened her?

And then she saw Cicely standing before the hearth, a tall, earnest knight at her side.

Diana moved through the steps of the dance and found herself seeing Cicely again. She wondered with sudden fear what her sister might do to have whatever she wanted.

To her surprise, she felt Bannaster's lips against her ear as she turned, heard him say, "I know where mistletoe hides in a secret alcove made just for lovers."

She deliberately stepped on his foot and smiled sweetly when he winced. "Then I suggest you go kiss yourself."

Chapter 12

Bannaster's bedchamber flickered with shadows cast by the dying fire's embers when Diana stepped inside and closed the door. She remained frozen, questioning herself once again, then dismissing her fears.

She was done being afraid, of waiting for the worst to happen.

She crept quietly across the floor, knowing how to pause before each step, to test each board for creaking. At first she didn't even realize she was doing it, so ingrained in her were the methods of the League. Halfway across the room, she realized that she had no need for secrecy—she wanted Bannaster awake.

Standing over his bed, she looked down at him. The coverlet and blankets were pulled high around his neck against the winter's cold. She could see the top of his dark head, his smooth forehead—

And his open eyes, glistening in the firelight.

He erupted from the bedclothes, grabbing her by the shoulders and twisting until she lay beneath him, trapped by the blankets caught around her hips, his forearm hard across her upper chest. When she felt the dagger at her throat, she lay still, not even considering moving.

"Who are you," he demanded, "and what—" He broke off, his narrowed eyes going wide. "Diana?"

She sighed with relief as the dagger moved away from her throat. "Aye, 'tis me. Or do men have the same shape as I do?"

He flung the dagger to the floor, but remained above her in the bed, half his face in shadow, the other half lit with firelight. And he was angry. His body held her down, his hands braced on either side of her shoulders as he stared down at her.

"I could have injured you," he said harshly.

"I would not have allowed it."

His eyes briefly closed and he spoke through gritted teeth. "And how would you have stopped me?"

She brought up her knee hard, but deliberately hit his thigh instead of his groin.

He flinched.

"Like that—only with perfect aim. Are you going to let me up and allow me to speak my piece?"

"You're in dark clothing," he said with exasperation, "your hair is covered. I could have hurt you!"

He couldn't seem to get past that, she realized. Frowning, she responded, "I did not want anyone seeing me come here. I did not mean to hide myself from you. And why would you care if you hurt me? Now let me up before *I* hurt *you*!"

She saw the change come over his face. One moment, he seemed angry and exasperated; the next passion rose in his hooded eyes. Were fighting and sex the only things men thought about?

"I did not come for *that*!" she said hastily.

"I told you I was going to seduce you, and here you are." His voice was a low rumble. "That was easy."

To her shock, he leaned down and pressed his face into her neck. She turned away and started to squirm in earnest, feeling his open mouth trace a wet path on her skin.

"I need to talk to you!" she cried, pushing up desperately with her hips.

But that only made him moan and press down into her. And there was something about that deep moan that sent shivers down her spine to tingle low in her belly.

"You promised not to force me!"

He moved lower down her body, his cheek coming to rest against her breast, which trembled with her frantic breathing.

He opened his dark eyes and looked at her. "I am not forcing you. But must I stop?"

"Stop!"

With a melodramatic sigh, he rose up on all fours over her. She tried to scramble out from beneath him, but the blankets trapped them together. With much tugging, she was at last able to free herself, but not before she saw that he was completely naked—and aroused.

She threw the blanket over his hips as she practically fell to the floor to escape.

He chuckled. "You did surprise me in my bed."

She groaned and got her feet, trying to banish the image of his nudity from her mind. But all she could think was—was *that* supposed to fit inside a woman?

But not in her—*never* in her.

She turned away. "Clothe yourself. I need to speak with you, and this was the only way to guarantee privacy. Cicely would do anything to interrupt us."

"Unless you plan to take me somewhere, I'm only going back to bed, so I won't don garments I don't need. But I am now covered."

She turned back to face him, and had to lick her suddenly dry lips. He was leaning back amidst cushions piled against the headboard. His upper body was still bare, all hollows and hills of flowing muscle, leading ever downward. A single sheet was swathed low across his hips, and the bulge of his arousal was unmistakable.

For a moment, she couldn't remember what she was going to say.

His grin was full of dark amusement. "Diana?"

Her gaze flew back to his face. How could she allow herself to be so flustered? He would not be the last man to use the threat of sex to intimidate her. He was the enemy, she thought, feeling a welcome calm settle over her. She could do this.

Whatever showed in her expression, it was obvious Bannaster recognized it, for his smile faded on a sigh. "What do you want, Diana?"

"I am tired of playing your games, wondering what your intentions are."

He arched a brow. "I have been perfectly clear about my intentions."

She rolled her eyes. "Not those intentions. You're a man, so I know I can expect no better from you."

"How flattering."

"You have done nothing but taunt me about what I've done to you. So toy with me no longer and be brave enough to tell me what you intend to do about your knowledge of me."

He rested his head back on his bent arm, and she tried to avoid looking at the long line of muscle from his elbow down to his ribs.

"Now you question my bravery?" he mused.

"'Tis a foolish tactic for one who is basically begging."

She put her fists on her hips. "Bannaster, just tell me if you're going to denounce me! I cannot stand the tension any longer. I need to make plans."

"You intend to escape here? To hide?"

Stiffening, she shook her head. "Nay, I cannot do that. I have nowhere to go." Lowering her voice, she said, "But I need to plan the best way to react to my brother's fury."

"Not Cicely's? After all, you did all this to keep me from her, did you not?"

She didn't like the speculative way he looked at her, as if he suspected more.

Quickly, she nodded her agreement. "Aye. She won't understand that I was protecting her."

His expression changed into one of amusement as he gently said, "I already told you my plans— did you not believe me? I'm not going to denounce you, not unless you give me a reason to."

Bewildered, she cried, "I do not understand you! Why are you not furious with me?"

He rose to his feet, letting the sheet fall away. His nudity was beautiful and awesome—and terrifying—as he came toward her.

"I was, but I decided it would be uninteresting to put a woman in a dungeon. I find that I'd rather put my energy toward something more rewarding."

She could not understand him. He backed her against the door, then came up against her, his erection touching her first, making her shiver with strange longings. It nestled hard against her stomach.

Leaning his forehead to hers, he whispered, "I mean to seduce you, to make you my mistress, to show you how I can make you feel."

"And that is a punishment?" she said, bewildered.

But at his triumphant look, she realized she'd said the wrong thing.

With satisfaction evident in his voice, he said, "So my touch is not repugnant to you. But then I knew that, by your every subtle reaction."

She jerked against him when his palm cupped one breast. He kneaded her gently, and she groaned, feeling her body—her very will—slacken.

Diana was trembling against him, and Tom felt a deep satisfaction to know how much he affected her. Her breast was warm and soft in his hand beneath her gown, and he watched her face as he used two fingers to coax her nipple into a hard point. He could still remember her taste in his mouth, smell the elusive fragrance that was her skin. As he looked into her eyes, for once her every expression was transparent to him: confusion and worry—and passion.

Her eyelashes fluttered, hiding and revealing the sparkling gray depths of her eyes. Would he have her now? Would just his declaration of his intentions make her surrender to him?

With his other hand he began to bunch up her skirt at her thigh.

And then she pushed him until he stumbled back. She fumbled for the latch behind her and escaped.

With a sound that was half laugh, half groan, Tom leaned both palms flat against the door and squeezed his eyes shut, mastering himself.

Though he would not seduce her this night, he did not regret telling her part of the truth. He had no intention of announcing to the world what they'd been doing to each other, whether it be imprisonment or foreplay. There would be too many questions he didn't want to answer.

And he didn't need any more notoriety.

He didn't want her in fear of him. Regardless of what she'd done to him, it wouldn't be right to force her out of her home. And he knew by everything he'd seen, that her brother might cut her from his life without thought if she angered him again. Tom wanted the challenge of facing her as an equal, matching his wits to hers, and feeling the satisfaction of besting her.

And he needed to understand her secrets.

At dawn's light, the castle attended early mass. Diana almost dozed through it, for she had had a restless night worrying that Bannaster would try to invade her bedchamber and continue where he'd left off in his seduction.

But instead she'd lain alone in peace and spent much of the night staring into the darkness, thinking of what she wanted to write to the League. But she hadn't begun the missive. Her ears had strained at every creak of the floor in the corridor, and she wouldn't have put it past Bannaster to swing in her window on a rope, just to return the favor.

Once again, he did not attend mass. Diana knew more about him, now, and thought perhaps that he could not thank God for his daily blessings when he felt that God had ignored him for so long. Or was his behavior really just a rebellion against all those years as a novice?

The men who were going on the Christmas hunt were eating heartily when at last Bannaster descended. Diana braced herself against her feelings, but to her surprise, the fear had gone. His revelation had freed her from it, and she could only admit that she was grateful.

But he still inspired so many other conflicting emotions. She would have to learn to master them.

Though she tried to ignore him as he greeted Cicely, she could not help noticing that his garments were simpler, warmer, breeches under a short tunic and shirt. He carried his cloak over his arm, and Cicely took it from him so that he could eat.

What did they talk about? Diana wondered. Surely he did not reveal much of his background to a woman he was courting, at least not in the beginning. Why scare her off? But then, would Cicely even care that he'd been suspected of murder? Probably not. And Diana couldn't imagine telling her sister something she herself was guilty of.

Cicely escorted Bannaster to the head table, saw that he had the best slices of ham and fat wedges of cheese. Cicely deliberately sat between Diana and him, chattering on about their plans to celebrate the beginning of the holiday that night.

"And since it is Christmas Eve," Cicely said at last, "I plan to try something different and accompany you on the hunt, Lord Bannaster."

Diana froze, her spoonful of pottage halfway to her mouth. A drop fell back into the bowl.

Bannaster smiled. "And here I thought I would spend the day pining for the company of the Winslow sisters."

Cicely didn't look at Diana, but Diana saw the stiffening of her back.

Cicely said, "Diana is much too busy today, are you not, sister?" She glanced over her shoulder at Diana, eyes narrowed in warning.

"Aye, the preparations for the feasting will

take much of my time," Diana said. Let them try to use a hunt as an excuse for courtship. Cicely would soon discover that baying dogs, galloping horses, and dying animals left little time for romance.

Cicely grinned at her, then went off to look for her maid to make preparations.

Bannaster slid over to the chair beside Diana. She stiffened, trying to ignore the traitorous way her heartbeat sped up. Was that the heat of his thigh that seemed to burn along the length of hers? And they weren't even touching!

"My thanks for the opportunity to be with your sister." His deep voice was casual and polite.

"You are welcome," she said pleasantly, breaking off a piece of bread and reaching for the crock of butter.

"I am sure she will find the perfect way to be alone with me," he continued thoughtfully. "She's been attempting that more and more."

It seemed that Diana's fears about Cicely's desperation were coming true. Her stomach began to churn with the slowly growing realization that her plans for the day were about to change.

"And I am only a man, after all," he continued with a sigh. "It will be difficult to resist her— especially because of a recent rejection," he added in a whisper. "She and I could practically be betrothed by the time we return."

She glared at him, and he laughed.

"Do you need my protection?" she asked, her quiet tone laced with sarcasm.

He leaned closer, and she stopped breathing as his thigh pressed even harder to hers.

"And you're so very capable of protecting me." His gaze roamed her face and settled on her mouth.

She found herself breathing too quickly, and then the inside of her mouth dried right up, and it took everything in her not to moisten her lips with her tongue.

They were too close together. Anyone could suspect what he was after, what he was trying to do to her. Cicely could return. But Diana didn't move away—couldn't. He slid his thigh gently against hers, back and forth. She felt trapped in the dark daring of his gaze. Beneath the table, his hand smoothed over her knee, and she jerked, breaking the spell. She turned away just in time, for Cicely came sauntering down the staircase, her beautiful green skirt rippling behind her.

"Good news!" Bannaster said when Cicely approached. "I have convinced Mistress Diana to join us. Why should she work hard all day while we enjoy ourselves?"

The trap so neatly ensnared Cicely that she could not refuse without seeming churlish. But when Diana later returned to her chambers to fetch her cloak, Cicely followed and slammed the door behind her. Diana whirled, hand already reaching for her dagger when she saw who it was.

"Cicely, that was unnecessary," she said, taking a deep breath to calm her nerves.

"And you intruding on my morning with Lord Bannaster was unnecessary, too!"

"You know I did not want to accompany you. But Bannaster felt too guilty leaving me here— unlike you, who always looks for an opportunity to saddle me with work."

"You know you are better at it than I!"

"And that's a good enough excuse for your behavior?" Diana demanded.

"You will not change your mind?"

"Do you not think he'd suspect my reasons?"

"I care not!"

To Diana's surprise, Cicely seemed even more overwrought than normal. Her blond curls were falling haphazardly around her splotched face. It was obvious that Bannaster's presence was her most cherished dream, so near she could almost touch it. And Diana felt sorry for all that she had to do to keep Cicely from what she wanted.

"Cicely," she began softly, "you must understand that Bannaster—"

"Do not tell me again that he will not suit me as a husband. You have seen how kind he is, how much he wants me."

Diana felt suddenly cold. "Has he tried—"

"Of course not. He is a gentleman. Just stay out of my way!"

Cicely slammed the door behind her, leaving Diana shocked and saddened.

Chapter 13

Christmas Eve proved colder than the day before. Tom pulled his cloak tighter, looking up at the swiftly moving clouds that mostly hid the sun. Near the castle, they passed goose girls driving geese across the field with cracking whips. Two dozen men—and two women—followed the course of the huntsman leading the way with his pack of hounds into the woodland that skirted the River Swale. Fox and hare were ignored as they searched for deer, though another party concentrated on those smaller animals. A third party had headed north, away from the river, searching for wild boar.

The dirt pathway was narrow, and Tom maneuvered so that the Winslow sisters rode together before him, leaving his man Talbot at his side. Cicely rode sidesaddle, a soft cloak over the gown that was too fine and lovely for a bloody hunt. Diana had changed into her breeches, with a sword in its scabbard hanging from her waist and a crossbow attached to the saddle. Something about this alerted and intrigued Tom, but he couldn't quite place why.

Talbot finally broke the quiet, speaking softly. "I do not envy you, my lord, courting two women in the same household." He gave a visible shudder.

Tom only smiled at him. "But such beauty is worth the effort."

"But only one maiden seems to want your attentions," he said awkwardly.

Tom's smile faded. "And which would that be?"

"Mistress Cicely, of course. Mistress Diana seems . . . cool toward you."

"And you are worried for me, Talbot?" Tom said, grinning.

Talbot's face reddened, but he good-naturedly said, "I know there is no need, my lord. But she is a curious woman. To think she thought to challenge me on the tiltyard."

"She did not defeat you?"

"Of course not!" He shrugged, his expression sheepish. "I simply know not what to make of her. Does she not wish to marry, to have the normal life of a woman?"

Tom looked ahead to Diana, riding so comfortably, with such grace and competence. "I know not what she wants, Talbot. But I find her . . . intriguing, even if she does not find me so." But that was only said for the benefit of Talbot. For Tom knew that Diana was drawn to him, and was fighting it as much as any wild horse resisting the control of a rider.

Suddenly, the baying of the hounds alerted the hunting party. And with a cry, horses were urged into a gallop. Tom watched Cicely look around her in confusion, even guide her horse to the rear, out of the way. But Diana took off, and he followed the party. She rode masterfully between the trees, ducking and swerving, racing wide of the field to herd the deer into the center, where men would be waiting with crossbows.

Two hours later, the party had slaughtered and gutted six deer, and Diana was beginning to let go of her fears that they would be unable to feed all of the expected guests. Surely the other hunting parties had been successful as well.

Hunters were busy lashing the carcasses to several horses brought along for this purpose. One of her men had started a fire so they could warm themselves, and she stood rubbing her gloved hands together near the crackling flames.

If she hadn't chanced to glance downhill, she would never have seen Bannaster and Cicely slip off alone between the trees.

Damn them, Diana thought. She wanted to leave them be, but knew she couldn't. She needed to know if Tom had lied to her about his intentions toward her sister—and needed to protect Cicely from her own folly. She began to work her way to the edges of the men, who'd gathered about to proclaim about the size of the deer antlers and debate the performance of the hounds.

At last she, too, was able to leave the clearing. It wasn't difficult to follow the trail through the snow, and she caught up easily. They had stopped near a small stream, and although they were only talking in low voices, Bannaster was rubbing Cicely's gloved hands between his own. Diana moved quietly through the trees, circling them to get closer, using every technique the League had taught her for avoiding snapping twigs and disappearing between the shadows of the trunks.

At last, Bannaster's voice came to her faintly, as he continued to rub Cicely's hands. "Mistress Cicely, you really should have dressed more warmly."

Between chattering teeth, Cicely said, "The sun was shining when we left. But I forgot how cool the woods can be when the wind blows."

Diana knew it wasn't *that* cold, but Cicely gave a masterful performance of shivering. Bannaster finally put an arm around her shoulders, and Cicely turned into him, lifting her face as if for a kiss.

Here was his chance, Diana thought in that frozen moment. Surely he would prove that he'd lied to Diana, that he would take whatever a willing woman would give.

But he stepped back, and Cicely opened her eyes in surprise.

"Mistress, I cannot take advantage of our time alone," he said in a gentle voice. "I am honor bound to your brother to respect your virtue."

"But surely a kiss—"

"If I allow myself even that, I will want more. You are far too beautiful for a weak man such as myself to resist."

His words seemed to mollify Cicely, and at last they started back to rejoin the party.

He'd kept his word, Diana realized, leaning against the trunk of a tree to hide herself. He could have taken anything he wanted from a desperate Cicely, but he hadn't. Or was Diana praising him too swiftly? Mayhap all he wanted to do was convince Cicely that he would make an honorable husband.

Honorable? Diana thought, leaning her head against the bark and closing her eyes. He'd decided to devote himself to seducing Diana. And she'd welcomed his attentions. Who was honorable here?

But she always knew that although the League's goal was justice for the weak, they'd had to do questionable things to achieve it. She herself had had to kill a man to protect the women of Castle Bannaster.

Her behavior made Bannaster, a man who wanted to satisfy his own pleasures, seem almost harmless.

Tom was shocked when on the way back to the clearing, he realized that someone had been following them. He hadn't even known, hadn't heard a sound, and only found one slim boot print in the snow that was not either his or Cicely's. It could only be Diana's.

When they reached the clearing, she was already there, innocently warming herself near the fire, but he wasn't fooled. There were traces of snow caught in her woolen cloak, which wouldn't be there if she'd remained near the fire.

He ignored Diana, fetching a goblet of warmed wine for Cicely.

How had Diana done it just now and even last night, when he hadn't heard her until she'd stood over his bed? She could have easily killed him! He had always prided himself on his sense of hearing, honed from years of listening for his tutor priest's arrival. Someone had taught Diana rare skills, and they weren't something she could learn on the tiltyard with only her father's permission.

Could Diana be the real connection to the League of the Blade? Tom felt a chill of recognition move through him.

Perhaps she herself was some sort of auxiliary member—or could she be an actual Bladesman?

A Blades*woman?*

Had there ever been one before? After his brush with the League at Castle Alderley earlier in the year, he'd done some investigating of his own, had spoken to men among the king's councillors who considered themselves knowledgeable about the League. None had ever mentioned stories of a woman member.

But had there ever been a woman like Diana Winslow? Had his cousin King Henry known about her when he'd sent Tom to Kirkby Keep?

Nay, but he was getting ahead of himself. No one had ever come up with proof that Tom had murdered his brother. He had thought himself untouchable as the viscount, but perhaps it wasn't so.

He had to discover if Diana really was the first Bladeswoman.

When all the hunting parties returned to the Keep by early afternoon, Diana began to oversee the distribution of the meat to the kitchens. She noticed that Cicely remained beside Bannaster, who was watching the organization solemnly. Diana tried to ignore them both, but at last the servants before her hesitated, looking past her. She turned to find Bannaster right behind her.

"Aye, my lord?" Why was he distracting her?

"Your sister wishes to show me the village, and since it is Christmas Eve, and you have servants to prepare the meal—"

"My lord, I simply cannot," she answered, interrupting him. "As you pointed out, it *is* Christmas Eve. Most of the villagers will be arriving soon for supper."

"But not for several hours yet," he said. "We still have daylight left."

Cicely approached and slid her arm into his. "Lord Bannaster, I told you that my sister is much too busy for such leisurely pursuits. You know she doesn't even believe in enjoying oneself," she added in a low voice that carried well past Diana.

"She is correct," Diana said with a perfunctory smile. "Even on Christmas, food must be prepared." And he'd already said he would not tell her secrets, so she was safe refusing him. It was a good feeling.

"Then we should remain here," Bannaster said to Cicely.

Cicely's leg twitched as if she wanted to stomp it in frustration.

"Mistress Cicely," he assured her, "I would understand if you need to assist your sister."

Diana could not miss the horrified looks of several of the servants. When Cicely was around, the work pace always slowed.

The cook hurried forward. "Mistress Diana, it is Christmas Eve! I have more than enough help. Go and enjoy your young man."

Cicely whirled around and started for the gatehouse, and Diana knew that her sister was trying to suppress her fury. Though Diana did not feel like starting a new argument, she also had pity on the servants.

"Then let us go, Lord Bannaster," she said wearily.

The walk down the sloping, snow-covered lane was filled with an awkward silence. Bannaster asked questions about the countryside and the village, and although Cicely's answers were vague, at least she was speaking. They passed many families who were on their way to the keep, and there was much wishing of good cheer. Diana thought more than one man had already begun to settle into a drunken relaxation.

Just as they reached the outskirts of the village, they heard laughter only a moment before a large clump of snow hit Bannaster in the face. For a long moment, both Diana and Cicely gaped, hearing nothing but the eerie sound of the wind.

From behind the snow-covered well on the village green, they heard laughter quickly muffled. Then calmly, Bannaster began to wipe his face off with his gloved hands.

What would he do? Diana wondered with apprehension. Surely he realized that it was only little children at play. They meant no harm.

But Bannaster had had no childhood to speak of. Did he even know what "play" meant—and how to respond to it?

Cicely picked up her skirts as if to walk forward alone. "How dare those children strike a peer of the realm!"

Before Diana could even move, Bannaster caught Cicely's arm and put a finger to his lips. After glancing at the well, from behind which no one had yet emerged, he bent over and gathered up a large amount of snow. Wearing a grin, he tiptoed forward—which was surprisingly grace-ful for such a big man—and with a loud "Aha!" jumped behind the well and dumped snow on his assailants.

Two little boys shrieked and ran from him, shaking clumps of snow from their hair as they went. While Cicely seemed stunned, Bannaster only laughed. His face was still damp and red from the snow, but his eyes were so merry that Diana felt a tug of envy—and then admiration. After how he'd grown up, he could still understand—and participate—in the merriment of children.

"You must be freezing, my lord," Cicely said awkwardly. "If you need to return . . ."

But he was ignoring her, gathering up more snow.

Cicely sighed with frustration. "Really, you cannot possibly catch those children."

And then he dumped his snow on Cicely's head. Diana could only gasp—and then begin to laugh helplessly as snow soaked her sister's hair, and a large drop plopped on her nose. Diana didn't remember the last time she'd indulged her amusement. She really had nothing to laugh about—her life was yet full of the danger of Bannaster, her strange feelings about him, and her future with the League.

With a shriek, Cicely shook her head before her, almost like a dog, then began to take long, angry strides back toward the keep.

"Mistress Cicely—" Bannaster began, but then he only glanced at Diana and shrugged.

"I had best see to my sister," Diana said, before he could get any ideas about her own participation. She was not going to play with him—not anymore.

Diana busied herself in the kitchens and out in the kitchen courtyard, where a large boar was already roasting in a pit for the Christmas Day feast. Several other outside fires were being used to cook meat for the anticipated crowd. The Yule log had been dragged in while the hunting parties were gone, ready to be lit in celebration that night. Villagers had been streaming in all day, bringing their offerings of bread and ale and hens for the feast, and many women gathered in the kitchens to prepare mince pies, fruit tarts, and custards.

More trestle tables had to be set up for so many extra guests who had wisely brought their own wooden trenchers and spoons. The Yule log was lit with great fanfare and the sounds of Christmas carols rose to the high ceiling beams overhead, along with shouts of, "Wassail!" Between each course of food, the singing continued. A beautiful carved Yule candle was placed at the head table, and Diana stared mesmerized into its flame, letting the good cheer wash over and cleanse her troubled soul.

This was her favorite time of the year, when everyone was in good spirits. Throughout the evening, the minstrels continued to sing and mummers performed their silent skits for the children. She could almost forget about her troubles, pretend that these were happier times.

Until she caught sight of Bannaster, playing Tables with her steward. She turned her back when he caught her looking, determined to ignore him for the rest of the evening.

But soon she heard a hush spread through the great hall, and she could pick out the strumming of a lute by a solitary musician. And then she heard a man's pure voice, low, flowing like warm honey. She closed her eyes, pretending she didn't know who it was. But at last she had to turn around, and although she stood closer to the kitchens than to the group gathered at the hearth, she could see Bannaster strolling through the crowd, playing a lute and singing a Christmas carol.

"God rest ye merry gentlemen, Let nothing you dismay."

He stood before Cicely and sang to her, causing her cheeks to redden with excitement. She had been rather dour through the afternoon after Bannaster's rejection of her kiss and his teasing her with a snow fight, but his romantic singing was obviously resurrecting her joy.

"O tidings of comfort and joy," he sang, so suggestively that the crowd roared with laughter as Cicely pinkened.

And then he caught sight of Diana, and though she tried to press backward into the crowd, hands on her back pushed her forward, so that she was forced to meet Bannaster face-to-face as he sang to her. She kept her expression politely pleasant, but inside, his voice reverberated, setting off little explosions of pleasure that she worried might betray her.

Tom let his eyes become languorous as he stood before Diana and sang, enjoying her discomfiture. He could tell that she did not like being the focus of a man's attention before all her people—before Cicely. Diana's cheeks were red as an autumn apple, but her stormy gray eyes met his with no false demureness. She showed no challenge, but he sensed it was there, banked like a fire at night, just waiting for a breeze to fan it back to life. What else did she hide behind those eyes? Was she part of a plot to trip him up,

to prove him a murderer? She'd had him in her
dungeon already, but he'd outwitted that plan.
Yet she couldn't have gotten what she wanted
with him in solitary captivity. Nay, there was
more going on here.

When the last chords of his song faded away,
the hall shook with applause and cheers, and he
felt the good wishes of these people who were
still strangers to him. He wondered if they cared
which Winslow sister he married, as long as he
made one of them happy.

Next, Tom saw the caps and scarves and mittens
given by the Winslow sisters to all of their servants
and tenants. He had already discovered the orga-
nized piles of food and firewood to be taken home
on the morrow when they all departed. Though
Kirkby Keep had little, the Winslows made sure
their people had a happy Christmas.

Tom did not need to wonder who was behind
such generosity, who had probably sewn with her
maidservants all year in preparation for this day.
Perhaps he did Cicely an injustice, but since she
seemed bored with the proceedings, and Diana's
eyes shown with excitement, he imagined his as-
sumptions were accurate.

But Cicely's own eyes lit when she unwrapped
the long blue silk fabric he'd brought for her. The
deep green silk he'd given to Diana, and although
she was more reserved, she had offered her thanks
as well.

When Diana went off to the kitchens, Tom was easily able to have Cicely alone before the hearth, their words private though a hundred people filled the hall.

"My lord, you did not need to give me a gift," Cicely said coyly.

"I wanted to. I have something else for you on New Year's Day, but I wanted you to have the cloth early in the holiday."

"That is so generous of you. Mayhap we should start a new tradition of giving gifts on Christmas Eve as well."

"We had other Christmas Eve traditions in my home," he said. "Do your people tell stories on this night?"

"Nay, music and dancing have always been our favorites. I'll admit, Kirkby Keep had few traditions when I arrived, but I made certain to hire the best minstrels each year, and the holidays have become merrier."

"'Tis a good thing you do for your people."

"What kind of stories do you tell?" she asked, falling right into his plan.

"One of our favorites is any new tales of the League of the Blade."

"Oh, I have heard of them," Cicely said with confidence. "But some say they are but a legend."

"So they've never helped anyone you know?"

She shook her head. "Diana mentioned them

once or twice in our girlhood, but she always did like unladylike fantasies."

Tom grew tense with anticipation. Had Diana deliberately searched out the League after growing up with the legends? "I have met a Bladesman," he confided softly, looking around to make sure Diana wasn't near. "Earlier this year, they helped the daughter of the earl of Alderley reunite with her childhood betrothed."

Cicely studied him. "Diana told me you tried to force a woman to marry you. Was that her?"

He straightened uncomfortably, deciding honesty would work best. "Aye, it was. I had hoped to marry her, but her betrothed arrived at last, and King Henry agreed to enforce the old marriage contract."

Cicely grinned and leaned toward him. "I am glad, for I would not have met you."

Surprised, he said, "You are unusual sisters, that is for certain. You are the clear beauty of the family, yet Mistress Diana has her own unusual skills."

Though Cicely had stiffened at the mention of her sister, Tom decided to plunge ahead.

"Has she ever competed in a tournament?" he asked, thinking that this would have been the best way for someone from the League to know of her. "I am certain people would come from far and wide to see a woman challenge men."

Cicely hesitated, obviously weighing how she

would be affected by revelations about her sister.

"Once, when she was seventeen," she said at last with obvious distaste.

Satisfaction eased through him. His guess had been correct.

"Our parents had already died, and Archie did not care what she did, as long as she did not shame him by appearing as a girl."

"She disguised herself?"

Cicely nodded with eagerness, as if she thought this made him think less of Diana. "As you must have noticed, her figure is rather boyish. She competed in the dagger and the sword against squires, for she could not obviously compete against armored knights."

"I have seen her train. I imagine she won the dagger."

A furrow appeared on her brow. "Aye, she did, but not the sword fighting. When I saw a stranger speaking to her, I almost thought we were ruined, that her deception was about to be discovered. But she told me later that he was only congratulating her on her talent, and that her disguise had not been penetrated."

Had that been her first contact with the League? Tom wondered.

"And then Diana angered Archie by going off to stay with a friend for several months without his permission. When she returned, he sent her here in punishment."

"Did she not visit friends again?" he asked, wondering if these "visits" were when she'd been with the League. "After all, that was several years ago."

Cicely shook her head. "Archie forbid it, and I am certain someone within the household kept him apprised."

Although Tom wanted to talk about Diana's disappearance, he sensed that he'd reached the end of Cicely's usefulness—and patience—on the subject. He made himself say, "You remained with your brother?"

"Aye, until he married the next year. After that, his wife wanted to be the only beauty in the household, and I was forced to join Diana in this remote place."

"But the rumors of your beauty continue, mistress," he said, smiling. "Why else would I have come?

Cicely's answering smile was truly stunning, and for a moment he let himself be caught in it. But Diana had reentered the great hall, and he looked at her cool competence with the servants, the graceful way she moved among her guests, treating them all as equals, from the poorest farm laborer to the landed gentry of a neighboring manor. He felt the satisfaction of knowing that she would not remain a mystery for long, that he might have guessed correctly about her.

If Cicely was to be believed, Diana had never

again left Kirkby Keep. It was the one thing that made him suspicious of the truth, for had he not heard that the League used its members at least once a year?

Once, he had heard his royal cousin mention a medallion that identified members of the League to each other. He had seen no unusual necklace about Diana's throat, but she would not display such an item. It might be hidden somewhere in her bedchamber.

"Lord Bannaster?" Cicely said in a teasing voice.

When his focus returned to her, she was pointing upward at the mistletoe that hung above the hearth. Before he could even move, she leaned forward and kissed him on the lips, then ducked as if feigning shyness. People around them smiled, and he added his own chuckle, although inside, he thought he should feel more when a beautiful woman kissed him.

He glanced across the hall and saw Diana swiftly turning away, busy with another chore. Or trying to prove that she hadn't glimpsed him kissing Cicely.

He felt a momentary pang, knowing he'd told her he would not seduce her sister. And he wasn't, he insisted to himself.

And besides, she was the one doing the lying. And he would have to prove it.

Chapter 14

L ate that evening, overly full of rich foods and exhausted from a productive day, Diana retired to her bedchamber, still carrying her gift from Bannaster. The green silk cascaded from her hands to ripple across her bed coverlet. It was a beautiful color, and seldom had she seen fabric so delicate and fine. There was enough material for an entire gown. Had Bannaster purchased it for Cicely, and then decided to share his generosity with Diana? Or had he thought of it as bribe for her affections?

Regardless, it had been a handsome gift, and she had had nothing for him. Cicely had given him several handkerchiefs, which were her specialty. Of course, Diana had not known that she was to share his attentions with her sister.

And then she spotted a dark object on the cushion at the head of the bed. She lifted it into the circle of candlelight and saw that it was the book of poetry that Bannaster had had in his saddlebag.

He had spent his life longing to read books such as these, he'd told her. She knew he had originally meant it for Cicely. But he had given it to her, all part of his seduction, of course.

Opening the book, she ran her fingers over its smooth pages. "And I looked like a fool for having nothing for him."

She felt a sudden prickling up her back, a wariness, then a certainty that she wasn't alone. All of her training swept through her, and she had the dagger out of her girdle as she stared into the dark corners of her bedchamber. From behind, a man grabbed her wrist.

"Shall I twist and make you drop the dagger?" Bannaster spoke into her ear. "It seems we are forever disarming each other. It makes for an interesting courtship."

With a deep sigh of relief, she let the tension drain from her muscles. "Oh, 'tis you, Bannaster."

"And you're not even concerned," he said as if hurt. "'Tis a shame when my very presence in a deserted bedchamber doesn't inspire worry."

Her lips twitched in a smile at his foolery, but she didn't let him see her amusement. Sliding the dagger away, she turned to face him. In the dark room, the single candle only illuminated half of his face, highlighting his broad jaw and the curve of his lips. His smile faded. His eyes were deep and dark, and he looked at her far too closely. The inevitable thrill of his regard shot through her, curling her toes.

"'Tis a shame I have no mistletoe," he said, taking a step nearer.

She didn't retreat, only lifted her chin. "I will leave that to you and Cicely."

"Ah, if you were watching, then you saw who instigated that kiss. Believe me, I do not betray you with your sister."

"There is nothing between us to betray," she said, trying for indifference.

He grinned. "Then why did you just wish you had a gift to give me?"

"That is not what I said." Her mouth was dry, her voice betrayed her with huskiness. They stood barely a breath apart, and she thought if she could somehow remember to inhale deeply enough, her breasts would touch his chest. "I simply said I looked a fool for having nothing to give you after you have offered not one, but two gifts."

His gaze focused on her mouth. "I can think of a simple way to show your gratitude."

She was looking at his mouth, too. Her awareness had been reduced to only the circle of candlelight, where he stood half in shadow, his big body a warmth she'd already experienced—and wanted to again. She blinked, trying to remember how to speak. "You promised not to force me into anything."

"I am not. Did I not prove my good intentions to you last night?"

His voice rumbled in his throat, making her stomach flutter with heat. She had to move away, to resist the sinfully wonderful way he made her feel.

"But what am I supposed to think about your intentions," he continued, "when I discover you've been spying on me?"

Her stomach seemed to sink to her feet, weighted down with dread. Fearful that she'd finally been discovered, she could only whisper hopefully, "When I saw you and Cicely under the mistletoe?"

"Nay, in the woods this morn."

She could have staggered with her feeling of relief. Staring up at him, she tried to force her foggy brain to remember. "You left the hunt to be alone with Cicely."

"And as you saw, it was harmless."

By rote, she said, "I have to protect my sister."

"Are you certain of that? It would seem to me that the two of you would be happier living apart."

"And do you want to take her away with you?"

He lifted his hand, letting the back of his fingers caress her cheek. She felt the shock of it burn through her, igniting a dark need she'd never imagined she could feel. Each time he brought it forth in her was a fresh shock.

"I don't usually think about your sister," he murmured, letting his thumb brush along her lower lip. "Diana, give me a Christmas gift."

He took a step nearer, and the brush of his chest against her breasts made her moan. She went weak with need, and almost reached to hold him, as if he were the last solid thing in her world. But somehow she held back. He bent his head down to her, his lips just above hers. Their breaths mingled, and it was the most erotic sensation. She waited eagerly for his kiss, but he did not grant her one.

"If it's to be a gift," he whispered, "it must be freely offered."

Her only kiss with him had been fierce and hungry, wildly exciting—and had begun with *him* taking her mouth. Now she hesitated on the verge of a new experience, wanting more, forgetting everything she thought mattered.

"Call me Tom," he said, when she hadn't moved.

"Tom." The word was just a breath of sound as she lifted onto her tiptoes to press her lips to his. The kiss was achingly gentle, a moist promise of tenderness. She felt . . . lost, needy, out of balance, and at last she put a hand on his chest as if she'd fall without him. His heart pounded rapidly beneath her palm as his lips gently explored hers.

She parted her lips, the better to taste him, and the kiss began to deepen.

She was leaning into him now, her head tilting back against his shoulder. His arms came around her, holding her to him, and it was she who first entered his mouth, licked her way across his tongue to explore. His groan filled her with both need and satisfaction. He was the first man to ever treat her like a woman, wanted her for the femininity she hadn't known she had. His reaction to her made her confused about everything she'd ever wanted in life.

But for so many years she'd had one goal: to be a useful member of the League of the Blade. And now she was kissing the man she was assigned to investigate! She was questioning her entire life.

She broke the kiss in confusion, turning her head away. Tom did not release her immediately. His hands were low on her back, holding her to him, their hips pressed together. She could feel the long, hard length of his arousal beneath his tunic, knew with heady certainty that he wanted her.

"Might I have another Christmas gift?" he said against the hair at her temple.

She shook her head and stepped away to turn her back, almost disappointed when he allowed it. Was she supposed to lead him on, use his passion for her own benefit as she discovered all she could about him for the League? But wasn't that what a real courtship was about, learning to understand each other?

Watching him court Cicely wasn't working. She told herself that allowing him these intimacies would certainly keep him away from her sister.

Diana was so confused. "I am tired, Tom. And there is so much to do tomorrow."

He put his hands on her arms from behind. "I like the way you say my name. That is also a gift."

He left her then, and she sank onto the bed, staring at the book of poetry.

In his bedchamber, Tom found himself pacing, wishing he could send for a cold bath instead. But it was late Christmas Eve—and Diana had freely kissed him.

It had taken everything in him to leave her. If he'd stayed, he would have wanted more, and he didn't want to scare her, as he had the last time he'd let his passion control him. Now at least she knew he respected her wishes.

But was she lying to him about her identity, about her purpose in his life? Could she be a Bladeswoman, yet have no mission that involved him? Perhaps her connections only told her to doubt him, to keep him away from her sister.

He had to know the truth.

* * *

On Christmas Day, the snow softly fell. Diana knelt on the cold stone of the chapel and looked for God's peace, but it eluded her. Bannaster—Tom— had once again avoided mass, and she vowed to introduce him to the priest, so that he could see that many men of God were good.

For the next twelve days, there would be no work. All would enjoy the holiday, and take turns with the few necessary chores. The keep was still filled with villagers and tenants, many of whom had wrapped themselves in blankets and found a spot on the floor of the great hall for the night. It had been a challenge stepping across sleeping bodies when she'd come down before dawn.

When she entered the great hall after mass, Tom was already there, standing with a group of men near the hearth. He met her gaze from across the room, and the connection between them was as powerful as if they touched. She glanced away, feeling shy but trying to pretend indifference.

What was she supposed to do about him? When this was over, he might be her brother by marriage. Or could she keep him distracted from Cicely? And if she "distracted" him, what more would he expect of her—and how much would she offer? The League would certainly assume she showed a lack of objectivity where he was concerned.

Nay, before this spun more out of her control, she would begin a missive tonight, while she could still be objective. It would not be a complete report, but she thought she knew enough about him to make a start. Eventually she would choose the best way to deliver it to the League.

The holiday passed in a blur of carols and games for both young and old. They played King of the Bean, and Tom found the bean in his loaf of bread and was declared king of the feast for that night. Diana suspected that Cicely had been involved in that outcome. But Tom was a gracious king, even accepting the next role they'd imposed on him: the blindfolded player in Hoodman's Bluff.

Many revelers formed a circle around him as the Kirkby captain, Nashe, tied Tom's blindfold on tight. Then he spun their victim, and the crowd roared with delight when Tom staggered once before righting himself. He began to walk cautiously with both arms held up, leaning precariously to one side, searching for someone he could recognize by touch alone. Women shrieked and darted away from him, while men simply gave him a push in another direction.

Tom caught one boy's collar, only to accidentally rip it off as the boy dropped to the floor and crawled on hands and knees through the legs of the crowd. Suddenly hands pushed Diana into the open circle that surrounded him. From the opposite side, Cicely staggered in a moment later, although Diana wasn't sure someone had actually pushed her.

"Who's here?" Tom called, his head tilted as if he would use his hearing rather than his sense of touch to determine his opponent.

While Cicely giggled loudly, Diana took the opposite tack and used silence, circling sideways like she did when facing an opponent on the tiltyard. Tom blindly turned his head, and she thought he was somehow tracking her. Why wasn't the crowd screaming when she needed them to? Instead there was smothered laughter, and the occasional "ooh," as Tom reached out with his hand and just missed her.

Diana ducked down beneath his raised arms and found herself behind him. The crowd reached forward with their hands to stop her from fleeing, so she was forced to turn and wait for his next pass.

Cicely was obviously through being patient. She was just slow enough that he easily caught her with the next swipe of his arm.

"Aha!" Tom cried. "Does this mean I win?"

"Nay, you have to name the person you caught," Nashe called.

Nashe was always a man who paid too much attention to the rules, Diana thought with exasperation. She just wished that the game was over.

Tom slid his hands down Cicely's arms. She gave a coy gasp.

"I believe 'tis a woman," Tom said.

"My, how intelligent you are," someone called.

People gasped and looked at each other in worry, as if a nobleman would take offense.

Diana was surprised to see that it had been Tom's man, Talbot, who'd offered the good-natured insult. But Talbot was grinning, and she saw Tom turn toward his voice and return the grin.

Tom put his hands on Cicely's head, fanning his fingers out through her hair. The ribbon came loose, and her long curls tumbled about her shoulders.

"I believe this is Mistress Cicely," Tom said, stepping back.

Cicely pouted when his hands left her. "How did you know?"

"No one else wears their hair the way you do. And your perfume marks you well."

"I am glad you noticed," she purred, tossing her head.

Still blindfolded, Tom turned about. "But there was someone else in the ring with us."

Diana, who'd been about to flee, found herself pushed back toward him again. She was tempted to say that the game was over, that he'd already won, but knew that her guests would be disappointed. She saw Cicely flash angry eyes at her; what was Diana supposed to do?

There was nothing distracting Tom from her now. Arms held before him, he moved toward her with purpose. Again she was able to speed by him, but he turned more swiftly this time and just missed catching her hair. The crowd gasped, and then one of the men caught him before he could reach the edge of their circle and turned him about in the right direction.

Diana wanted to cry foul, but this was a child's game, not a contest for adults. Winning shouldn't matter. Loyalty obviously didn't, she thought with mild irritation. But she was battling Tom, and defeating him was always a good motivation.

He came toward her again just as she'd allowed herself to get too close to the crowd. She couldn't dart past him, because cheering people were blocking her path on either side. As she was forced to drop down into a squat, Tom embraced the empty air above her. If she hadn't been wearing a gown, she would have rolled past him and back to her feet. As it was, she tried to remain in a squat and step sideways, but he was on to her now. His flailing hand hit her head, knocking her onto her backside, where she quickly yanked down her skirts before they could do more than show her bare calves. Everyone gasped, but Tom was already pulling her to her feet.

She said nothing, trying not to breathe too quickly, trying not to tremble with his hands on her as memories of his kiss swept over her.

"Did I hurt you?" he asked with concern in his voice.

She couldn't answer him without giving her identity away, so she covered her mouth with her hand, making everyone laugh.

He smiled with wicked chagrin when his trick didn't work, then smoothed his hand over her head as if soothing what his clumsiness might have injured. He seemed to be good at knocking ribbons loose, for soon her hair fell forward.

The crowd oohed and aahed, and she thought that more than one person stared at her in surprise, as if the shock of her loose hair had reminded them that she was a woman. She waited for Tom to reveal her identity, but he let a confused expression cross his face.

"And this is not Mistress Cicely again?" he asked with feigned innocence.

Everyone laughed—except Cicely, of course, who stood with her arms folded and wore a tight smile.

"Who else would wear her hair like this?" he continued thoughtfully.

And to her surprise, he let his fingers slide down over her face, smoothing her forehead, her nose, her cheeks. She couldn't seem to breathe as he tossed a big smile to the crowd and let his thumb trace her lower lip. Men started hooting, and Diana put her hands on her hips as if in exasperation—when really she was praying this would be over before she betrayed her confused emotions where he was concerned.

"Ah, I recognize you now!" Tom said in triumph. "For that is the mouth so good at giving orders. Mistress Diana!"

More laughter and cheers assaulted Diana's ears as Tom pulled his blindfold off with a flourish. She wanted to kick him, and instead gave a quick curtsy of surrender.

"Now you owe me," she said quietly as the crowd dispersed to find the next amusement.

"I won—how can I owe you?"

While he was still basking in his victory, she led him to the hearth and introduced their priest, Father Francis, who'd been asking to meet the nobleman who avoided mass. Father Francis was a good soul, and would not harangue Tom. When she left them alone, Tom was politely listening. Maybe he would see that not all priests had to remind him of his childhood misery.

After Diana had abandoned him to Father Francis, Tom was prepared for a sermon about the fires of hell waiting for him for missing mass. Yet the old man just seemed to want to talk, and Tom accepted the easy conversation for several minutes. Father Francis asked if Tom had seen the new church being constructed in London.

Since he still had a personal mission to complete, he soon made an excuse to leave the priest. He waited near the kitchens, and he was eventually rewarded by the arrival of the maidservant, Mary. He had already spoken to Cicely, and now it was time to speak to Diana's friends. Diana had trusted Mary enough to help kidnap him, so the two women had to be close.

When Mary had set down saltcellars at several tables, she headed back down the kitchen corridor. Tom followed and called her name.

She turned around in surprise, and when she saw him, she could not hide her momentary look of guilt and fear. He had never wanted to see that kind of look directed at him again.

"Peace, Mary," he murmured, saying nothing until several curious servants had passed. "Is there a private place we can speak?"

Obviously used to subservience, she bowed her head and led him through an intersecting corridor, down a set of stairs and out into the kitchen courtyard, where outdoor cook fires sizzled beneath roasting rabbits and birds for the large Christmas crowd. Several kitchen boys glanced at them without interest and went back to turning the spits. Beside the water well, snow-covered furrows of a kitchen garden waited for spring. At last the maidservant turned to face him, hugging herself, as if expecting the worst.

"Mary, you do not need to look so frightened," he murmured. "I have told no one what you and your mistress did. I know it was a foolish mistake on her part."

She nodded, but did not lift her eyes. "We are grateful, milord."

"You know that I came here to court Cicely. To antagonize your mistress, I also included her."

Mary only nodded again.

"I was still angry about being imprisoned, and thought I could find a way to punish her. But over the last few days, I have come to know her better." He deliberately softened his voice. "It is easier to overlook what she did to me, because I'm so drawn to her."

Now Mary's brown eyes lifted to his, as if searching for the truth. And he wasn't lying, at least not where his attraction to Diana was concerned.

"Tell me something about her, Mary. Tell me why I should choose her over her sister."

Mary's face brightened momentarily, she opened her mouth, but then a look of consternation flashed through her eyes. Again she bowed her head. "I know not what ye want me to say, milord."

"How can I trust she'd make a good wife, when I see that she has so many skills of a man?"

"She's strong, milord, and she has a mind that always needs to find new things to learn. Though she chose the tiltyard, she has a woman's heart."

"But why the tiltyard?" he asked with growing exasperation. "What would she possibly use those skills for, when she will eventually have a husband to defend her?"

Mary said earnestly, "Mayhap she never thought she'd find a husband. Mayhap she feared she alone would be called on to lead the defense of her castle."

"But she was only a young girl when her father permitted it. Surely she never thought she'd be running any castle someday without a husband."

Mary only shrugged, and looked longingly past him to the keep. Tom sighed as he realized he wasn't going to learn anything else from her.

"Forgive me, Mary. I am simply trying to learn what I can about each sister, to make the decision that will benefit us all. Go back to your duties."

With a grateful nod, she escaped, leaving him frustrated, yet still determined. It was time to look for positive proof about the League. If Diana had the medallion, the mark of the League, it would be in her bedchamber.

And on Christmas Day, he imagined she would not return there until nightfall, leaving him plenty of time to search it.

Chapter 15

Through Christmas afternoon, Diana enjoyed watching the merriment of her people, glad they did not have to work overly hard. Villagers and tenants took turns with the castle servants helping to prepare for that night's feast when such an immense crowd would be served.

But somehow, she'd lost track of Tom's whereabouts. He wasn't with Cicely, who sat sewing with her maidservants, laughing at something Talbot was saying to the group.

Diana hated this feeling of relief that Tom wasn't with her sister. Should she add jealousy to her many sins?

"Mistress Diana?"

She turned to see Mary hurrying toward her, her expression worried. "Aye, Mary, is something wrong?"

"'Tis Lord Bannaster."

"I do not see him," she said, once more glancing about the hall.

"I just spoke with him in the kitchen courtyard. He was askin' questions about you, mistress, why ye wanted to learn a man's skills. I said nothin', of course," she hastened to add.

Diana put a hand on her shoulder. "I know you didn't, Mary. Do not worry yourself. He has been suspicious of me all along, with good reason after I put him in the dungeon, so this is nothing new."

But although the maid went away satisfied, Diana was not. She'd seen Tom talking to Cicely earlier, and now he'd gone to Mary. Had both conversations been about her? What would he do next with his suspicions? He might be beginning to remember her. He might be ready to rid himself of everyone's suspicions about his brother's death.

What would she do in Tom's place, if she had suspicions about *him*?

She would search his bedchamber, looking for something out of the ordinary.

Would he do the same to her?

She slipped out of the great hall, walking quickly up the stairs without looking back, in case someone tried to catch her eye. At her bedchamber door, she didn't pause, worried he'd hear her in the corridor. She simply opened the door to her own bedchamber—

And found Tom Bannaster kneeling on the

floor before one of her coffers, his hand on the closed lid.

He looked up at her, and betraying not a bit of guilt, gave her his slow, arousing smile.

She shut the door. "Why are you here?" she demanded coldly.

"I have been waiting for you," he said, coming to his feet and sauntering toward her. "We have more Christmas gifts to exchange."

Part of it was a lie, part of it was the truth. She knew that he wanted to dally with her, wanted her in his bed. Was that what it would take to dissuade his suspicions?

"If you were so confident in your powers of seduction," Diana said, "you would have been waiting in my bed instead of going through my things."

He put his hand on her shoulder, ran it slowly down her arm. She let him, telling herself she was distracting him.

Distracting herself, too.

"I was not going through your things," he said, his low voice an intimate murmur. "Well, not all of them. I was looking for the perfect gown for you to wear tonight, something more festive and feminine."

"I am not fine the way I am?" she asked, arching a brow. If she was toying with him, why did she let his words hurt her?

He clasped her hands between his and spoke earnestly. "I have never said that. You need no special gown to emphasis your womanliness. It is very obvious to me."

His behavior had always shown that to be true. But then why was he looking into her coffer?

He pulled her closer, moving very slowly, as if waiting for her to refuse.

Inside her brain were two very different voices, one telling her to push him away, the other slyly reminding her that she needed to keep him off guard, keep him distracted, while she finished her mission. Was he a man the League—and the king—could trust? She didn't even know if *she* could trust him, and here she was, letting him touch her.

As his hands cupped her hips and slowly moved up her sides, she told herself that she was being practical, doing her duty for the League. But her eyes closed, her body swayed, as her logical mind began to fade away.

Another desperate part of her said that this wasn't the way to keep him from Cicely.

But she no longer cared. Her world had become his hands, sliding now around her back, beginning to tug on her laces. She felt the press of his mouth just beneath her ear, tongue licking, teeth nipping. She groaned and tilted her head, giving him more access. His wet tongue rasped a path ever downward, and her garments, loosened, seemed to wilt down her body, giving him an invitation to take what he wanted. Her arms came free of her sleeves as her bodice and smock pooled at her waist.

She stood still, swaying with the pulse of desire that moved slowly through her blood, heating it. Leaning back, she grasped the bedpost in her hands, put her back against it, because she would have fallen without support. A cold breeze touched her bare chest only a moment before his mouth was there, warming her. He held her breasts in both hands, lifting them to his lips. She arched her back, trembling with the exquisite darts of pleasure that shot through her. Beneath lowered eyelids, she watched the concentration on his face as he licked slow circles about her nipple, teasing and taunting, leaving her to gasp her disappointment when he lifted his head, only to renew his attentions to her other breast.

Inside, she burned hot, centered between her thighs. She felt restless and needy, greedy for more, as if her skin quivered on its own. She could no longer pretend that she was not a willing part of this; she let go of the post and touched his broad, hard shoulders, holding them for support, then sliding her hands up into his hair to keep his head against her. His hair, soft and exotic, curled against her fingers.

Once more, she felt his hands low on her back, felt the laces give way, and his hands pushing on her garments. The last of them suddenly slid to the floor, leaving her wearing only her stockings and shoes. She stiffened, not sure she wanted him looking at her entire body, so different from other women's, with its scars and bruises and long lankiness.

But he only moaned against her breasts, let his mouth move up her body to meet her lips. His kiss swept away the last of her fears, and his arms drew her against him. She could feel the smoothness of his silk doublet against her flesh, the warmth of his thigh easing between hers, separating her. His kiss deepened, roughened, became all the more exciting as his tongue mated with hers. Distracting her, she knew, from the strange, new, thrilling things he was doing to her.

Suddenly, he grasped her waist and lifted her up to sit on the edge of the bed. He was kissing her again before she could even protest, stepping between her thighs, separating them even farther. She felt suddenly out of control, wanting to pull him harder against her, needed to feel him deep where the hunger seemed unappeasable.

"Wait, wait!" she said against his mouth.

He stilled, and lifting his head, looked down at her. In that moment, she knew she could stop this, that he would do as she wanted. His eyes searched hers, burning with urgency and promise, but he was leaving the choice up to her. In this at least, she trusted him.

"You are wearing too many garments," she found herself saying breathlessly.

A relieved grin stole over his face, and then he was tugging at the buttons of his doublet, at the laces of his shirt, pulling them both off over his head. His wide chest was scattered with dark hair, hard with muscle that rippled downward.

His smile faded with her intense regard. Hoarsely, he said, "Touch me, Diana."

And she did, smoothing her trembling fingers over his hot, firm chest. Beneath the skin his muscles were as hard as if forged by a blacksmith, and he inhaled sharply when she rubbed her thumbs across his nipples.

"Do you like this?" she asked.

He groaned and came down over her, forcing her back onto her elbows, her knees on either side of his clothed hips.

"Wait, wait!" she cried again, this time biting her lip to hide her laughter. She hadn't known lovemaking could be playful as well as passionate.

Again, he stilled, although this time he trembled as he met her eyes, waiting as she'd ordered. She let the moment drag out, enjoying the anticipation, the press of his groin against hers. At last she could not hold back, and did the brazen thing she'd been dying to do. She rolled her hips against his, groaned with the undying pleasure of it, and cried, "You are still wearing too many clothes!"

He stared at her as if he'd been expecting rejection, and the expression on his face when he dropped his hose and codpiece was primitive with a satisfaction that made her feel all woman. She'd reduced him to a man who needed her, needed what she could give him.

He came over her again, hands braced on either side of her shoulders. As she felt him hard and heavy between her thighs, she stiffened, closing her eyes, ready for his bold entrance, knowing that it might hurt.

But instead she felt his mouth pressing delicate kisses on the tips of her breasts, his fingers sliding in a slow caress down her inner thigh. Her eyes opened wide when he touched the moist depths of her, tracing the feminine folds no man had ever touched. She trembled and tensed, not knowing what she was supposed to do.

"Relax, Diana," he murmured against her skin. "I wish to give you the pleasure you've given me."

"I've given you pleasure?" She hated the neediness in her voice.

His expression was fierce. "Ever since we met, I have thought of nothing but touching and kissing you. Even when I was angry, I knew what I wanted."

She tensed when his fingers slid deeper, easing into her. She couldn't seem to breathe, didn't know what she wanted.

"Just touching you and being touched in return gives me pleasure," he murmured, leaning over her.

"But . . . I know not what to do," she found herself whispering at last, knowing she could reveal her inadequacies to him.

His grin was wicked, his brown eyes dark. "Trust me, you will learn."

His smile faded, and he only watched her as his fingers moved inside her. She should look away in embarrassment, but she was caught in his spell, in the intensity of their connection. And when his fingers slid out of her and moved higher, touching the small, hidden nub, she shuddered at the beginning of an explosion of sensation that only made her desires more urgent.

"Oh, please," she whispered, pulling at him, "Finish this!"

But this time he did not do as she wanted, only teased her lips with his, while his fingers caressed and circled, sometimes slowing until she felt mad with restlessness, other times moving faster, taking her higher.

And then he moved his hand from her, and she cried out, desperate, no longer caring what she sounded like.

Still standing on the floor, he pulled her hips to the edge of the bed, then sheathed himself inside her, going deep. The shock of pain was swift and faded almost immediately as he rubbed his hips slowly against hers, where his fingers had just been. Immediately, her passion surged again.

"Oh, yes," she said on a moan, trying to move against him, but feeling awkward and unsure.

Then he pulled almost all the way out, and surged into her again. Her body stiffened, and she flung her head back as his mouth settled on her breast. The world seemed to turn upside down as she reached the crest and rode the pleasure of his body, each even stroke of his erection inside her bringing on more shudders of pleasure. She didn't understand what she'd just experienced, but knew he must want the same thing, for he strove to move faster inside her. She pushed back against him, intuitively understanding the rhythm, taking it inside herself and wanting to give it back, to give him the pleasure he'd granted her.

She wrapped her arms about him, and to her shock, she felt the scars she'd only witnessed from a distance, long hard ridges that once must have hurt terribly.

And then he shuddered hard against her, his groan a release, and she held him until a damp, exhausted stillness claimed them both.

At last he came up on his elbows and looked down at her. She stared back, not really knowing what she saw on his face, the quiet gaze of his eyes, the slight curve of his mouth.

She'd given herself to him, another impulse she'd been unable to control. But in this peaceful moment, she found she couldn't quite regret it. That might come eventually, but she would find a way to deal with it.

Though winter's chill haunted the stone walls of her bedchamber, beneath Tom she was incredibly warm. Their skin was moist where they touched. Still joined most intimately to him, she reveled in the way he filled her, made her feel a part of him.

Tom didn't know what to think as he stared down into Diana's languid eyes. He hadn't imagined that she'd let him take her, was overwhelmed by how unprepared he'd been for sharing lovemaking with her. He'd never felt any joining so deeply, so movingly, as when she'd offered him her virginity. Had she felt so free because she assumed she wouldn't marry? It troubled him, the thought of her always alone but for her occasional surrender to her need for a man.

The heat of her surrounded him, pulled on him, and his thoughts faded away. He was overcome with the need to have her again. He moved inside her gently and felt the quick shudder that spoke of pain rather than desire.

He stilled at once. "Diana? Have I hurt you?"

Her smile was sweet and embarrassed. "I feel a little . . . sore." She looked away, dark lashes fluttering to hide the gray jewels of her eyes.

Regretfully sliding from her body, he climbed up beside her and collapsed on his side with a groan.

"You are hurt?" she asked in obvious surprised.

He propped his head on his arm and smiled. "Nay, just tired. You take everything out of me, but leave me well sated. Did I please you?"

He was surprised at her faint blush, for she always seemed so forthright and unflappable to him. Her skin continued to pinken, clear down her chest, and he traced the path with his fingers, causing her to tremble.

"You know you pleased me," she said in a low voice. "I could not disguise what I felt, and practically shouted it to the world."

"No one heard," he said, laughing and leaning over to kiss her. "All are busy celebrating."

She came up on her elbows. "I should be there. What will they say if they cannot find me?"

He kissed her shoulder, then the side of her breast. "I think they are too engrossed in their own enjoyment."

But she sat up, not meeting his eyes, looking about as if she didn't know what to do first.

He put his hand on her thigh and she stilled. "Diana, do not regret what we've shared."

She took his hand, and instead of pushing it away, she squeezed it gently and at last met his gaze. Something in him eased, and he realized what she thought of their lovemaking mattered to him greatly.

"I do not," she said softly. "But . . . I cannot think

now about what it means, or . . . or if it should even happen again. You might marry Cic—"

He reached up and covered her lips with his fingers. "Do not say it. You know that I will not marry your sister. You have won in that regard."

Her eyes widened and she ducked away from his hand. "You do not think that I . . . that I would let this happen just to stop you from—"

He sat up and put his arm around her. "Nay, I do not think that. You wanted me as much as I wanted you. But as for Cicely, what would you have me do? What will make things easiest for you?"

"I—I know not. You cannot hurt her by telling her that you do not favor her."

"That I favor you?" he asked wickedly.

Diana visibly shuddered. "Never say such a thing to her. I know not what she's capable of, and I feel that her desperation is overcoming her. Be kind to her."

"And what of you, Diana?" he asked, knowing her answer mattered so much more.

This time when she moved to leave the bed, he allowed it. She found her garments and, endearingly, could not meet his eyes as she drew on her smock and pulled tight the laces gathering her neckline. Now that her nudity was covered, he sensed that her usual cool nature was reasserting itself. She raised her calm gaze to him, and when she saw that he was still naked, her breathing hitched.

He rolled onto his side, his head propped on his hand, and she watched his body with wide eyes.

She licked her lips, but didn't look away. "What of me?" she repeated. "I . . . I will think on what this was between us. I did not plan it."

"I know you didn't. I am the one who surprised you in your own chamber." He hesitated. "You say you do not regret what we've shared, but you can barely stand to look at me."

She bent and picked up her gown, but he swiftly sat up and caught her arms, bringing her to him.

"Diana."

She looked at his mouth, and he saw the softening in her eyes the moment before she touched her fingers to his lips. "I cannot help my embarrassment. And I will not use this to discuss marriage, not when I never knew if I wanted it myself."

"You told me this before. Why would a lovely woman such as yourself not want marriage?"

She gave his question thought, and he wondered if she was debating telling him the truth— or concealing more of herself from him.

"I knew from childhood that I was different," she said quietly. "Most men want a very typical woman."

"Apart from your skills on the tiltyard, you seem like all women to me, if you can call any woman alike with another."

"But my skills are a part of me, and something I will not give up, not for any man."

She spoke urgently, firmly, and he knew that this, at least, was the truth.

"I understand," he said.

She pulled the gown over her head, and Tom knew he surprised her by turning her about and tying up the laces himself.

"I am very forthright," she said over her shoulder. "Now tell me if *you* regret what has happened between us."

"I am a man." He bit her softly on the neck, and she jumped. "We never regret such things."

"Only a few short years ago, you never thought you'd have such things." She didn't hide her curiosity.

Tom jumped lightly to the floor and began to draw on his own clothing. Hiding himself, he thought with sarcasm. "Aye, I would have given myself to the church, would have given up women with that vow, all because my family demanded it of me."

"Your family, or your father?"

He gave her a half-smile as he tightened the laces of his shirt. "And my brother, after my father's death. I thought I would be free to pursue my own life, but Nicholas decided otherwise."

"And to you, that was a double betrayal."

He shrugged. "I had already begun to see the kind of man Nicholas was, so I shouldn't have been so surprised. But I was young and naïve, and hoped for too much."

"Was he the one who ordered the lashing on your back?"

He was used to a version of this question from women he'd bedded. Once or twice, his disfigurement had sent a woman running before anything physical could happen between them. Other times, their pity drove *him* away. But Diana wasn't pitying him. Her solemn eyes studied him.

"The priest who tutored me," he finally said.

He saw the surprise in her eyes, but all she said was, "A man of God?"

He looked down her body, making light of the past. "When I was fourteen, he caught me eyeing a girl. He decided that pain would help me remember to deny my 'base nature.'"

"And your father allowed this?" she asked, not bothering to hide how appalled she was for him.

"My parents did not know until it was done. My father accepted it; my mother cried as she cleaned my wounds with her own hands."

"And this foolish priest thought such tactics would work with you."

He cocked his head, smiling. "You don't think it did?"

"Nay, you probably perfected the art of concealment more than anything else."

He caressed her cheek. "You already know me too well."

For a moment, they didn't speak. He looked into her eyes and saw a sweet softness that made him feel too good.

He shouldn't feel that way, not about her. She admitted she thought he'd mastered the "art of concealment" from a young age. He knew she was a master at it as well. He did not yet know if she was a Bladeswoman; he had found no medallion that would identify her. He'd seen a wax tablet deliberately smudged, but she could have been writing anything. And she'd put him in a dungeon, by God.

But once he was out of the dungeon, he'd found himself admiring her daring.

He put his arms into the sleeves of his doublet. "The priest's usual punishment was more original."

She reached for a bedpost and leaned against it, waiting quietly. He found he wanted to tell her so many things, but he had to hold back. How could he be thinking about trusting her, when she was still concealing so much?

"I knew from a very young age that I was supposed to be different from the other boys, not involved in worldly matters. But all I wanted was a sword, even the wooden ones the other boys had."

She smiled. "I had one."

He rolled his eyes. "Of course you did." Then he sobered. "One reason it was difficult to believe the worst of Nicholas was that he defended me when I was young. When the other boys taunted me, and I was forbidden to respond, Nicholas took them to task for me."

"He was a complicated man." It took everything in Diana to keep her face impassive, to let him talk without showing him the sympathy he didn't want. What must it have felt like to know that the brother who took care of you could turn around and abuse innocent women? "But you did not tell me the priest's usual punishment."

He cocked his head, studying her. "So interested in me?"

"And I should not be, after what we just did together?"

His smile was slow in coming, full of promise. "And to have my way with you, you'll make me tell sordid secrets of my childhood?"

"You began this."

He reached for her, pulled her close. She made herself relax in his arms, told herself that she would not allow more to happen.

"Nay, sweetling, *you* began this by putting me in a dungeon."

"And I would not have had to, if you had not deserved it. But you are still forgetting to tell me about the punishment."

He sighed, rubbing his cheek gently against her hair. She didn't move, wondering if he realized what he was doing, the very tenderness of the gesture. She felt safe in his arms, and that was so very troubling. For she was lying to him—betraying him, she realized with dismay. That was what he would think if he discovered her mission.

"When the priest caught me with a sword, he decided that I was far too active, that if I were tired, I would not be so inclined to amuse myself with something forbidden. At that time, my father was having a new parish church built near the woods outside the village. So the priest had me push blocks of stone at the site for hours on end. And while I did it, he wanted me to think about my sins."

"And as a young man, you had so many of them," she said lightly.

He smiled. "I must say, that hard work did pay off in the end, when I was newly the viscount, and had to prove that I could lead my men, even though I was not yet a knight. They saw my strength, and knew that it was just a matter of training."

She liked how he didn't allow bitterness to overcome him, considering the trauma of his childhood. Without thinking of the consequences, she let her hands trace his muscular arms through his garments, and then across the impressive width of his chest. He went still, barely breathing, and she looked up to find him staring down at her, all trace of amusement chased from his eyes.

She couldn't quite catch her breath. "So the priest did you a favor. I now understand why your body is so impressive."

He said nothing, only leaned down as if to kiss her.

She turned away, escaping the enticement of his embrace. "Nay, Lord Bannaster, my people are expecting me for the Christmas feast."

He caught her hand, forcing her to turn back to him.

"Lord Bannaster," he echoed dismissively. "Say my Christian name."

She wondered why it was so important to him. "Very well—Tom. It seems strange to say it, when you were 'Bannaster' in my head for so long."

"For so long? It has not even been a fortnight."

She smiled to cover what could have been a terrible mistake. "When you were in that dungeon, it seemed like forever."

He grinned. "Guilt?"

"Never." She tugged her hand away. "Be very careful when you leave. I cannot have anyone seeing you. I will follow after a decent amount of time has passed."

"One kiss."

"Go!" she said sternly, pointing at the door.

His face full of exaggerated disappointment, he opened the door carefully, looked both ways, and then left.

Diana closed her eyes and sank down onto a bench. She had just made everything more complicated. And she hadn't meant to! When Tom touched her, she could think of nothing else—not the League, not her future unencumbered by a husband—but how he made her feel, how much she wanted to pleasure him in return.

But . . . a buried part of her mind worried that she'd given in to his seduction only to best her sister. She hugged herself, a thousand thoughts darting through her brain. Nay, Diana had had his attention from the moment she'd imprisoned him, and Cicely had nothing to do with it.

She tipped her head back with a groan. He was a good man. She had never forgotten the shocked gratitude she'd felt when he'd allowed her to escape from his dead brother's bedchamber. He had taken the blame, suffering for what she'd done to protect her, a stranger.

And now she was spying on him in secret, betraying him.

But was it a betrayal, if she was defending him to those who did not trust him? Perhaps she could be the one to redeem him in the king's eyes! Telling herself to feel relieved, rather than worried, Diana took out her wax tablet and began to compose her ideas.

Cicely could not believe her eyes. She stepped back into a garderobe to avoid Lord Bannaster, who was coming down the corridor that led to her sister's bedchamber. She pressed herself to the wall until he'd passed, telling herself it meant nothing. There were other chambers, including her own, on this floor.

But his own bedchamber was above them, and there was no reason for him to be here. Yet Diana was not in the great hall.

In that brief moment, she'd seen his face, saw the lightness in his step.

What was happening?

Chapter 16

"A New Year's Day tournament?" Tom said two days later, when Diana proposed it.

She nodded cheerfully, staring down the head table at the midday meal, meeting her sister's suspicious eyes last.

"Cicely," Diana continued, "the weather has been mild for the Christmas holiday. The traveling would not be difficult. Our grooms can deliver the invitations. Surely the knights from the surrounding countryside would like a challenge. We can make it last only a day, so that the competitors can arrive the day before, compete the next, then return home to their families the following morn." *And not eat so much of their food supplies,* she thought.

She had seen Cicely's eyes alight when she'd mentioned "knights."

"But, Diana," Cicely said, "our brother has always said that he must be consulted if we wish to do anything beyond the ordinary here at his keep."

Diana smiled confidently. "But it will take so long to reach him, and the holiday only lasts through Twelfth Night. He will understand."

For once the two sisters agreed with each other. Cicely returned her smile. "Aye, he will. And 'tis not as if we've ever disobeyed him before."

At least this response was better than the coolness Diana had faced the last several days. Though Diana had been careful to keep her distance from Tom, lest her longing gaze betray her, Cicely seemed to sense something amiss. Conversations between the sisters had grown even more strained.

Diana knew that Tom had outwardly continued to spend time with both of them in the same manner. Just this morn, after he'd returned from the tiltyard, he'd taken Cicely on a long walk.

Diana had told herself this was a good thing. Whatever happened between her and Tom, she did not want to face Cicely's wrath until Diana could understand her own intentions.

And so far, Diana had no clue about what she meant to do. She had made it a point to never be alone with Tom. She felt confused and uncertain, things she was not used to feeling. What was their relationship supposed to be? Were they simply using each other physically? And if that were so, they could not allow it to go on, not and risk the possibility of conceiving a child.

Diana shuddered, imagining Archie's reaction to that disgrace. She would be banished from yet another home.

But the missive to the League was written, and the only way to see it safely into the correct hands at this time of the year was to have a tournament, where strangers would be expected to attend. The Bladesmen could easily participate, giving them a reason to be here. Then her mission would be finished.

But after that, if she expected a fresh start between her and Tom, she was fooling herself. With all the secrets that existed, how could they trust each other?

For the last two days, as she'd stayed away from him, she had wondered how he'd felt about her distance after their intimacy. But he'd been nothing but patient, not sneaking into her bedchamber, or trying to find another way to be alone with her.

But she could sense his focus on her, knew when he felt free to look at her unobtrusively. She could feel the force of his gaze like a touch that smoldered within her, ready to ignite. She knew what he wanted, and he was just waiting for her to make her decision.

He would not force her, would not persuade her. Part of her wished he would. But she understood that she was just looking for an excuse to blame him rather than herself.

For he was all she could think about. If they were training at the same time on the tiltyard, she could barely concentrate on her opponent, so drawn was she to watching Tom fight. He had an aggressive, yet quick style of attack that always left his challenger one step behind.

She'd sparred with him in bed; now she wanted to compete against him with the skills she'd spent a lifetime learning, where she felt more confident. Because a woman's skills did not come so easily to her.

Yet she was leery of training with him before her own men. It was hard enough hiding her emotions in the great hall. On the tiltyard, she might lose focus, be too distracted to pit her skills against his, to triumph over him, or be defeated.

But while she readied for the tournament, to begin four days hence, she kept her distance, not wanting to be distracted.

Two days before the tournament, Diana heard a quick knock on her door late in the evening, and put down the embroidery she'd been making a mess of. She tensed with excitement and worry, imagining Tom filling the doorway. What would she say to him? What would she do if he swept her into his arms—

But Joan scurried into her bedchamber, closing the door behind her. Diana knew a deep disappointment that worried her.

The maidservant leaned back against the door and took a breath, closing her eyes.

"Did you need to run?" Diana asked, smiling.

Joan shook her head. "Nay, mistress, but I seldom leave the kitchens, and when I do, I feel the need for quickness."

Diana sobered. "Joan, you know you have my apologies. When Tom—Bannaster leaves, you shall be free again. But . . ."

"Aye, I know, if he sees and recognizes me, it will not go well for you and Mary."

"Nor you, Joan, and the two of you concern me the most." Diana sighed and leaned on the edge of her bed. The lies never seemed to end.

"I came because I thought ye should know there's been talk among your people," Joan said, speaking almost hesitantly.

"Talk?" Diana responded, curious.

"Before Christmas, Lord Bannaster spent time equally between you and Mistress Cicely. But since then . . . well, folks are upset on your behalf, thinkin' he's neglectin' you in favor of your sister."

Diana barely kept herself from laughing in dismay, remembering Tom's form of "neglect."

"I know what ye're thinkin'," Joan hurried on before Diana could speak. "Ye didn't want his attention anyway, not after . . . well, ye know, what we did to him."

Diana nodded, trying to be solemn. "I know."

"And if ye just hoped he'd choose your sister
and be done with it, then this would be fine. But
ye want him to leave, do ye not?"

More lies, Diana thought. She could not tell
Joan—or Mary—what had happened between
her and Tom. "You bring up a valid point, Joan.
I cannot have people begin to question his lordship's conduct. And aye, he needs to leave—without Cicely."

Joan nodded and reached for the door latch.
"I'll return to me duties, mistress."

"My thanks," Diana said, reaching the door in
time to touch the maidservant's shoulder. "You've
been a good friend, one who does not deserve this
forced solitude."

Joan blushed. "I don't mind, mistress. I'll never
forget ye savin' me, when I had no one."

When the girl had gone, Diana resolved to do
better to keep her people's suspicions at bay.

The next day, the castle was in a flurry of excitement, preparing food for dozens of knights and
soldiers and any family who might attend. Rooms
were aired out; pallets were laid so the bedchambers could fit several people each.

At the midday meal, Diana took a deep breath
and looked past Cicely to Tom. "My lord, would
you grant me the favor of examining the lists and
the tiltyard, so that you may give me your exper-
tise?" Before he could answer, Diana said to her

sister, "You did have his attention in the lady's garden this morn."

Diana hadn't been able to imagine what they'd been talking about, sitting on blankets on the cold stone bench. But she'd glimpsed Cicely pointing to the various plants, and she wondered if her sister had been expounding on her knowledge of the flowers that slept until spring.

"Very well," Cicely said primly. "The maidservants have need of me in the sewing chamber. We're almost finished with the banners that will decorate the castle," she said proudly to Tom.

"I look forward to seeing them," he said.

Then he looked back at Diana, who felt her stomach flip upside down. This is what she'd been avoiding for so many days. How long could she keep this polite façade believable?

After retrieving their cloaks, they walked outside together, their breaths puffing before them. The day was gray with the threat of snow, but rather today than tomorrow, when their tournament would begin.

Diana felt the stares of many, but when she glanced around, people quickly acted busy.

"I am surprised at your request for my presence," he said quietly, looking ahead rather than at her. "You have been avoiding me."

"Aye, 'tis true," she murmured.

"Yet you could not miss the way your sister looked at you just now."

"I suspect she is suspicious about my motives. But it is the rest of my people we also need to placate." She told him of Joan's visit.

"So I am allowed your attention, for everyone else's sake?"

She glanced at him, but she could read no emotion on his face. "I . . . feel confused."

"Well, I do not," he said.

They came to a stop on the far side of the gatehouse, just outside the castle. The villagers had done an impressive job setting up lists for riders to joust against each other, complete with benches for spectators.

In that moment of solitary stillness, where it was just the two of them, he murmured, "I am not confused. All I can think is that I want to hold you and taste you—everywhere."

She shuddered and closed her eyes. "Your kisses are—"

"I have barely begun to show you kisses, sweetling."

Her mind, always so active, now churned through imagined events. As if it hadn't been difficult enough to forget the way his hands pleasured her, or his body fit so rightly to hers. But now his tongue . . .

"I have so much to do," she found herself saying, as if from a great distance.

Slyly, he said, "But will not your people wonder why we leave each other so quickly?"

She felt like she was *breathing* too quickly, as if she couldn't get enough air.

"Let us continue our walk," he said, beginning to amble toward the lists.

She had no choice but to follow him. But inside her seethed a wealth of confusing emotions, as she wondered how she was supposed to feel about him. How was this supposed to end?

Did she *want* it to end?

During the following day, New Year's Eve, Tom spent little time with Diana. Competitors arrived for the small tournament, sometimes on horseback by twos and threes, and other times with family following behind in carts. Cicely dealt well with the ladies, showing them to their chambers, inviting them to embroider with her near the warmth of the large hearth in the great hall. Once Tom had overheard Cicely discovering the marital state of the men in attendance, and he had to smile. He understood her urgency, since she lived in a place as remote as Kirkby Keep. Though she would not be the woman for him, he thought if she were kept happy, she would make a man a good wife. It was a shame her foolish brother did not see that. But then Cicely saw Tom lingering near, and her radiant smile jolted him. He was still her primary target.

Diana dealt with the men, and Tom found himself remaining on the fringes of whatever group she was with. It was obvious that many of these men were her neighbors, and had known her for several years. More than one man asked what competition she would be entering, playfully suggesting he did not want to go up against her.

Other men, strangers, stared at Diana with expressions ranging from displeasure to shock to curiosity. Tom received a few of those stares himself, when his identity was made known.

But he was curious about Diana, too, just like some of the other competitors. He assumed that her skill at a tournament had probably won her the attention of the League. The last few days, he'd found himself forgetting his peril where the League was concerned, all because of his preoccupation with Diana. But at a tournament full of Yorkshire men, most of whom he did not know, would there be some from the League? All he could do was remain on guard. He was used to living his life that way, even though his title and relation to the king usually protected him.

Would Diana know if some of her guests were Bladesmen? He could not believe that she wished him ill. But how well did he really know her?

Alone in her bedchamber late that night, Diana reflected with satisfaction on the first day. Among the many strangers present, one or two were surely from the League. They had been ready for her call to tournament. Her encoded message to them was already hidden within the stables, a place agreed on before hand, available to all, and well marked in a way that only a Bladesman would recognize.

After supper, the music had seemed to shake the very foundations of the old keep. Her guests danced with abandon, joining hands and moving through complicated dances. When Tom had pulled Diana into a dance, she could hardly protest. Soon she'd been laughing as he'd lifted her into the air. His hands had been so strong that she'd felt as safe as a bird in flight. The only thing that had marred her enjoyment was knowing that Mary had come down with a winter cold, and had gone to bed early.

Suddenly, Diana's door was thrown open, and Cicely entered, fists on her hips.

Diana's feeling of accomplishment faded away on a sigh. "Aye, Cicely?"

"You danced with Lord Bannaster more than I did," she said coldly.

With a tired voice, Diana said, "It was not intentional."

"And I did not like the way you stared at him! What do you want people to think?"

"That I want my guests to enjoy themselves. And he is our *guest*, Cicely, not simply your plaything."

She took a step forward. "I am going to win him."

"Are you trying to intimidate me?" Diana asked in disbelief. She was so surprised and frustrated that she spoke without thinking. "Do you not understand, Cicely? He is not the right man for you. I have told you how he tried to force a woman to marry, and you did not care. But he has also long been suspected of his brother's murder. Is that the kind of man you want?"

No sooner had the words left Diana's mouth, than she wished she could call them back. How could she have used a crime she herself had committed to make Tom look bad?

Aye, it was to Cicely, but that did not give Diana the right to treat him as others did, as if she only gossiped. And during the commotion of arriving guests, she had seen more than one man's scowl upon hearing that Viscount Bannaster was in attendance.

Cicely only lifted her chin with determination. "I know what kind of man Lord Bannaster is. And do you think I have no ears, that I would not listen and understand everything about him? I also had heard what kind of man his brother was. It sounds as if he deserved to die— although I do not think Lord Bannaster capable of such a deed."

Nay, but I am, Diana thought sadly.

"I want my time with him, Diana," Cicely was saying. "My friends are here, and they will expect it."

"Just go," Diana said, pointing to the door. "I will be so busy that you will be able to do as you please."

Cicely nodded and marched out the door. Diana sank down on the bed. Her secrets were weighing on her, and were beginning to feel unbearable. But she was so afraid of what would happen, should the truth come out.

During the next morning, the ground thundered with mounted men jousting each other at the lists. The sound of lances against armor or shields was like a crack of lightning, and voices shouted encouragement. The weather was brisk, on the ground patches of snow and mud, the spectators full of good cheer.

Within the curtain walls, Diana watched the dagger-throwing competition, awaiting her turn. She wore her breeches and jerkin over a heavy woolen shirt, and knew that many women gave her a second, surprised glance. Though she seldom flaunted her unusual skills before strangers, she was used to the stares.

In fact, the last time she had competed in a tournament was when she was seventeen, and the League of the Blade had taken notice of her, seeing beneath her disguise as a boy. They were here again, she assumed, studying her, determining if she was worthy to remain a member. She had successfully completed her mission; now she would abolish her opponent.

When she looked at the displayed parchment with the competitors' names randomly matched, she saw that opposite her, a neighbor's name had been scratched out, and in its place was Tom's name.

Surprised, she looked around to find out what was happening and found Tom watching her, casually tossing a dagger into the air. He never looked at the blade, only caught it smoothly by the hilt and sent it aloft over and over again.

For Cicely's sake, Diana had meant to avoid him during the tournament, but she couldn't very well protest his rearrangement without drawing too much notice. She arched a brow at him, and his grin turned wicked.

As if he did not think of besting her at daggers, but at something far more intimate.

She enjoyed him, she realized. How could she want this to end? Her days would return to boring drudgery without him. She could not ask a man to marry her, but would she be content as his mistress?

But even that relationship would suffer without the truth between them.

A large wooden board had been set up, and

like the archery competition, there was a target drawn with smaller circles leading into the center. Though the dagger competition was often fought with opponents battling hand to hand, she had decided to make this one more about skill with the blade, and her captain of the guard had agreed with her.

Now she and Tom stood side by side, at a marked distance from the target. It would be the best throw out of three, and if they tied, they would retreat several paces and start again.

They tied with daggers in the center ring, and had to move back for another round. Young grooms excitedly returned their daggers to them each time, and the crowd began to grow. Diana did not let thoughts of the spectators—or her sister—distract her. This time, two of Tom's throws hit the outside circle, but he still hit the center on his third, to match all three of hers in the center.

"'Tis the single best out of three!" Tom called, when someone shouted that she'd already won.

The crowd roared with laughter. They backed up another ten paces, farther than any competitor yet, and this time, none of Tom's hit the center of the target, and one of hers did. She had advanced to the next round.

Tom found himself impressed with her skill, but not surprised, and he bowed to her as if she were the finest lady at the king's court. People laughed and applauded, and he was rewarded with her adorable blush.

She had the sort of single-minded dedication that made her succeed at anything. Even the League, he thought. But it could not only be her skill with a dagger that had impressed them. He hefted his dagger and faced her, curious to see more. She too faced him, a small smile curving her lips, and the tension between them was like a physical thing, a shimmering wave of mutual passion and understanding. Around them the crowd watched and whispered.

Tom thought Diana would be uneasy being the center of attention, but she twisted the dagger slowly, flashing it in the sunlight. *Did she mean to spar?* he wondered in pleasant surprise. After losing to her, he would welcome the second chance for a victory.

"You need swords!" another voice called from the crowd.

Diana's captain of the guard, Nashe, spoke up. "My mistress did not enter the sword-fightin'."

Diana said evenly, "But I will challenge Lord Bannaster."

Tom slowly smiled with anticipation. Before he knew it, the two of them were being outfitted with breast and back plates, helms, and dulled swords. The crowd had swelled with spectators coming over from the lists, as the morning's competition came to an end.

Nashe, looking as if he disapproved, called out, "If there is not a clear winner with a sword point touch to the armor, then the victor will be the one who keeps his sword."

After nodding their acceptance, Tom and Diana moved out into the open, muddy ground of the tiltyard. He could not easily see her face through her visor, and when she began to circle him, tall and lean, holding the sword two-handed, he could almost forget who faced him.

But those legs encased in woolen breeches were hard to miss. And as he admired them, she made her first thrust, and he barely had time to parry it before she almost hit his armor to win immediate victor.

The shouts and laughter faded as he focused his concentration on her. "Very good," he said as they circled once more.

"You are too easily distracted."

Her voice sounded coolly amused. This was a Bladeswoman, strong enough to challenge a man. And he wanted her right now, so desperately. But first he would defeat her. He attacked, slashing twice as she backed away, and on the third stroke, she jumped his blade, then hit him hard in the shoulder with her padded elbow. He staggered in surprise and almost went down on one knee. The crowd gasped, but he righted himself.

"You will not win so easily, mistress," he called out in a cheerful voice.

She said nothing, only attacked again. Their swords met and held on high, glittering in the sun. He caught himself just before he would have kneed her in the groin, as he would have to a male opponent. With a twist of his wrist, he released his blade from hers and backed away again.

"Do not ignore your instincts," she said, her breath coming a little harder now. "I will not."

"So you wanted to be kneed in the stomach?"

"I would have blocked it," she said with confidence.

For several minutes, they circled, tested each other's defenses with a feint or a thrust. At last, Tom was able to lure her to commit, and he came up under her arm with his sword, scraping against her breastplate. Their eyes locked and held, stormy gray and solid brown. Tom felt as if he could discover everything about her and it would never be enough to sate his need to possess her.

"Winner!" shouted a voice.

And then suddenly Nashe was between them, separating them, as if he was worried they would continue fighting. Tom thought that in another moment, it wouldn't have been fighting everyone would have witnessed. He removed his helm, and then watched as Diana removed hers. Her hair had come unbound, and now streamed and tumbled slightly damp about her shoulders, glinting as brilliantly in the sunlight as their swords had. Nashe unbuckled her training armor, and Talbot removed Tom's. The attention of the crowd turned to the next match, and Tom found himself facing Diana alone.

"I need to wash before dinner," she said, her voice almost distant.

But those eyes never left his.

"I will accompany you to the keep," he answered, and they fell into step beside each other, not touching. But his senses were so very aware of her, it was as if they moved as one, each footstep the same, each sway of their arms identical. He wanted to brush his shoulder against hers, but did not dare, so fragile was his control.

"We will enter through the lady's garden," she said, then added, "It is the closest entrance."

He said nothing, fixed on keeping himself from grabbing her. No one was in the garden, bare in winter, with the occasional drift of melting snow just off the gravel paths. The door into the keep was beneath a trellis, its vines withered overhead. Tom took the door from her and closed it behind. The corridor, though lit by far-spaced torches, was deserted.

And then he could not stop himself. Taking her arm, he turned her about until he could pull her into his arms. To his pleasure, she did not resist, only threw her arms about his shoulders and moaned as their mouths met in a passionate kiss. She tasted as fresh as the outdoors, and the heat of her body from their sword fight only made him want to give her other reasons to be hot. They slumped against the wall, as if they no longer had the strength to stand after resisting each other for so long.

At last Diana lifted her head on a gasp. "Nay, anyone could find us here! I do not want you forced into making a decision that you don't want."

He spread kisses along her jaw. "What decision? Never mind, just tell me where we can be alone, and say you'll go with me."

For a long moment, while their hearts pounded in unison, and they stared into each other's eyes, Tom thought she would refuse, would come to her senses and realize the danger.

But she didn't. She licked her lips, watched his mouth, and at last whispered, "There is a staircase down to the undercroft just ahead."

"Why not the dungeon? You could shackle me to the wall and do as you pleased." He had had more than one fantasy about what he would have done with her in his cell.

Her eyes went wide. "But . . . all of the stores in the undercroft would have been retrieved early this morn to prepare dinner." She leaned forward and kissed him swiftly. "And 'tis right here."

"Aye," he said against her mouth. "Take me there." *Take me.*

The door opened onto blackness, and Diana reached for a torch from its bracket in the wall and brought it with her, leading the way. Below, the air was noticeably cooler, and Tom could smell grains and ripening fruit. Barrels were piled high beneath the arched ceiling that faded away into blackness as it held up the very keep itself.

As soon as Diana secured the torch in the wall bracket, Tom was on her, pressing her to the wall with his body, his hands in the wonderful silkiness of her hair.

He gripped her hair firmly, just enough to tilt her head back. Her breath on his face made him roll his hips into hers. "Facing you in battle was one of the most stimulating moments of my life."

She gave a groan mixed with a laugh, and held his face in her hands, stroking him with her thumbs as she kissed him. "We both like a challenge. And won't this be one?" she added doubtfully, looking about them.

The floor was cold, packed earth; lumpy bags of grain were piled high.

With dismay, she said, "Where will we—"

He caught her beneath her hips and lifted, spread her thighs as he pressed her body against the wall.

She gasped. "We can . . . do this?"

When he felt her long legs wrap about him, he groaned. "We can, but not through so many garments."

He lowered her to the floor, and they began to untie each other's breeches, reaching around each other, stealing kisses.

"I want to see your breasts," he said against her mouth, cupping them through her leather garment. "But we can't."

When their legs were bare beneath their upper garments, Diana seemed almost shy, but Tom did not give her a chance to change her mind. Once again he picked her up and pressed her back against the wall. Between her thighs, she was so hot and already so wet, that for a moment he simply let the length of him be cradled against her. He rubbed up and down. She gave soft, little, panting moans, locking her legs about him, thrusting against him.

This was what he wanted, only the excitement and intrigue that was Diana. He wanted her in his bed every night of his life; he wanted the surprise of wondering what new challenge she'd conquer every day; he wanted her to wife. Had he fallen in love with her? That would change everything. He could wait patiently to learn her secrets, for he knew she would eventually tell him.

He sank into her, and it was like finding peace at the center of a whirling storm. Moving in her, he put his mouth against her ear and whispered, "I want to know everything about you, Diana. Confide in me."

But she only kissed him, and he lost himself.

Chapter 17

Diana moaned with the bliss of being cradled in Tom's arms, suspended, fearless, with his body deep inside her, rocking her ever closer to a pleasure that when later remembered, might seem like a tale of fantasy. Above them, the world and their responsibilities seemed far away. Down here, beneath the arches of the ceiling, was another world, one where passion and secrecy ruled. She could only hold on and let him do as he wanted with her, giving herself up to him, trusting him.

Inside her body, the world stilled and she was suspended on the brink. She heard his harsh breathing, felt the strength of him moving, and was lost, tumbling through a shuddering web of pleasure, knowing she took him with her.

When at last, he eased away from her, setting her gently on her feet again, they both slumped back against the wall.

Diana gave a shaky laugh. "I . . . I know not what to say."

"I say—magnificent."

"You were?" she asked innocently.

He leaned to kiss her. "*We* were."

They both pulled on their garments, and the easy silence between them lengthened. Overhead, they could hear the distant noises of the castle, but layers of stone separated them from the real world. Diana wanted to stay here forever, pretend there was no past between them.

But she remembered his words of a moment ago, asking her to tell him everything. Inside her chest, her heart seemed to twist painfully. She would lose him if he knew.

"It is surely time for dinner," she said at last.

Tom sat down on a sack of grain and tugged on her hand. When she tried to sit beside him, he turned her so that she was sitting sideways on his lap.

"We should spar more often," he said, pressing his face against her throat.

She laughed. "Our behavior would become rather obvious, should we keep disappearing." She put her hand on his, where it rested on her thigh. "You were quite impressive on the tiltyard. One would think you'd spent your entire life training."

"Instead, you had more training to be a knight than I had," he said with a smile.

"Ah, yes," she said, feeling wistful, "and though I had the satisfaction of accomplishing my goal—at the expense of ever having a decent relationship with my brother—I became practically a squire in the eyes of men, not a man, but not a woman either."

"You only think they were uninterested in you. They wanted to see you in those tight breeches."

She tilted her head at him. "But—"

"And besides, were they not your soldiers, for the most part?"

"Well . . . aye."

"They can only show you respect, not affection, because of your place above them."

"Oh. And what about you?"

"Oh, I respect you." He let his hand slide up her thigh, beneath her jerkin.

She slapped at his hand, and before he could persuade her to stay, she rose to her feet. "We must go. They'll be suspicious if we are not there for dinner."

They stood looking at each other in the flickering torchlight as their smiles died. Very gently, he cupped her face in his warm, callused hands, and kissed her lips.

She waited, aching, part of her wondering what she waited for. A declaration of . . . what? She had just finished spying on him—she'd killed his brother and let him take the blame. How would she tell him those things?

She couldn't. She turned away. "I'll go up first, you bring the torch with you. If I slam the door, it means someone is up there, and you should wait before coming out."

As she ascended the stairs, she pretended she didn't hear him call her name, pretended that her eyes weren't stinging, pretended that what they had could actually continue.

Cicely carried a covered tray back into the depths of the keep, where the servants had their bedchambers. She fumed in silence, furious with herself for letting this happen. She'd heard that the maidservant Mary had taken ill. Diana, who always saw to the illnesses of the servants, was nowhere to be found. Surely she was out proving how unwomanly she was on the tiltyard.

Cicely had foolishly offered to bring dinner to the sick woman, only to realize that Lord Bannaster wasn't in the great hall to see how kind she could be. To keep this from being a wasted effort, she would just have to make sure he heard about her benevolence later.

At Mary's door, Cicely didn't bother knocking. She went inside and found the woman lying on the floor beside her low bed, as if she'd fallen out of it. Her face was red with fever, and although her eyes were closed, she mumbled unintelligible words. Disgusted, Cicely looked about, but the other three women who shared the chamber were gone.

With a clatter, Cicely set the tray on the table and went to stand above Mary, hands on her hips. "Can you get up?" she called in a loud voice.

Mary gave a small moan, her head rolling weakly. Heaving a long-suffering sigh, Cicely knelt down and gripped both of her hands, pulling the woman into a sitting position. Mary slumped against her, and Cicely could feel the damp heat wafting off her skin.

Grimacing with distaste, she put an arm behind the maidservant's back and pulled. Somehow, Mary got her feet under her, and Cicely was able to dump her back into the bed. But her touch seemed to upset the woman, who mumbled and pushed at her hands when Cicely tried to cover her.

"Nay, touch me not!" she said weakly, her head thrashing back and forth.

"I am certainly not going to continue touching you."

"Mistress Diana, ye saved me!" she cried, her eyes opening briefly.

She was looking right at Cicely, but it was as if she didn't see her. "Saved you how?" Cicely asked with reluctant curiosity.

Mary thrashed again, and Cicely, seeing the basin of water nearby, wet a facecloth and stroked her heated skin. To her relief, it seemed to ease the maid.

"They won't find you, mistress," Mary mumbled. "I tell you we've left . . . Bannaster land."

Cicely gasped. Surely this was the fever talking. When had Diana ever been to Castle Bannaster?

Mary lifted a hand weakly. "He deserved to die for how he treated us all . . . They'll never know what ye did to save me."

"Who deserved to die?" Cicely demanded.

But Mary's lips had stopped moving, and she seemed to sink deeper into sleep. For another half hour, Cicely bathed her face and arms, trying to encourage her to speak again. Had Diana killed someone at Castle Bannaster? Cicely wouldn't put it past her, with those deadly skills she'd insisted on learning. But who had deserved to die? The only person she could think of was the late viscount, who was notorious for abusing his servants—although many of them had probably thought they would be rewarded for giving in to him.

But hadn't Diana just said that Lord Bannaster had been suspected in his brother's death? And if he was suspected, then the true murderer had never been caught.

Cicely straightened, letting the cloth fall from her fingers onto the edge of the bed. Had Diana killed him to save the women he'd been abusing? Years ago, Diana had returned from a several-month visit with a friend, bringing both Mary and Joan, two new maidservants for the keep.

That was when Archie had been infuriated by her conduct, and banished her to Kirkby Keep.

Mary's eyes began to flutter.

"Mary?" Cicely asked softly. "I have brought soup. Would you like some?"

It took great effort for the maidservant to focus on her, and she looked startled to see her.

"Mistress . . . Cicely?"

Cicely smiled, uncovering the tray and lifting the bowl into her lap. She spooned some of the broth. "Open wide."

Obediently, Mary did, swallowing several spoonfuls.

"Mary," Cicely began, trying to keep the excitement from her voice. "Where did you and Joan live before Kirkby Keep?"

"I . . . in a castle, mistress."

"But where? You just now told me that you came from Bannaster lands."

The woman was obviously too weak to hide the sudden terror in her eyes. "I—I did?"

"Never mind," Cicely said, feeling a deep satisfaction. "I must have misunderstood."

She was feeling so happy that she fed the maidservant the half of the soup before getting to her feet. "Sleep well, Mary. I will send someone to look in on you this afternoon."

"I . . . thank you, mistress."

Cicely was late for dinner, but she did not mind. She felt as light as a butterfly, and her future seemed to stretch before her with happiness. She would be able to put Diana in her place. No longer would Cicely have to watch Lord Bannaster's gaze settle on her sister, while she felt helpless and outraged and confused. It had been like childhood all over again, where no matter how perfect and lovely she was, her parents focused on Diana and her manly exploits.

Diana would now have to stop encouraging Lord Bannaster, or suffer the consequences. ·

Just after dinner, Diana and Cicely opened the package sent by their brother in time for the holiday. For once Archie had thought of them, and sent them each a necklace—of common stones, it was true, but Diana was grateful to be remembered.

Diana had made Cicely a headpiece and veil, and Cicely had embroidered several handkerchiefs for her. Tom had once again surprised them each with a gift, little gold cups. He had not had those in his saddlebags when Diana had searched them. As Diana thanked Tom, Cicely graciously waited her turn, not intruding as they spoke about the workmanship of the cups. Diana felt unsettled.

During the afternoon, Diana moved through the rounds of the dagger competition and took first place. She thought of what Tom had said, that the men she'd trained with had been men who wouldn't consider themselves her equal, could never treat her as anything more than the mistress of the castle. But there were other men here, not beholden to her, and several even looked . . . impressed.

But she found that the only man who mattered was Tom, and he looked at her with pride and even a glimpse of tenderness, which he quickly masked. It struck her heart in a way that made her catch her breath, which worried her.

Diana was in her bedchamber changing for supper when the door opened, and as usual, Cicely sailed in.

Diana knew it was useless to ask her sister to knock. Dryly, she said, "You are just in time to tighten the laces of my gown."

Cicely's smile was radiant. "Of course!"

Diana felt a shiver of unease. When her sister was this happy, it usually boded ill. "Go ahead. Tell me what you came to say."

"Lord Bannaster is finished courting you."

When the laces were tight, Cicely sank onto Diana's bed, leaning back on her hands, her skirts puffing around her.

Diana eyed her and carefully said, "I thought he'd decided to treat us equally."

"He had, but you will now dissuade him."

"And why would I do that?"

"Because I know you killed his brother to save Mary and Joan."

The truth of her words struck Diana like a
blow to the stomach. She had spent so many
years fearing discovery, then gradually relaxing
her vigil, then ramping it up again when Tom
had arrived.

But hearing it like this, from so unexpected a
source, had shocked her.

She called on every bit of control to say evenly,
"Whatever are you talking about?"

"Do not blame Mary. She is so ill, and you were
not here to take her a dinner tray."

Because I was with Tom, Diana thought distantly.
"Poor Mary is still ill?"

"I fed her most of a bowl of soup, so I think she
is beginning to recover. But first, she was feverish,
and quite talkative. I found it so fascinating. To
think you rescued her from the evil Lord Bannaster. I am so proud of you!"

Diana could only stare down at her sister, sitting on the bed like a queen, her beautiful face
animated with pleasure.

Cicely tsked and shook her head. "But what
would *our* Lord Bannaster say? You murdered
his brother, and allowed him to accept everyone's
suspicion."

Diana couldn't even think of a response, just
watched her sister with vague puzzlement, not
understanding how they could even be related.

"I am certain that you murdered him to save
every woman in the castle, and that was noble of

you. But perhaps Lord Bannaster—or the king—will not see it that way."

"What do you want, Cicely?" Diana asked coldly.

"No explanation, no denial? I am so disappointed. I don't even know why you were *at* Castle Bannaster."

Diana linked her hands behind her back, afraid she would slap her sister.

"I can see you are in no mood to satisfy my curiosity," Cicely said with grave disappointment. "So I will simply repeat what you seem to have forgotten. You will tell Lord Bannaster that you no longer wish to be courted. I freely grant you permission to make up any story that you'd like, as long as he believes you. Then I will have him for myself, and soon, you and I will never have to see each other again. I'll be free of this dreadful ruin of a castle."

"And you think it will be that easy to convince him to marry you?"

Cicely's smile was slow and gleeful. "He is a man, is he not? It will not be difficult to be alone with him, to allow him certain . . . liberties. And after that, honor will demand that he marry me."

"If you think it will be that easy, then why do you even need me to dissuade him? It sounds as if you plan to attack him."

Cicely's smile vanished, and she rose to her

feet. "Just do as I say and I will not have to tell everyone what you did."

Until her sister had gone, Diana held herself so stiffly that it seemed she had to uncurl each finger from her tight fists. Her shoulders and neck ached with tension as she sat down very carefully on a bench.

She had known that the hidden truth would always be between her and Tom. Perhaps it was better this way, she told herself, her eyes too dry for tears. Her rejection of Tom would be over with quickly, and he was too proud a man to beg her to return to him. After all, he hadn't even offered marriage. They had just been two people enjoying themselves.

But now it was over. She had the League, which was all she'd ever wanted.

After Tom and Diana's pleasant afternoon together, and his realization that he wanted to marry her, Tom had been anticipating supper. He had not figured out the best way to let Cicely know he'd made his decision, but he would find a way to do it gently.

He still did not quite know how he'd gone from angry prisoner to besotted lover, he thought with amusement. He sat down at the head table, which was now crowded with other visiting noblemen. As he spoke about the various matches of the day, he looked about idly, waiting for Diana. And then he saw her, dressed in a dark wine-colored gown, her lithe figure delicately rounded. She would make every man here who thought of her as just another competitor remember that she was a woman.

He wasn't surprised when Cicely again forced Diana to sit on the far side of her, away from Tom. What did surprise him was that Diana avoided even speaking or looking at him the whole meal. He knew she was having difficulties with her sister. Perhaps she was even feeling guilty for their affair, though she should not. He had exchanged no promises with Cicely.

But Diana's face was almost . . . pale, too somber, which was unlike her. He remembered his earlier concerns about the League infiltrating the tournament. If she were a member, she would think she couldn't tell him. He was confident that he could eventually persuade her to share everything with him.

After supper and into the merriment of the evening, Cicely never left his side. She constantly touched his arm, leaned into him as she pointed out a juggler, or proclaimed about the sweet voices of the minstrels.

Diana remained on the opposite side of the hall. Hadn't she recently told him that her people were upset he wasn't courting the sisters equally? Then why was she avoiding him, giving him no chance to spend time with her?

Though Cicely tried to keep his attention, he could not miss that Diana danced repeatedly with the same man, Sir Bevis of Richmond. For the first time in his life, Tom experienced the ugliness of jealousy where a woman was concerned. Just this morn, he had been inside of her, pleasuring her, imagining asking her to be his bride.

Something was wrong, and the fact that she didn't confide in him was his true worry.

If she left the great hall that evening, he never saw it, so he was unable to find her alone. At last he was forced to steal a moment of her time when she was speaking to a servant near the entrance to the kitchens. She turned around and came up short when she saw him waiting for her.

She didn't meet his eyes. "My maidservant, Mary, is ill. I will be going up to visit her."

"Diana, what is going on?"

Her gaze lifted, but she looked past him. He saw her eyes narrow, her jaw set. He looked over his shoulder and saw Cicely watching them. But instead of wearing her usual pout when she felt herself ignored, Cicely only smiled and waved, turning away in confidence.

Tom frowned down at Diana. "What is going on between you two?"

"I cannot . . . be with you anymore," she said woodenly.

Furious that she had not discussed her change of heart, he said, "Look at me, before I put my hands on you before all of your people and give you a good shake!"

She lifted her gaze at last. He saw the cool gray of her eyes and could read nothing.

"This morn I realized that you might be thinking of me as more than a mistress," Diana said in a low voice. "But you see that my passion is in tournaments, not in the foolish duties of a wife. I thought you understood that before, but our time alone this morn made me see that I needed to make clear our situation."

He blinked at her in surprise. "So . . . you want to be my mistress, not my wife."

She shook her head, and he saw a crack of exasperation break through her impassive mask.

"It was a brief affair. Surely you have had those. And it is done." She went to move past him, and when he reached to take her arm, she drew back, saying with fury, "Do not touch me."

And then she was gone, and he was left to stare at her stiff back.

She could not possibly believe he would accept such nonsense. She was not a woman who trusted easily, and granting her body to a man had required her utmost trust. Something had happened to make her behave this way, and he would find out what it was.

Chapter 18

Diana moved through the rest of the evening in a blur. Somehow she spoke to people, called, "Wassail!" at the appropriate times, kept her guests entertained, and oversaw the servants. She knew Cicely sparkled like the crown jewel of the tournament, but Diana paid her little heed.

Because Diana's heart was breaking.

Having to tell Tom those terrible things had torn her up inside, and she would never be the same again. She'd seen anger and confusion in his face, but she sensed he was not ready to believe her. She would have to do even more to convince him that she was finished with him, watch his face as she hurt him again and again, until at last, he would only feel disgust for her.

To make everything worse, she saw when Cicely led Tom from the great hall, as if they were looking for privacy.

Diana fled to her bedchamber, barely holding back the tears until she was alone.

* * *

When the castle had at last settled down for the night, Tom stood outside Diana's bedchamber, deciding how to approach her. He knew she'd watched him leave with Cicely, and yet she'd allowed it, as if she thought he would bed two sisters on the same day!

Whatever was going on between them, he did not want to make it worse, so he'd been gentle when he'd refused Cicely's attempts at seduction. He'd talked about her being a nobleman's daughter, and how he respected her. He'd left her with the implication that he was still open-minded about his future. And although she'd been understanding in her manner, he knew she had not been pleased.

He knocked on Diana's door.

"Who is it?" she called in a pleasant voice.

He walked in and firmly closed the door behind him. "Not your sister or your servants, so you can put away the false demeanor."

He heard a shocked gasp, but for a moment, all he could focus on was Diana, dressed only in a night rail, long linen that skimmed her figure. She stood near the bed, which had been turned down for the night.

Then he realized she had not been the one who gasped.

A maidservant whom he didn't recognize stood at the washstand, holding a cloth to her chest as if he'd shocked her. Which, of course, he had. But if she was here with Diana, then surely she was loyal and would say nothing.

"Joan, you may leave," Diana said quietly. "This rude viscount will be on his way soon."

The girl turned her face away and hurried from the bedchamber. For just a moment, Tom felt an unusual tug of familiarity, but since he'd spent over a fortnight at Kirkby Keep, he'd surely seen her among the servants.

Diana did not break the icy silence between them, so Tom folded his arms across his chest and watched her. She pretended to plump the cushions on her bed, then moved to the washstand to dampen a facecloth.

Tom snorted. "You cannot believe that I will leave just because you're ignoring me. Not after those foolish things you said to me in the great hall."

She gave a heavy sigh. "Tom—"

He strode forward and stopped before her. "You saw me leave with Cicely, and you *allowed* it. I felt like a New Year's present from one sister to another."

Red crept into her cheeks. "Was I supposed to scream your name with jealousy? Did you spend so many years without a woman that you demand our constant attention?"

He flinched, but realized that she did, too. He took her shoulders and found that she was trembling. "Diana, tell me what is wrong," he said softly, urgently. "You know I do not want Cicely. I want you."

She shrugged off his hands. "Well you cannot have me."

"Diana—"

"Do not continue this conversation," she cried, "or I will have to tell you things you do not wish to hear!"

He was taken aback by her passion. "No longer should you keep your secrets from me. Tell me now."

She moved away from him, and he let her. Hugging her arms, she kept her eyes averted, and then suddenly gave a bitter laugh. "When you first arrived, I thought you'd finally discovered the truth after all these years. And that's the main reason I locked you in that dungeon."

The tension and uncertainty crawled up his back, but he said nothing, not wanting her to stop.

"We met six years ago," she said softly, "at Castle Bannaster."

His mouth fell open. "I would have remembered you!"

With a shake of her head, she sadly said, "I looked different—I was different. Beneath you. Just another of those poor women in your household. I'd heard about them in London, heard how your brother treated them. And I was so full of my own skills, confident that God had given me a man's talents for a reason. So I disguised myself as a maidservant to encourage them to demand better treatment."

Cicely had inadvertently confirmed some of this story, by saying that Diana had been gone several months. And then he realized what she was trying to say.

"It was me, that night in your brother's bedchamber," she whispered harshly, closing her eyes. "I had saved Mary from him, but could not escape. And then he tried to rape me, and I was forced to kill him."

He flinched, remembering the flickering light from the hearth, the image of the woman on the floor beneath his dead brother, her face turned away in shame.

"You set me free, saved me," she went on in a dull voice, "and like a coward, I repaid you by allowing you to take the blame. This is what Cicely just discovered, what she is now holding over me."

Something wasn't making sense, but it wouldn't come clear to him. All he saw was the guilt and pain that she'd been carrying with her for six years. "I made the decision to let you go. I thought you were a maidservant. They would have hung you for the crime, regardless of what my brother had done to you. Surely you understand that!"

"But I wasn't a maidservant. If I would have

stayed and accepted the blame, I probably could have made them see—"

"They would have at least imprisoned you, demanded that the king see to your fate. You would have been ruined, your family shamed."

She covered her face with her hands. "Instead *you* were shamed. And when you arrived here, I panicked. I thought you had discovered my identity. And how could I have allowed you to court my sister, when I had killed your brother?"

Had he been wrong about everything, about the League? If her reasons for kidnapping him had really been so personal, then the League had never been involved.

"Nay, this does not make sense," he finally said. "Everyone knew what my brother was like. I would have understood what you'd done; I would have helped you."

"How could I have known that?" she demanded. "I was frightened and not thinking clearly. And you know how impulsive I can be—our relationship is fraught with the mistakes I've made when I didn't take the time to think things through."

He advanced on her until she was forced to back up against the bed instead of retreating farther. "Diana, you are not telling me everything. I do not believe that a young girl of—what, seventeen?— could have taken it upon herself to travel across the country alone, disguised herself and risked her life for women she'd never met before."

"You know what I am like!"

She spoke with heat—and too much desperation.

"Aye, I know. I know you're a talented woman who first showed her skills at a public tournament. Was that when the League contacted you?"

She betrayed not a single emotion but confusion. Oh, she was good at lying.

"What are you talking about?" she asked. "Why are you bringing up something that is only a legend?"

"We both know it's not a legend. I worked with them just this year. I know they come when justice has been denied, when nothing can be done to stop the powerful from hurting the weak. You with your skills would appeal to them. A woman—a Bladeswoman—would be perfect to place within my brother's household. A maidservant would never be suspected of having plans against a viscount. But I do not believe your assignment was to kill him."

She said nothing, but this time he saw the fleeting emotions in her eyes, the panic, the sadness, the secretiveness that made him wonder if he would ever know everything about her, if she would ever trust him. He thought she would have fled if he hadn't trapped her up against her tall bed, where she'd have to touch him to escape.

He stepped back. "I shall speak with Mary. She was one of the maidservants, was she not? And that girl who was just here. I recognize her, too."

"Do not involve them," she said between clenched teeth. "They are innocent. Even after what your brother did to them, they are still innocent."

It was his turn to remember the pain of helplessness and betrayal, all his conflicting emotions about his brother. "I won't hurt them. I am glad you have taken such good care of them. But I need the truth."

"Damn you, Tom, can you not leave it alone? This is none of your—" She broke off.

"None of my affair? Is that what you meant to say? My brother made it my affair, long ago."

She groaned. "Yes, yes, you are right about everything. I am a Bladeswoman, and I was assigned to persuade your maidservants to rise up against your brother, to convince the local sheriff that terrible things were going on. If your brother was taken to task by men more powerful then he, even the law court, he could have been stopped."

"But it didn't happen that way," he said softly.

Diana was swamped with the regrets of her past. There were so many of them. She didn't see Tom or her bedchamber, but Mary's tearful face as she ran from the viscount, the white, pinched expressions of the maidservants as they scurried from duty to duty at Castle Bannaster, always wondering when it would be their turn to have the viscount's attention.

Softly, she said, "I have spent these six years telling myself that I had made the only decision I could, that those women were safe now."

"You cannot possibly think I would have wished you to allow yourself to be raped."

She glanced at him in surprise. "Perhaps not, but there must have been many days when you wished you had not let me go."

His expression clouded. "Aye, there were some. But I knew I could bear the scrutiny better than a maidservant. I was the viscount now, and there was no proof I'd murdered my own brother. Does the League know?"

She nodded. "I told them from the beginning what I'd done."

"Then they never suspected me, were not looking to prove I was a murderer."

She shook her head, but felt uneasy. She could not reveal everything to him, not if she wanted the chance to remain a Bladeswoman.

Bitterly, she added, "They said I had handled the situation poorly, that I was too young and impulsive. They said they'd made a mistake, that they would someday reevaluate their decision about admitting me, but until then I was to wait."

"And you're still waiting."

She said nothing. She had never thought she'd have to choose between the League and a man, but apparently she really had been too young when she'd agreed to join. She had never considered how it would feel to fall in love.

The first tear slid down her cheek. She had to be in love with Tom, because lying to him hurt so badly. She'd thought unburdening herself of some of the guilt would have helped. But he'd . . . generously understood what she'd done, and didn't blame her. She kept telling herself that she'd help exonerate him in the eyes of the League and of the king. But it didn't make her feel any better.

She gave a start when he cupped her cheek, used his thumb to wipe away her tear.

"I know you worked hard to be a Bladeswoman—the first, and that is an incredible accomplishment. But if they don't understand what you had to do, perhaps you are not meant to be with them."

She shuddered.

He let her go. "Think on it. I have not turned you away like they did."

When he left her bedchamber, she could only sink onto her bed in wonder. He did not blame her for the troubles he'd suffered after his brother's death. He was a hero in every sense of the word.

But now she was further confused—to whom did she owe her ultimate allegiance: to the League, or to the man she'd fallen in love with?

* * *

Tom returned to his bedchamber, although he'd wanted nothing more than to stay with Diana, convince her that she could trust him.

But he knew she still didn't, knew she was hiding something. Because after an hour of pacing, sorting through everything he'd learned tonight, putting aside his growing feelings for Diana, he'd finally realized that it was still too much of a co-incidence that King Henry had suggested he visit the Winslow sisters.

The League of the Blade was somehow still in-volved. And he wanted Diana to freely tell him all of it.

Chapter 19

Early in the morning, before mass, Tom knocked on Cicely's door. The castle was only just beginning to rouse after an evening of Christmas carols and dancing, and no one had seen him come up. And he knew that Diana was already awake and below overseeing the servants preparing for the final meal before their guests' departure.

When at last Cicely opened the door, a dressing gown wrapped about her, her face broke into a lovely smile.

And beneath that smile lurked an ugly cruelty, for to have what she wanted, she'd threatened her sister with disgrace—and even death, if Cicely had thought that far ahead. He hoped she hadn't.

Spreading her arms wide to welcome him, she practically purred as she said, "Come in, my lord."

He did, and then slammed the door shut too hard, causing her cloak to jar from its peg beside the door and fall to the floor. Her smile faltered, and she took a step back in retreat when she looked into his face.

Tom said, "Diana told me everything."

"I know not what you—"

"All about how you blackmailed her over my brother's death."

She still must have thought she had the advantage, for the lines on her troubled forehead smoothed away. "She can deny it all she wants, but there are witnesses." Her voice was so cold, as if she were speaking about a stranger, rather than her sister.

"*I* was a witness."

She paled.

"I did not know who she was," he continued, "and I never saw her face, but I found her beneath my brother's body. He was trying to rape her. Did you ever wonder how that felt? Your sister, so talented and confident, about to be violated, after she'd saved a woman from that same fate? What would you have done in her place?"

"I—I—"

"I will tell you what *I* did. I let her go, told her to flee. I never even saw her face. I knew she would have suffered far more than me if the truth had come out."

"Well . . . that was simply foolish on your part," she said, pulling herself together. "She did not need you to risk yourself in her defense. If I were her, I would never have allowed myself to be in such a position."

"That is because you never would have agreed to help innocent women by putting yourself in grave danger."

Tom knew Cicely might not be able to understand another's pain, but she certainly knew when she was being insulted. Her eyes flashed with anger, but he gripped her shoulders, and she stumbled over her words.

"I will tell you how this will go," he said in a low, deadly voice. "I will not shame you before your people, telling them about your betrayal of your own sister. Not for your sake, of course, but for Diana's. I want her."

Outraged, she cried, "How can you want—"

"You will do well to listen, and be rewarded for it."

She was sulky, but quiet.

"You have done all of this for the sake of having a husband. Some of the blame lies at the feet of your brother, for denying you and Diana your rightful place with him and at court. Now you will let the past lie. You will say nothing about my brother's death, and in exchange, I will sponsor you in London."

Her eyes went wide.

"You will have your own house, your own servants, new clothing," he continued. "Soon I will convince Diana to be my wife, and she'll be a noblewoman. If you speak of what you know, she will be protected, and you will lose everything. Now do you think you can find yourself a husband in London? My generosity will not continue forever, though I will even grant you a dowry if you need one, for the sake of your sister."

She seemed so stunned, that the words wouldn't even come. At last, she began to slowly smile. "Aye, my lord. We have an agreement. And of course you know I will find a very wealthy husband."

"You put great stock in your beauty, and rightly so," he said, feeling almost tired with relief. When she preened, he added, "But beauty is fleeting. You need to cultivate your other talents to make a man happy for a lifetime."

She looked as if she didn't want to believe him, but he no longer cared. He left her bedchamber, knowing she was too smart to ruin the agreement between them. Cicely might consider that she'd won, but Tom didn't think so. He wanted Diana happy, and knowing that her sister was taken care of would relieve any of Diana's guilt when he took her away from here.

Diana spent the day alternating between feeling relieved that some of the guilt had been lifted from her shoulders and wondering what Tom now expected of her.

He knew about her membership in the League, and seemed . . . proud of her accomplishment. There were many men who might feel slighted that a mere woman had taken a knight's place within the order, but he was not one of them.

She didn't think he understood how deep a commitment one had to make to the League to be a member. She had broken the vows of secrecy by admitting her membership to him, but he'd deduced it, left her no choice.

But how could she tell him that he'd been the subject of her assignment? Long ago he'd protected her identity as a murderer, suffering in her place, and she'd betrayed him—more than once. The League would never forgive her if she revealed her mission—and perhaps the mission was something Tom would never forgive either. Though she felt she'd helped him in the end, he might not see it that way.

Would she have to make a choice between him and her membership in the League? Could she not be both things, a Bladeswoman and . . . a wife?

She'd seldom imagined herself as a wife, beholden to a man. Her ambitions were so unwomanly, she never thought they could be compatible with marriage. But loving Tom had made her rethink all of that. How could she go back to a life without the intimacy of his regard, his conversation—or his bed?

It was all too much to take in. She spent the day seeing to her departing guests. Tom never pressed her for a decision about their relationship. Only once did he approach her in a moment's privacy to explain that he'd taken care of Cicely, who would not bother either of them again. They'd been interrupted almost immediately, so she'd had no time to ask what he'd done to make her sister change her mind.

And yet Cicely spent the day looking so full of herself, like a hound that had eaten the fox.

Diana tried to let it all go. She had a day's respite, she thought, and sometime she would have to begin to think on her future, on what to do next.

She slept fitfully that night, and awoke the next morning to find another surprise: Tom attending mass.

He grinned at her before bowing his head for the prayers. Was he trying to say that if he could change, so could she?

But by late afternoon, she knew her day of uneasy peace was over. Her brother, Archie, and a small company of men had been sighted on the approach to Kirkby Keep.

Diana saw the moment Cicely entered the great hall. Her sister hurried right to her, as if ugly things had not been said between them.

"Is it true?" Cicely demanded. "Archie is here?"

"And why do you care?" Diana was surprised to hear herself say. "Aren't you going to tell him what I've done?"

Cicely rolled her eyes. "Why would I risk what I've won?"

"Won?"

"Did not your precious Lord Bannaster tell you of our agreement? He is sponsoring me in London! So let me handle my situation with Archie. Do not interfere."

Diana gaped at her. "As if I don't have enough to talk to Archie about." In a horrified voice, she added, "London?" It sounded like her sister was far from being punished for the cruel things she'd done.

But Diana was guilty of her own sins. How could she judge another?

Archie and four men-at-arms entered the great hall, stomping snow from their boots into the rushes scattered on the floor. Their brother was a tall, broad man, given to a bit more paunch than muscle, but then he'd never been diligent in his training. He dropped his hood back onto his shoulders, revealing his unruly blond hair. To Diana's surprise, it seemed to have retreated a bit on either side of his forehead. She was trying to remember the last time they'd spoken, when he saw her and Cicely standing near the hearth.

He strode toward them with great deliberation, a frown dominating his face. "You dared to have a tournament without asking my permission?" he bellowed.

Archie always did enjoy bellowing. "A happy New Year to you, too, brother," Diana said.

He blinked.

"Thank you for your thoughtful gift," Cicely continued. "Did you receive the handkerchiefs I sent?"

He cleared his throat. "I did. My thanks." Then he seemed to remember why he'd come, and his light brows plummeted over his eyes. "Do you have an explanation for this tournament?"

"Aye, the tournament," Diana said calmly. "If we'd have asked your permission, it would have been weeks before we heard your answer." *And it would have been "no,"* she thought grimly. "The holiday would have been over, the mild weather gone. How were you able to come so quickly?"

He took a tankard of ale from a waiting servant and gulped deeply. "We spent Christmas in York."

Being so close, Diana thought, a normal brother would have sent for them. She knew Cicely thought the same thing, but with her newfound future, Cicely only shrugged as if Archie's good will didn't matter anymore. When Archie took another drink, Diana gave Cicely's arm a squeeze, trying to warn her not to speak until they knew why their brother was here. Although Cicely gave her an impatient look, she did remain silent.

Archie looked Diana over, curling his lip. "And I imagine you embarrassed our family once again."

"By winning the dagger competition?" she asked sweetly. "Why, yes, I did."

Archie scowled.

"But you will be happy to know that I lost the only sword-fighting match I entered."

"Who defeated you?" Archie demanded.

"I did."

Tom's voice rang through the great hall. He and his men were just coming in, after having exercised the horses. His face was red from the cold, his dark hair mussed when he removed his snow-covered cap. Yet Diana felt a shiver of lust that went clear to her soul.

"And who are you?" Archie was bellowing again.

"Thomas, Viscount Bannaster."

To Diana's amazement, Archie didn't look surprised. And then she realized that the tournament wasn't the only reason that Archie had decided to pay them a visit.

Tom arched an eyebrow in amusement, adding, "And I do believe we've met, Winslow."

Rudely ignoring him, Archie turned back to his sisters. "When do we eat?"

Throughout supper, Archie remained in a bad mood. When Diana asked about the health of his wife, his answers were mere grunts as he contin-

ued eating. He kept flashing dark looks at Tom,
and she knew that an explosion of temper was in
the offing.

Diana may have had trouble being impulsive,
but at least she realized it and attempted to curb
it. Archie did anything he wanted, the moment he
thought about it. When he was young, he would
have gotten along far better with their father if
he would have simply known when to keep his
mouth shut. Now he glared at Tom down the
length of the table, where he sat between Cicely
and Diana.

When Archie was finished with his custard,
he set down his spoon with a thump, and Diana
jumped. Tom put his hand on her thigh, but if he
thought to calm her, then he didn't understand
what his touch did to her.

Archie's eyes narrowed as he looked at Tom. "I
heard you came to court Cicely. You never asked
my permission."

"You do not allow your sisters to live with you,
Winslow, so why should I ask your permission?
It was the king who suggested I come. I took that
as my permission. And 'court' is an inappropriate
word. I came to meet both of your sisters and see
if we suited."

Archie ignored his reference to King Henry, as
Diana knew he would.

"Both sisters?" Archie bellowed.

Diana flinched as the great hall grew even quieter. She prayed that Tom would not bring up their relationship, when nothing had been decided.

Tom cocked his head, his expression confused. "Are not both young ladies eligible?"

"They are," Archie answered, looking around as if he realized that everyone was staring at him. "But Diana—"

And then he simply stopped. Diana kept waiting for him to say she was more a man than a woman, one of his favorite taunts, but he didn't.

At last, Archie said, "Which woman you're here to chase is not as important as your unsuitability to marry into my family."

Tom's smile took on an edge. "I am a viscount, cousin to the king, wealthy beyond what you can imagine."

He looked around the great hall of Kirkby Keep as if judging it, and Archie's face reddened.

Tom continued pleasantly, "And how would those qualities make me unsuitable?"

Archie slammed his hands onto the table. "You know damn well why you cannot find a wife, why you had to journey into the north away from London. Your brother may have been an ass, but you were supposed to be a priest. And that wasn't good enough for you. You had to murder your own brother and take everything he had. I will not allow one of my sisters to marry into such a scandal."

Diana held her breath, and now it was her turn

to put her hand on Tom's thigh, pray that he could hold his temper. But she forgot that he'd spent six years doing just that. He had taken abuse from so many people, had made some foolish mistakes, it was true, but he had not allowed it to make him bitter. He still wanted a wife and a future and children.

She herself was furious on his behalf, wanting to shout at Archie that the late viscount was worse than an ass. If Archie wanted scandal, she could give it to him, proclaiming the truth about the viscount's death before all. But Tom's hand covered hers and gave it a gentle squeeze. He had taken the blame for her, and obviously wanted to keep on taking it. She felt humiliated and miserably guilty.

"You'll be happy to know," Tom said mildly, "that no decision about marriage has been made. Yet Mistress Cicely and I have decided that our relationship is best kept as friendship."

"Then she's smarter than I ever gave her credit for," Archie said, pushing to his feet. "What about Diana?"

Diana's jaw hurt from clenching her teeth so hard.

Tom smiled at her intimately. "We'll see."

He'd just openly proclaimed his sole interest in her.

Archie reddened. "You cannot force a woman to—"

"That is enough!" Diana said, rising to face her brother. She knew Tom had tensed at her side. He was a different man now, and she was proud of him. "Lord Bannaster is our guest, and I will not listen to another word of inhospitality."

Archie stared at her in astonishment. "How desperate do you have to be to think that he—"

Now Tom slammed to his feet, the look in his eyes murderous, his hand on the hilt of his sword.

"Please find your bed, Archie," Diana said firmly. "You must be exhausted."

Archie opened his mouth to retort, but instead looked around again at the unfriendly faces watching him. Stiffly, he said, "I am thinking of you, Diana—and you, too, Cicely. I am your brother and it is my duty to protect you."

Perhaps in his strange way, he thought he was being considerate of them. The threat of scandal had a lot to do with it, of course, since he had a wife and a title to protect. But the old Archie would never have admitted to caring about his sisters' well-being. Perhaps their long separation had changed him, if only slightly.

Diana glanced at Cicely, then said in a quiet voice, "Archie, I thank you for your concern. I understand your objections. I am certain Cicely and I will give it great thought."

He had their dowries, and could have brought the money up to control them, but he didn't. Instead he only turned away and walked upstairs.

"Hmm," Cicely said thoughtfully. "He seems to have mellowed."

Tom looked between the sisters in surprise. "That behavior was mellow?"

Cicely only shrugged and left the table. "Good night, Lord Bannaster."

Diana frowned as she watched her sister ascend the stairs. It was still early in the evening for Cicely.

"I am ready to retire as well," Tom said, his face grim. "Sleep well, Mistress Diana."

He walked stiffly up the stairs, and Diana stared after him, feeling hurt and angry on his behalf. But Archie wasn't the only one who'd hurt him.

And she could not let him suffer.

Chapter 20

I n the middle of the night, the only light in Tom's bedchamber came from the low embers of the hearth. Diana leaned back against the door, waiting, but her entrance must not have disturbed him, because he didn't move in his bed. She did not regret coming here; this was where she needed to be, at Tom's side. She went to the hearth and added more wood, watching with satisfaction as flames caught and flickered.

Then she rose and slowly walked across the carpeted floor, letting her dressing gown fall from her arms and puddle on the floor behind her. Nude, she lifted his coverlet to slide in beside him and saw the sheen of his open eyes.

"I wondered at your plan," he said softly, looking down her body with appreciative eyes that narrowed with rising passion.

"Oh, Tom." Shivering, she slid beneath the warmth of his blankets, encountering a cocoon of heat and the faint, masculine scent of Tom, so arousing to her.

Naked, he pressed against her side and she moaned with sheer delight, as if she'd been denying her hunger for him for an eternity instead of days. She loved him, and she didn't know what to do about it.

And then she felt his open mouth on her neck, a gentle sucking that made her shudder. He explored her skin with soft kisses, tender caresses. Her breasts ached for every touch he teased them with, her thighs spread as if she wantonly begged for him. Beneath the blankets that surrounded him, he rose up over her body, but only to reach more of her with his kisses. He scattered them down her belly, across her thighs, the trailing silkiness of his hair making her shudder. She touched him, tried to coax him into taking her, but he ignored her wishes and concentrated on his own purposes.

And although she'd come to offer herself in sympathy and love, his purpose was obviously giving her pleasure.

She stiffened when his mouth moved even lower on her body, as with gentle fingers he parted the curls at the joining of her thighs.

"Easy," he whispered.

His breath in so private a place made her gasp, and she almost resisted in embarrassment as he spread her thighs farther. But then he licked her, his hot tongue a rasp that made her stifle a cry of ecstasy. She couldn't bear the pleasure of it, squirmed and rolled her head back and forth with every stroke, arching her body off the bed as her climax seemed to explode inside her.

Barely a heartbeat later, Tom used his body to separate her thighs even farther and buried himself deep inside her, as if he could wait no longer. She loved his need and his passion, and held him to her, stroking his skin, leaning up to kiss his chest, his neck, and at last his mouth. They lost themselves in each other, the ecstasy of their joined bodies, the sweet fulfillment that they reveled in.

He came so quickly that she flung her arms wide and laughed with the knowledge that he could not control himself in his desire of her.

With a groan, he collapsed atop her, and she enjoyed his weight and the firmness of his slick muscles.

Into her neck, he said, "You are a witch, to make me lose myself so."

She wrapped herself around him, arms and legs, almost humming her satisfaction.

Sated and tender, yet still uneasy about her motives, Tom rolled to the side, then propped his head on his arm, thinking that he could look upon Diana forever. "But why did you risk so much to come to me tonight?"

"My brother was terrible to you, even though

you'd declared your interest in taking me off his hands. I had to come."

She thought it was about her brother? He tried not to feel disappointed, but told himself if he ever needed patience, it was now.

He settled his hand on her breast, unable to be near her without touching her.

"We seem to have problems with our brothers," he said, hoping that this topic would lead to others.

"Surely Archie cares more about his reputation and pride than about Cicely and me. That is the only reason he came."

"I don't know about that. I almost thought he did not know how to say that he was concerned for his sisters."

Her eyes grew thoughtful, as if she'd considered that but had disregarded it out of long habit.

"People change," he added softly.

She rolled onto her side to face him, breasts touching his chest, her arm looping over his waist. "We both know that."

"I'm not sure *my* brother could have."

She tensed.

"Nay, do not think I am still angry with him, for I have put that behind me. And I'm not talking about his death either. 'Tis about what he tried to do to you. You were a virgin when I took you, so I know that he did not . . . but it must have been terrible for you."

She caressed his face. "Why bring up the past, Tom? It is over with."

"I think it is a ghost between us yet, and I don't know how to change that except by talking."

She kissed him, nuzzling her nose to his. "You sometimes talk too much."

"Aye, but I can change. You did see me at mass the other morning."

She giggled. "Father Francis almost tripped on the altar when he saw you. Why did you come?"

Shrugging, he said, "Because you introduced me to him. He seemed like a good man, more interested in his flock than in his divine authority. And you once said that God had not caused my problems; I have finally understood that you were right."

He rolled onto his back to look at the shadowy ceiling, and she nestled into the crook of his arm, her head on his shoulder.

"I was always quick to judgment and resistant to changing my mind," he continued. "My brother protected me when I was a boy, therefore, I assumed he could not do anything bad. I convinced myself of that for a long while. Even as a man I clung to my opinions, blaming the church and priests for what one man had put me through. And when I decided I had to marry, needed a wife and an heir, I was ready to persuade the first woman who met my standards. And 'persuade' is too nice a word for what I did to her."

"People change," she repeated.

"You showed you did, last night."

"What do you mean?"

"Well, when I first came here, you threw me into a dungeon."

She groaned and covered her face, but he pulled her hands aside to kiss her.

"And when your brother came here," he said, "you wanted to confront him in righteous indignation on my behalf, but you controlled yourself."

"Because of you. And it seems I also have you to thank—or blame—for Cicely's bliss."

He arched a brow in mock offense. "That does not sound very good."

Ignoring his playfulness, Diana said, "She was too happy today, and she finally admitted that you were paying her to go away. Tom, after everything she's done—"

"Do you not want to be happy?"

"Well, of course, but—"

"How long do you think it would have been after I did not choose to marry her that she would have tried to use you and your secrets to get what she wanted?"

"Well . . ."

"Exactly. It was a small price to pay to keep her from bothering us. And we know with her beauty she'll find a man who will take her off our hands."

"Aye, that's true. But she thinks she won!" Diana added in frustration.

"Let her. *You* have won, because you will not have to deal with her frustration anymore."

She groaned. "How did you become so important to me?"

"I like being the one you need."

He heard the sharp way she inhaled, knew she probably wasn't ready to hear the words, but he had to say them.

Looking into her distraught eyes, he said, "Diana, let me be always at your side. I love you. Marry me."

It had taken a lot of self-examination—and mistakes—to learn how to say those words correctly, to understand that one had to mean them, to be ready to sacrifice anything for them.

But Diana's eyes turned misty with tears, and they weren't the joyful kind. Her secrets were still between them like a dark shadow in daylight.

Before she could speak, he covered her mouth with his fingers. "Think on my words. I do not need an answer tonight."

She flung her arms around his neck and held on. "I must go," she whispered.

He rolled until she was on top of him, kissed her swiftly. She could not miss that he wanted her again, would always want her.

She groaned and pressed her belly against his erection. "I cannot linger. If my brother decides to come persuade me against you, he won't care what time it is."

"Then go. Just promise me you'll think on my words, and believe that I love you."

She stared at him for a moment, eyes baffled and full of tenderness all at once. Then she whispered, "I will," and slid from the warmth of the bed.

She practically hopped to her dressing gown and pulled its folds about her for warmth, but her feet were yet bare, as if she hadn't even thought of her comfort in her haste to see him.

"Hurry, before you freeze to death," he admonished.

She blew him a kiss and fled his chamber.

With a sigh, Tom lay back with his hands clasped behind his head. After so many years of anger against God, he found himself praying to Him for a miracle.

When Diana was alone in her bedchamber, she donned her warmest night rail, dove beneath the blankets, and shivered until at last her bed was warm. When she could think again, she stared at the ceiling in shock.

Tom loved her. He wanted to marry her. Most women would have gladly shouted to the heavens their affirmative answer. God above, she wanted to do the same.

Squeezing her eyes shut, she rolled onto her side. But other women weren't keeping secrets of betrayal from the man they loved.

Once again, like a tired refrain, she told herself she'd helped clear his name. That she could just put it behind her. But could she put the League behind her? Did she want to?

She loved Tom, and that should be enough for her. But he wasn't the one asking her to choose between him and her dream, was he? Nay, it was her own nature that was forcing a choice.

Late the next morning just before dinner, Tom finished sparring at the tiltyard with his men. He'd taken a lot of good-natured kidding about his relationship with Diana. They all kept giving him advice, from laughing insistence that he compose a sonnet to her, to suggestions that he ride high into the dales to gather wildflowers for her—In the winter? he pointed out.

"I am surprised Winslow is not out here with us," Tom said, as Talbot helped him remove his training armor. "One would think he would want to show me his skill, hoping I'll back down from my pursuit of Diana."

"Let him become used to you, my lord," Talbot said. "Surely he wants his sister happy."

"What is he going to do, deny me a dowry? I certainly do not care. And Diana is a woman grown, not a girl. When we marry, there is nothing he can do about it."

"When?" Talbot echoed innocently, a smile at the corners of his lips.

Tom only shook his head. How could he explain that he was not Diana's only choice in life?

When he went inside to wash for dinner, Mary hurried toward him. The worry in her face made his smile fade.

"Milord," she said, "have you seen Mistress Diana?"

"She did not come down to the tiltyard with me, Mary. I assumed she was working inside this morn."

Mary shook her head, beginning to wring her hands in a display of nervousness. "She is nowhere within the castle. I've spoken to all the servants and we have not seen her since mass. I did not see her within the ward."

"Did you question all the servants working outside?"

"Nay," she said, looking hopeful. "I will send the valets."

"I'll go, too."

Finally, after a half hour of questioning everyone Tom could find, a young groom stammered to him that Diana had taken her horse and gone for a ride.

Tom would have felt better about knowing what she was doing, but she'd left hours before.

The wind was picking up, and the sky threatened snow.

"Where is Lord Winslow?" Tom asked the groom.

"He's gone, too, milord. He said he was visitin' the village."

"By himself?"

"He took two of his men."

Uneasiness roiled inside Tom. Diana did not owe him every detail of her whereabouts, but he couldn't believe she'd be gone so long without leaving word. In winter, no less.

But the fact that Winslow was also absent turned Tom's uneasiness into anger. Was Winslow so determined to keep them apart that he'd kidnap Diana?

Riding always soothed Diana's restless thoughts. The mechanics of guiding a horse through hilly terrain required a concentration that took her away from herself, let her thoughts churn in the background, instead of obsessing over them.

The day was cold, the wind smarted her cheeks, but the exertion of riding warmed her stiff muscles. And the scenery was beautiful, a long, sloping valley leading up to the flat tops of the moors. Here and there she could see bonfires in the farmers' fields, and knew that all were celebrating Twelfth Night, the last day of the Christmas holiday.

After several hours riding along the winding bank of the River Swale, deeper into the wooded heart of the dale, she turned around to go back—

And saw four cloaked men on the trail behind her. Diana reined her mount to a halt and waited, her hand at her waist where her dagger was concealed. She hadn't thought to strap a sword to her saddle, hadn't meant to leave Kirkby land, but somehow her ride had gone on longer than she'd meant it to.

Each man watched her somberly, their cloaks thrown back to show the broad chests and thick arms of warriors. She met their gazes, lifting her chin.

"Gentlemen, are you following me?" she finally asked.

"Mistress Diana." The blond man who spoke rode out several paces before the others, speaking her Christian name not as a question, but as a certainty.

"Aye," she said, because what was the point of denying it? "What is your business with me?"

He lifted a hand to his throat, and she found herself stiffening, hand on her hidden dagger, wondering what he hid beneath his cloak. But he only reached under the neckline of his shirt and pulled out a familiar medallion on a chain.

They were members of the League of the Blade.

The air went out of her lungs in a rush, and the tension in her shoulders eased. "You are looking for me, Sir Knight?"

"I am Sir David," he said impassively, not offering his surname, as was League custom. "We received your missive."

"Why have you come to find me? Do you not believe I have fulfilled the terms of my assignment?" She hoped he'd deny it, saying how well she'd done, and that they were prepared to accept her back.

Instead, Sir David said, "We need to discuss it."

That was not a good sign. "And I do not suppose that you wish to get out of the cold by accompanying me back to Kirkby Keep?"

The knight shook his head. "We know of a nearby farm, tucked away up the valley, that has been long abandoned."

"It sounds warm," she said dryly.

He lips curved in a ghost of a smile. "We will make it so. Will you accompany us?"

She had no choice. They had identified themselves as Bladesmen, and knew about her assignment. She rode to join them, moving into the lead at Sir David's side. For another hour no one spoke, as the horses climbed higher up a winding path. It was a good thing that Diana didn't mind silence. These four quiet men could have unnerved another woman.

But she was a Bladeswoman. She was one of them. The fierce pride in her accomplishments could not be denied. She could not give this up. She wanted to help people who had no one else to turn to.

At last they reached the cottage, and although the door hung crookedly from its leather hinges, the window shutters were still closed and the earthen floor was dry. One man began a fire with the tinder and wood left behind, and the other two went searching for more wood.

Sir David stood with Diana before the small fire.

"Am I allowed to speak of my mission before your men, as well as you?" she asked.

He nodded. "I would appreciate if you would wait for their return so that we may all hear together."

She stood at his side and silently stared into the fire, feeling the comfortableness of two people sharing the same goals. He was so much taller than he'd seemed on the horse. She thought his hair must brush the dried herbs still hanging from the ceiling beams.

At last, all four men were gathered. They found a lopsided stool for her, and two crude benches for themselves, and soon they were all seated, warming up before the welcome fire.

Sir David said, "We received your missive, and my superiors are grateful for your detailed report on Lord Bannaster. His attempts to improve himself are laudable, but . . ."

"But?" Diana echoed. Had they discovered her foolish kidnapping of Tom?

"But . . . although you give us plenty of opinions, with facts to back them up, your wording suggests that you cannot be considered objective where Lord Bannaster is concerned."

Sir David looked a bit embarrassed, as if he was repeating a message he did not find easy to discuss.

"But if I've given the facts, and you believe them, then how am I not being objective?"

"My superiors are concerned that you and Lord Bannaster have developed a relationship."

She eyed him, trying not to take offense, trying to think through her answers. "We have, although I do not yet know how it will be between us. Are you saying it was obvious in my missive?"

"Not obvious, but my superiors were concerned that—"

"Let me address their 'concerns.' I have fallen in love with Lord Bannaster, that is true." She could not believe she was saying the words aloud to strangers, when she hadn't even said them to Tom. But they felt so right. "But the reason I did so, was because he's a good man. He had a hard life, raised by a zealous family to be a priest. He has been suspected of the terrible crime of killing his brother, which he didn't commit. Your superiors know who did." She did not bring up her own responsibility, for it was the League's decision to decide who should know. "He had to learn to be a knight and viscount all at once, quickly, with no training in his youth. He has made mistakes. We can all say the same. But he has learned from them, and not become bitter. He approaches everything in life with determination, and he is loyal to his king. Did you know that he even helped all the women his brother harmed?"

Sir David studied her, his mouth not quite a smile. Diana thought he might actually approve of her, even though she was defending Tom more than might be necessary. She noticed that two of the men nodded to each other.

"Your arguments are persuasive, Mistress Diana. I plan to recommend to the League that your report about Lord Bannaster be the last one necessary."

"He can be trusted, Sir David, by both the League and our king."

"And how did he react when he learned of your mission for us?"

"He does not know."

Sir David nodded. "That is as it should be." He slapped a hand on his thigh as he looked to his men. "Could you see to the horses, and to disguising our presence here? I have a last message for Mistress Diana that is to be given in private."

Diana blinked as, unquestioningly, the other three men left the cottage. She turned back to Sir David, who looked almost . . . uncomfortable.

"Is there something wrong?" she asked.

He sighed and returned his serious gaze to her. "I did not want to speak in front of the others, because you have satisfied your assignment for the League. But personally, I am worried about how your relationship with Lord Bannaster will be affected—and how that will affect you. There are those who say that the League's secrecy must be honored in every way. But I have heard rumors of marriages among us withering because of rigid adherence to this doctrine of secrecy, even among spouses. If you love Lord Bannaster, and he you, you might want to think about what you're keeping from him."

Inside her, her heart constricted, but she had to be strong. "It would be a betrayal of the League." She spoke simply, from the center of her beliefs.

Sir David looked at the fire and said, "Secrets in a marriage usually fester and worsen over time. Does he know about your involvement in the League?"

She was not tempted to lie. If she wanted to be a Bladeswoman, she had to speak the truth. "Due to my involvement in his brother's death, he deduced my League membership. But he is the king's cousin, and he would never—"

Sir David held up a hand. "I am not questioning Lord Bannaster's loyalty. *My* mission is to discuss *you*. Speaking as a man, not a Bladesman, I suggest you think long and hard before marrying a man who does not know he was the subject of your assignment. And of course, if someone asks you what I said, I will deny it all." His mouth twitched in a smile.

Diana said nothing, her eyes burning as she looked into the fire.

"Thank you for your honesty, Sir David," she said at last, rising to her feet. "I will consider your words. Now I have to leave before it grows too dark to travel."

When the fire was put out, and the cottage left as they'd found it, Diana mounted her horse. The Bladesmen stood respectfully watching her, and she felt again that surge of pride and satisfaction. She had acquitted herself well, had not gotten angry or defensive with their personal questions. And if the League thought her answers were not to *their* satisfaction, then she'd done all she could. She bowed her head to Sir David and his companions, then guided her horse in a circle and down the lane, heading for home.

Several hours later, when she was near the village, she was spotted by some of her tenants, who looked shocked to see her. They'd been running from the direction of the keep, and that made her heart pick up pace in unease. She trotted the last distance down the hillside to the village green, with its squat stone cottages perched on the slopes above the River Swale.

The two people who'd come from the keep spoke to others, and then a woman walked swiftly toward Diana. She recognized the woman immediately as the local brewer.

"A happy Twelfth Night to you, Matilda," Diana said.

"The same to you, Mistress Diana," the woman said, struggling now to catch her breath. Her pale face had splotches of excited color. "Forgive my boldness, mistress, but while ye've been gone, there's been a terrible quarrel at Kirkby Keep. I fear your brother and Lord Bannister will come to blows soon! The lads have come from the castle to say that men are donning armor, and 'twill not be used for training."

"My thanks, Matilda," Diana said with urgency. "Tell the villagers that there will be no battle today."

Chapter 21

T om was dressed for a winter's ride into the village to find Winslow and Diana, when the baron and his men-at-arms returned. Tom marched across the snow-covered ward toward the stables, his fury boiling his blood. He knew Diana, and she would have fought her brother if he'd tried to steal her away. By God, if he'd harmed her—

Winslow was just outside the stables, talking to his men, when he glanced over his shoulder and saw Tom approaching. His expression changed from wariness to anger.

"Where is Diana?" Tom demanded.

Winslow faced him, hands on his hips, close to the hilt of his sword. "What are you talking about, Bannaster?"

"She has been missing most of the day. Her groom said she'd gone for a ride alone, and she has not returned. Coincidentally, you were gone at the same time."

Winslow glanced between his men, an amused smile tilting his lips. "So she has rejected you."

"By leaving her own home?" Tom asked incredulously. "She is a strong woman. She would have told me to my face if she wanted nothing more to do with me. I think you've tried to force your opinion on her."

"Leave my sister to me. It is obvious that you believe there is more between the two of you than she does."

Tom felt a momentary pang of uncertainty. Could Winslow be right? But nay, he remembered Diana in his arms, the way she'd come to comfort him last night. A woman did not offer herself if she didn't feel something. He would convince her that they were in love.

If he got the chance.

"I think you are interfering, Winslow," Tom said. "Diana is a grown woman who deserves the chance to decide her own future."

"As you've given other women that chance in the past?" Winslow said with a sneer.

Tom punched him hard in the jaw, and Winslow flew backward. Only his man catching his arm kept him from tumbling into a snow bank.

Tom stepped closer, ignoring Winslow's soldiers who reacted defensively, hands on their swords, several beginning to unsheathe them.

"I care not what you say about me," Tom said,

"but the things you've done to your sister are beyond the bounds of decency."

Winslow snarled, "For assaulting me, Bannaster, I challenge you to defend yourself as a knight!"

"I will—and gladly. Don your armor, sir, for I shall not use a dulled sword. I will force you to tell me where your sister is."

Tom stalked to the armory, a wooden structure built against the curtain wall near the tiltyard. A dozen people came behind, talking excitedly. More would soon follow, he knew, but he did not care.

Talbot caught up with him. "My lord, is this battle wise?"

"You heard him. He will not tell me where Diana is. If I have to humiliate him before his people, I will."

"Do you think he has harmed her?" Talbot said, opening the door to the armory.

Tom unbarred several shutters and opened them, letting in light. "He is not a fool. He merely wants his way. Where is the armor I've been using?"

Talbot held up breast and back plates. "But should you not wear more protection?"

"I'll take the gorget around my neck and the gauntlets for my hands, but I do not think more will be necessary. I've heard of his lack of skill.

Comes from lack of practice, the fool. He'll tell me what I want to know before long."

When he was ready, Tom strode out of the armory and came up short. The tiltyard was lined with spectators, two and three deep though snow was beginning to fall. More people were coming down through the inner ward from the gatehouse. How quickly had news of this foolishness spread across the countryside?

Winslow was already waiting at the tiltyard, and he wore more armor than Tom, vambraces on his arms, pauldrons covering his shoulders, tassets draped over his abdomen and hips. Tom thought Winslow looked discomfited to see his opponent so lightly dressed. But Winslow said nothing, only narrowed his lips.

Tom held his own helm beneath his arm. "Are you prepared to reveal Diana's location?"

Winslow's answer was to don his helm. Tom did the same. Talbot handed him his sword, and he went out to face Diana's brother.

When Diana rode beneath the gatehouse, she was shocked by how deserted the inner ward looked. No children chased geese or rolled toy hoops, no dairymaids carried buckets of milk into the Keep. Even the blacksmith's anvil was silenced. Snow was falling softly, blanketing everything.

A cheer rose up from the rear of the ward, and her stomach took a sickening twist. That had come from the tiltyard. But she didn't hear the sound of sword fighting. Panicked that she might be too late to have prevented an injury, she urged her horse into a gallop and raced past the stables. A crowd had gathered about the tilt-yard, blocking it from view. Boys dangled from the few trees planted near the garden, and they leaned out for a better view between the bare branches.

Suddenly, Diana realized that Cicely stood in the lady's garden, well cloaked and hooded, but far enough away that she couldn't possibly see what was happening on the tiltyard.

"Cicely!"

Her sister lowered her snow-flecked hood. "Oh, 'tis you," she said, with little interest.

"What is going on?" Diana demanded.

"Archie and Lord Bannister are about to fight. I hope it doesn't take too long."

"They're fighting with *swords*?" Diana cried. "They could kill each other!"

"You do not have to worry. Lord Bannaster is clearly a superior swordsman. He won't kill Archie."

"Can I worry about my brother, too?" she asked with sarcasm. "Or the state of Tom's soul if he should *accidentally* kill him? Quickly tell me what this is about, so that I can put an end to it."

"Archie came storming in, said Lord Bannaster had offended him, and it was time to end it."

"That cannot be all that happened," Diana said in surprise. "Did you hear what Tom supposedly said to start this?"

Cicely shrugged, rubbing her arms against the cold. "Everyone in the castle spent hours looking for you. I heard from someone that Lord Bannaster thought Archie had kidnapped you to keep you away from him, so when Archie returned, words were exchanged."

Diana could only gape at her. "Tom thinks I've been kidnapped? By my own brother?"

"I hear Archie did not deny it. He always did like to goad people." Cicely eyed her in disapproval. "You *have* been gone most of the day, without leaving word. Rather disrespectful of you, was it not?"

Closing her eyes, Diana nodded. "It was. I did not mean to be gone so long. I only needed a ride to clear my head."

She suddenly heard the ringing of steel on steel from within the crowd. There was a collective gasp, then applause, all interspersed by the sounds of two men battling with swords.

Diana drew back on the reins and guided her mount toward the tiltyard. When she reached the spectators, she slowed her horse, but did not dismount. "Make way!" she shouted.

The people at the rear of the crowd began to turn her way. One at a time, their eyes went wide, they whispered to their neighbors, and at last began to move back. Yet strangely, their smiles seemed glad and relieved, and Diana now understood why. They had been worried for her, and she was touched.

But they also probably didn't want her to stop the sword fight. It would be an amusing piece of gossip to relive when winter was at its bleakest.

Tom and Archie circled each other, swords raised, faces obscured by their helms. But it was easy enough to recognize the combatants by their stance alone, and the snow was not yet thick enough to obscure them.

"Hold!" Diana cried, but neither man heard her.

The crowd buzzed with excitement, and Archie lunged forward, the thrust of his sword aimed at Tom's heart. Diana lost her breath in that instant, but Tom easily parried the sword aside and slammed the edge of his blade across Archie's helm.

She rode right into the middle of the battle, forcing both men to stumble back.

Tom had his helm off first, and his face was split with a broad grin. "Diana! You escaped!"

She gave him a smile, but aimed a scowl at Archie as he removed his helm, and she dismounted. "I was never held captive by anyone, including my brother."

Tom took a menacing step forward. "Why the hell did you not simply deny the accusation?" he demanded of Archie.

"It did not deserve a response," Archie said coolly, deliberately avoiding Diana's stern gaze. "I wanted to finish this battle between us once and for all."

"And if I really had been kidnapped or hurt," Diana exclaimed, "you were keeping Tom from helping me!"

Archie looked only a bit sheepish. "Well, 'tis true, but you've always taken care of yourself."

She wanted to gape at him. "Did you think I always could, even as a young girl? Did you think that that was the kind of relationship I wanted with my brother? Mayhap I would have enjoyed you occasionally taking care of me!"

Archie stared at her, his bewilderment giving way to anger. "What do you think I have been doing? *This* is the man"—he pointed at Tom—"I want to protect you from! And are you thankful? Nay, you are not! You want everything on your own terms." He tossed his helm onto the ground, and then turned away from her. "Ale for all in the great hall," he called.

The disappointed murmurs turned to cheers

and the crowd began to flow back toward the keep. Diana followed, leading her horse until she spotted a groom, who took him for her.

"Take good care of him," she said tiredly. "He has had a long day."

"Doing what?" Tom caught her elbow. "I think you owe me an explanation."

"I do," she said, bracing herself.

"Then I want to hear it now." Tom drew her into the abandoned lady's garden, away from the crowd. "Tell me everything."

"Out here?"

"I cannot wait until the night, when we next have a moment alone. Tell me where you went without leaving word with anyone."

"But your armor—"

"It can wait. Now tell me."

She took his hand in hers and squeezed. "I only needed to think, to be alone. I often go for a ride just to be away from everything. I thought I would be home by dinner, but I rode farther than I meant to."

"That is all?" he asked, confused.

For a moment, the ramifications of whatever she chose to tell him weighed her down. Would he accept her, accept what she did for her life's passion—accept what she'd done to him in the name of duty?

He was so good, so concerned. She gently caressed his cheek with her fingers, hoping this would not be the last time she did so. She wanted to tell him of her love, but that would only distract him from what he needed to hear.

"Nay, that is not all," she said quietly, full of worry and fear and resignation. She looked around, caution long engrained in her. But they were alone. "Four Bladesmen met me to discuss my last assignment."

His brows lowered in confusion. "You have not told me of anything other than your mission against my brother. But I know that the League insists on secrecy."

"Aye, and that was going to be my excuse to never tell you this, but I cannot marry you with this secret between us."

He gripped both of her hands now. "I have been waiting for this, sweetling. Just tell me."

"After I . . . locked you in the dungeon, I received a note from the League, one that had been delayed by bad weather. They informed me that they were sending you here so that I could get to know you, to evaluate you."

The puzzlement in his face was slowly changing to wariness. "To evaluate me?" he asked, his voice impassive now.

She nodded, swallowing, trying to clear the lump from her throat that only kept getting bigger. "The League wanted to know if you could be trusted by the king. You had made errors in judgment, and they wanted to determine if you were susceptible to the plots of treason that whirled around the king."

"The king, my cousin," Tom said woodenly.

"Aye," she whispered. The wind caught her cloak, tugged at her hair. But even the snowflakes melting on her face were not as cold as the paralyzing feeling squeezing her chest.

"And all this time, you have simply been spying on me, using me to satisfy your assignment to the League." He pulled his hands away.

She wanted to grasp for them, as if Tom himself were slipping away from her. "That is not how it was! Well, it was at first, of course, but not when I came to know you. And is that not what courtship is about?" Her voice was beginning to sound desperate.

He blinked. "Now you're saying you were courting me?"

"Ohh!" She covered her face momentarily with her hands. "Nay, but I was coming to know you, like a courtship. And I learned that you're a good man, worthy of trust. I told the League so!"

His dark eyes flashed. "And what did taking me to bed tell you about my character?"

She gasped, feeling nauseated. "Nay! You cannot think I would use you in such a manner! You know that I never meant more to happen between us. I was trying to keep you from my sister because of what I had . . . done to your brother."

"So you bedded me to keep me from your

sister. A bonus to your assignment," he added with sarcasm.

She didn't want to cry, mustn't cry, but the tears burned her eyes trying to escape. "Oh, Tom, you know that is not true. I am not saying any of this correctly. Six years ago, you saved me at the expense of your own peace of mind, and I have repaid you terribly."

"No wonder you've been so evasive," he said, his eyes losing focus as if analyzing everything she'd done in these last weeks.

"I have been so torn!" she pleaded. "For six years I have done my duty to the League. I did not know what choice to make, but I know now. I owe you the six years of suspicion that you've suffered on my behalf. That is the only thing that will make it right. I will tell the king and court that I was the one who killed your brother defending myself. They will know that you are innocent."

He looked at her, his eyes at last betraying surprise more than anger.

"Diana!"

Diana recognized her sister's voice instantly. *Oh, not now!*

"You are not traveling with me!"

That was Archie, who sounded exasperated.

Cicely came to the half wall of the lady's garden, pulling on gloves. She looked brightly between Archie and Tom, then said to her brother, "Lord Bannaster and Diana offered me a gift to celebrate their upcoming wedding: they're sending me to London and will provide everything I need to live on as I look for a husband. And I do not wish to wait, so Archie, I'm leaving with you."

Why did Cicely have to complicate everything? Diana wondered with exasperation.

In the silence that followed, she saw that Archie didn't know who to look at first, Cicely or herself. She herself wanted to shout "Wedding?" at her sister, but it would only make matters worse.

Finally, Archie rounded on Diana. "You're getting *married* to him? I thought it had not been decided."

"I—" What could she say? Tom had asked her, she hadn't answered, and now he might withdraw his proposal all together.

Tom simply crossed his arms and stared at the three Winslow siblings, as if waiting for the next act of a play.

Archie ground his teeth and turned on Cicely. "I have not agreed to any of this!"

"I do not need you to. I can rent my own house. Lord Bannaster?"

Tom nodded. "We made a bargain. I will hold to it."

Hold on to the lies that Diana had begun so

long ago? Why would he want to go on keeping these secrets? She was going to tell the truth!

Or was he just trying to get rid of Cicely? Diana was so confused.

"And how do you propose to live?" Archie bellowed at Cicely. "You cannot rent a house with *his* money." He jerked a thumb at Tom. "I will not have you looking like some man's leman. You will stay with me."

Cicely arched her brows in obvious surprise. "Well . . . what a kind invitation, brother dear. Then I can use my newfound money for an even better wardrobe, to attract a handsome, wealthy nobleman."

"Do not forget the dowry," Tom said.

Diana was gaping now, staring at all of them like they were mad.

"You already have a dowry," Archie said angrily. "And it is substantial. I was furious at how generous Father was."

Cicely grinned. "Good. Then we will travel together."

"And you," Archie said, rounding on Diana. "You will not marry *him*!"

That was one order too many, and Diana felt her hard-won control give way. "That is enough!" she cried, finding her hand reaching for her dagger as if she meant to draw it.

On her brother? Was this what she wanted for

her life? Always fighting Archie, always losing control of her temper? In many ways, she was too like him.

She had spent her life trying to be different from other women, going after what she wanted using the fighting instincts of a man. It was now time to go after what she wanted, but using the ways of a woman.

She lowered her hand. "That is enough," she repeated in a quieter voice.

Tom still said nothing, simply folded his arms over his chest and watched her with narrowed eyes.

"Archie, I am not going to fight you over this. I am in love with Tom Bannaster." She didn't look at Tom, was too afraid of what she might see in his eyes.

Cicely gave a dramatic sigh of boredom.

"It is my dearest desire to marry him, but I no longer know if he wishes to marry me. I've spent my life feeling like an outsider within my own family, within my very womanhood. But he has made me realize that I have a home where I belong, and it is at his side, wherever that may be. He is nothing like his reputation. He is a man who would have done anything for his family, who was true to them even when they betrayed him. But I have done unforgivable things, and I need to tell—"

"This doesn't concern him," Tom suddenly

spoke in a firm voice. "If your brother has a problem with me or my reputation, we can meet at King Henry's court to discuss it."

For the first time, Diana felt a flicker of hope. She gazed at Tom, no longer caring who saw her longing.

Archie frowned at him, then glanced at Diana. "You do whatever you want. You will anyway." Muttering, he added, "I . . . give you my permission. And I'll be too busy to worry about you. My wife is expecting a child."

"When were you going to tell us this?" Cicely asked with exasperation.

He shrugged and stalked away.

Following their brother, Cicely looked over her shoulder and met Diana's gaze, giving a single nod. Surprised, Diana nodded back. Then, squaring her shoulders, Diana turned back to Tom. Bare branches creaked against each other in the wind, and the daylight was draining away into the gray of twilight, mixed with the swirling snow. It looked as bleak as her soul felt at the thought of a life without Tom.

"You should have let me tell him about what I did to your brother," Diana said. "Delaying it will only—"

"You are a fool," Tom interrupted, suddenly gripping her arms. "Six years ago, I knew that if it were discovered that you had killed Nicholas, you would suffer greatly, perhaps even be put to death. Do you think anything you've said today would make me change my mind? You can't believe I want to punish you for what has happened between us. You have suffered enough for what was not your fault."

Tears slipped from beneath her lashes as she briefly closed her eyes. "Oh, Tom, just tell me what you want, how I can prove my love to you."

"You have proven it," he said softly.

When he gathered her into his arms, his armored chest proof that he'd even go to war for her, it was all she could do to keep from breaking down and crying.

"I know you spent your girlhood with the dream of accomplishing more with your life," he said quietly. "I know what it's like to want something so badly you feel that you'll do anything to have it. Things outside of my control gave me my freedom, but you—you made your dreams come true. How can you think I would not admire what you did, training yourself, coming to the League's notice and then grasping the chance to belong?"

"But . . . I betrayed you." The words seared her throat.

"I was angry at first, and in that anger I said things I regret. You may have started out using me. And I began our relationship by deciding that I would discover your secrets and find the perfect punishment for you because of my imprisonment.

But from the beginning, I felt torn, because there was always something about you that attracted me, and I spent far too long trying to pretend it was simply lust."

"Oh, I felt the same!" she cried, cupping his face in her trembling hands.

"And then I fell in love with you," he continued, a smile slowly transforming his face, "and I forgot that we were enemies, and wondered if we could have a future together."

"I thought so, too, Tom. I did not know how I could satisfy the League—and I needed to do that. They are important to me, and I cannot give them up."

"I know, and I would not ask you to change what you are."

She dropped her head to his chest for a moment in relief. "But Tom," she said at last, "I told myself that I could make things right, that my report to the League would tell the truth about you, what a good man you are and how you've learned from your mistakes. But how could I tell you? I felt it was disloyal to the League to reveal their assignment, and disloyal to you to withhold it. How could I marry you with a secret like that? A husband and wife are supposed to share everything. That is why I went riding today. I had to make up my mind. You had not asked me to choose between you and the League, but I was worried that I was.

Then I met the Bladesmen. One of them was kind enough to talk to me about the festering of secrets in a marriage. I realized then that the League would not expect perfection of me. And what I share with the man I love is none of their business. Then I returned, only to find you battling my brother for me—"

He leaned down to give her a gentle kiss, and she inhaled the welcome scent of him in the cold air. It was like coming home.

"I love you, Diana," he murmured against her lips. "You've said those words before your brother and sister, but not yet to me."

"I love you, Tom," she breathed, kissing him gently, reverently. "I want to be your wife and bear your children."

"And be a Bladeswoman?" He smiled down at her.

"Only once a year," she said quickly. "And when our children are born, I will excuse myself from assignments while they are young."

"And I, too, will have to do dangerous things to support you and my people, to defend our way of life. We will both have to suffer as we worry about each other."

"But we'll always have each other to come home to." Her happiness could not be contained, and she threw her arms around his neck. He picked her up off the ground and hugged her so tightly that her ribs creaked. She'd never felt at home with her family, had been banished by her brother, but she'd made her own home here at Kirkby Keep. With Tom, she would gladly make a new home again.

"Let us marry soon," Tom said. "The priest can be convinced to hurry the banns."

She leaned back to stare into his face. "But your own home, your people—"

"I want you to spend this time with *your* people, the ones who've become your family. And do you not wish your brother and sister to share our happiness?" He grinned.

"Cicely is already happy, but Archie . . ."

"He's already given his blessing. And he's not going to be able to travel in this snow. Kirkby Keep will hold a special place in our hearts, the place where we found each other again, the place we fell in love. We'll visit whenever you'd like. It will be a welcome change after Castle Bannaster. My home is . . . slightly larger." He grinned.

"And how will your people react to me? They will not know that I'm a Bladeswoman, but I will have to continue to train."

"You'll be the viscountess. You can do as you please."

"People will have even more reason to talk."

"Let them. We're used to that. We will have

each other. And love. And children."

She leaned her head against his chest. "Aye, I want nothing more than a life with you."

He kissed her temple and whispered into her ear, "We've already begun."

Unforgettable, enthralling love stories,
sparkling with passion and adventure
from Romance's bestselling authors

At Avon Books, we know your passion for romance—once you finish one of our novels, you find yourself wanting more.

May we tempt you with . . .

- **Excerpts** from our upcoming releases.

- Entertaining **extras**, including authors' personal photo albums and book lists.

- Behind-the-scenes **scoop** on your favorite characters and series.

- **Sweepstakes** for the chance to win free books, romantic getaways, and other fun prizes.

- Writing **tips** from our authors and editors.

- **Blog** with our authors and find out why they love to write romance.

- **Exclusive content** that's not contained within the pages of our novels.

Join us at
www.avonbooks.com

AVON

An Imprint of HarperCollins*Publishers*
www.avonromance.com